Twisted by Desire

Lust, Desire, and Love Trilogy (Book 1)

Desiree A. Cox

ISBN-10: 069232268X

ISBN-13: 978-0692322680

Published by Desiree A. Cox

Cover Art: Kellie Dennis at Book Cover by Design
www.bookcoverbydesign.co.uk

Editor: Melissa Gray Editing
www.melissagrayediting.com

Dedication

I am sending a silent thank you and special dedication with lots of love to my Dad. He may be gone but will never be forgotten. He has been with me every day, in my heart and in my mind, since his passing.

I have always said 'like Daddy, like daughter' and this book is proof that I was right, no matter how many times he told me to stop saying that.

Acknowledgment

I would be remiss if I didn't pay homage to the fantastic people who supported and believed in me before I believed in myself.

You have all encouraged me to write and keep writing. You've allowed me to bounce ideas off of you, get your feedback, and even have read the works in progress, excerpts, or chapters for me. Thank you all.

To my husband, whom I am still madly in love with after all these years, you are wonderful. I was the lucky girl to win your heart, and I'll never let you go. I tell you every day I love you, but my words can't express the magnitude of the feelings in my heart. You have supported me for many years – you are my rock and my best friend. I am nothing without you. We are in this life together, forever.

To my very good friend, Ron. You planted the 'write a book' seed in my mind years ago. This genre is a *little* different than what we talked about many times in your office, but your encouragement got my wheels spinning. I love you and Holly, and thank you for giving me the push to explore writing for real.

To my three amazing kids, technically adults now, but always my babies; each of you are fantastic in your own unique way. I loved raising you, you were perfect, no troubles, no sassiness, and ... aw, who the hell am I kidding. I wanted to string each of you up at some point along the way. I'm glad I was able to restrain myself. I love talking to each of you, and not only being your mother, but also being your friend. I am proud of you all and love you all so much.

Thank you to my two brothers and my sister-in-law for telling me to just go for it and write about whatever I want when I began second-guessing myself. Through writing and conversation, I have come to understand my family is still cool as hell. Yolanda - thank you for reading my draft copy for me. I love you all.

Thank you, Monique, for reading my manuscript and providing feedback. You have been a great person to toss ideas out to and your suggestions have helped me more than you will ever know. I truly appreciate you, too. The wedding is coming in book two.

I have a special thank you to Dorothy F. Shaw for helping me understand the craft of writing, especially show, don't tell. Thanks to Kelli Dennis for my cover design, Melissa Grey for the editing, and Cyndi at Bookswagbag for my awesome swag.   Thanks for helping me pull everything together.

Thank you to the ladies at Book Partners in Crime Promotions, for everything you've done to help me from cover reveal to release.   And a huge thank you to all the bloggers and reviewers. I appreciate you all!

For everyone that has offered encouraging words, votes of confidence, and kept me sane – especially Debbie and Al, thank you.

For my two special muses, you are both so beautiful and I love the hell out of you both.

And last but definitely not least, thank you to my Mom and Dad. I hold in my heart decades of cherished memories that I could have only gotten from the both of you. I didn't get to pick my parents, but if I could, I'd pick you both all over again. I love you and wouldn't be here if it weren't for you both. I appreciate your love and support growing up, and throughout my life.

If I forgot anyone, I apologize. There have been so many people that have offered words of encouragement or helped in some way to keep me going, I certainly don't mean to leave you out.

Chapter 1

I used to believe in fairy tale romances where a princess was swept off her feet by a prince, they got married, and lived their happily ever after. Great story.

After my six-year marriage ended up in divorce court, I wasn't sure what to believe in anymore, but I knew that fairy tale shit was for the birds. And whoever came up with the saying 'all you need is love' didn't realize utility and cellphone companies won't take an 'I love you' for payment.

I hated the idea of being single again, but I planned to be smarter if I remarried again, if there was even going to be a second time. I had no clear idea how to go about dating; I had been out of the game for over six years. Times had changed, situations had changed. I wasn't in college anymore, where the men were easily accessible. Hell, I didn't even know what I was looking for in a man. To make things more difficult, I still loved my ex, Skylar. I held a special place in my heart for him and still craved his touch. Every single man I talked to or looked at ended up being compared to him, and then crossed off the list for one reason or another before they were even given a real chance.

After my divorce, I spent a few months moping around, looking like someone had stolen my puppy. My mom and friends were quick to offer plenty of 'why don't you try' advice about getting onto an on-line dating website. Even if I did, which site would I sign up for? There's like a bazillion of them to choose from. I've heard plenty of horror stories about some of them, too. Yeah, that's just what I wanted in my life.

I couldn't bring myself to create a profile and run the risk of having random, creepy single men looking for a quick hook-up, or married men looking to cheat, messaging me. Plus, the thought of meeting someone sight unseen didn't appeal to me one bit. Sure, we could exchange pictures, but what if I met him and instead of him being tall, dark, and handsome like the picture he sent me, he was short and Quasimodo hideous? It would be just my luck to get cat-fished, stalked, or worse. What if the guy was a serial killer? I didn't want to end up on Investigation Discovery like on those dating-gone-wrong stories.

So I chose to ignore them and stick with what I did best. For me, I took the safe route. Friday nights after work, I had a standing date with my co-workers. Candace,

Georgia, Robert, Carla, and Tristan made up the regular group. Happy hour at the restaurant/bar down the street from our office had become my weekly opportunity to get out of the house for socialization, while trying to find someone worth dating.

I liked the bar scene; it was easy, and I felt like I was in control. I could flirt without commitment. If they were interested and I was interested, we could talk or whatever. There was always someone that sparked at least a smidgen of interest and they normally showed plenty of interest back. But the night I met Jeff was different.

****

The place was jam-packed, like every Friday night. The hostess's waiting area was crammed tight with people squeezed together on the seats, holding their coaster-like buzzers in hand while others stood waiting shoulder to shoulder. The outside area was every bit as crowded, with a sliver of space just wide enough to walk inside when a group was called.

Georgia and I had left work around four-thirty, like we usually did on Friday afternoons, to beat most of the influx. We put our names on the list and were able to get seated while we waited for everyone else to join us. We were regulars at this spot. We got seated at a great table near the bar, making it perfect for us to see quite a bit of the restaurant. Being early was ideal for us; it gave us a chance to check out all the guys before the rest of the group -- well, Candace really -- showed up and tried to play matchmaker for us. As we scanned the place, we each doled out our ratings.

"Look at the two geeky-looking guys at the bar." Georgia laughed.

"Oh, jeez, no way." I giggled with her. "They are real nerds, probably discussing an upcoming Comic-con event or Star Trek convention."

"Pocket protectors for everyone." We both laughed as we continued to look around.

"What about the third-wheel guy sitting at the booth across from that couple?" She nodded her head in the direction she wanted me to look.

"Uh, he doesn't meet the height requirement for me, but I guess he isn't bad looking. He's actually kind of cute. What do you think?"

"He's not bad. I'd talk to him."

"His feet barely touch the floor." We both laughed.

We spent the next few minutes continuing our critiques. Today was the same as most other days; there wasn't anyone in here that was worthy of pursuing, and the couple of guys who had potential were sitting next to a female.

The rest of the team showed up and joined our party by five fifteen. We were all happy Jack had decided against coming out that night. We liked him, but since he was our manager, we didn't feel comfortable enough to speak as freely in his presence.

Everything seemed like a normal Friday until we heard voices get loud and stern. There was a lot of commotion by a group of patrons up near the hostess stand. "Are you freaking kidding me right now?" a female voice shrieked.

We all turned our heads. Robert and I stood from our chairs to see who was getting bitched out.

"This is total bullshit!"

Everyone in the restaurant and bar area within earshot turned to see what the uproar was about. I watched as a fiery, petite woman with her eyebrows furrowed tight and her face reddened, shook her index finger in the face of the hostess at the podium. "That's no way to treat us. We've been standing here for-fucking-ever!" she screamed. We were all up on our feet watching the scene play out by now.

Pretty much everyone in there was aware of how pissed she was. She stormed out of the restaurant in a huff, with her friends following close behind her. She shoved the door open, snatching it out of the host's hands, then grabbed it. Once her last friend cleared the door, she pushed back on it with all her might in a failed effort to slam it. I couldn't help the large smile on my face as I watched her enraged exit.

The chaos at the front of the restaurant almost overshadowed the two suit-clad men who walked in the double-door entryway and were immediately seated. They were the banes of everyone waiting's existence and the eye candy I had been waiting for. As they strode past our table following the hostess, my attention and eyes darted from the activity in front to following them like radar as they were seated just on the other side of the half wall that separated the two tables.

Bingo! We have a winner, folks, I thought.

I wasn't the only one who noticed them when they walked through. Candace made sure to point them out -- I mean literally point at them -- and whisper to Georgia and me how 'hot' they were. I took a sip of my drink, all of a sudden feeling parched. I almost choked when she suggested we go introduce ourselves. *That's not going to happen.*

He caught my attention with his long strides through the bustling restaurant in his fit-his-body-like-a-glove black suit, cream-colored dress shirt, and black tie. He looked like he had been peeled off the pages of GQ magazine and had life breathed into him. He was so tall, towering over everyone, with brown, somewhat disheveled hair. He had a very tight, serious, all-business look on his ruggedly handsome face, adorned with a salt and pepper low-cut beard, but no smile. His skin tone was a beautiful tan, a clear indication he wasn't all business. He was panty-soaking perfect from head to toe.

He looked like the men I labeled as untouchables. The guys who look perfect but are off limits because they are with someone, are famous, or make way too much money to know I even exist. He came in with another man who seemed much more relaxed and outgoing; he was talking, laughing, and carefree.

"I don't think *hot* is an appropriate description for mature, professional men. They should have a more classy description."

I liked to save hot to describe the thirty and under men, and both of them definitely looked over thirty to me.

They also appeared to be higher-ups in the corporate world. My ex-husband, Skylar, was under thirty and was hot.

"So how would you describe them?" Candace asked.

"I don't know... maybe something more majestic sounding like, they exude sexiness, a certain je ne sais quoi."

"Yeah, like I said, they're hot." We all laughed.

He *was* hot -- damn was he ever. An unmistakable confidence and sexiness dripped off of him like water off a duck's back.

Georgia, the only other single woman in our group, and I were again encouraged to go introduce ourselves. That's part of the matchmaking crap we dealt with every week; they spot them then tell us to go introduce ourselves.

Introducing myself went against one of my rules; don't introduce myself first. I had learned that lesson while I was in college, after my near-catastrophic freshman mistake. Not only had I been humiliated with the rude rejection after introducing myself to one of the starting football players, but I came close to getting beaten up by his girlfriend. I'm sure she would have kicked my ass; I'm not a fighter. After that little debacle, I created that rule and tell people I don't want to make myself look desperate. I want a man to notice me, then be the initiator and introduce himself to me.

Georgia and I both fell for it once and felt like complete asses when we found out the two guys, good-looking as they were, were a gay couple. I was so mad and embarrassed that I had let them talk me into doing that. But that night, I had dropped my guard and let myself end up looking like a fool.

I had a couple of other rules that I tried to stick to when it came to men: don't make the first phone call; don't act like a stalker; don't be materialistic; don't be in a rush to tell a guy I love him; and don't, under any circumstances, settle.

Georgia wasn't willing to run to their table either. She was more than happy with where she was in her life and not in a rush to have a man impose on her personal freedom. She rarely dated. She had high hopes of Mr. Right falling from the sky for her one day, but wasn't rushing it. She's thirty years old, not a spinster, not a beauty queen. She's an average-looking five-foot-four-inch girl-next-door type of woman carrying about thirty pounds more than she should be, but she's comfortable in her own skin, and I admired her for it.

The longer I sat in my chair, the more restless I became. I needed a closer look at this guy and decided a trip to the restroom was in order because that was a direct path past their table. I pushed my chair back away from the large round table and stood to straighten my clothes, combing my fingers through my waist-length blonde hair.

Tristan's eyes popped open wide as he watched my mirrorless primping. He stared at me from head to toe, running his tongue over his bottom lip. Our eyes met when I glanced over at his boyish freckled face across the table. Tristan is a young Ron Howard look-a-like. He reminded me so much of Richie Cunningham from the *Happy Days* reruns. I turned away, avoiding any lengthy connection to him.

My eyes caught Tristan's again just in time to see him mouth 'sexy' to me. My nose wrinkled, and my lip curled as I tried to fight the onslaught of saliva that was flooding my mouth. I turned my eyes away from him in hopes he wouldn't see the pained expression on my face.

I shuddered at the thought that I had ever considered dating him long-term. He had been good for a drunken, horny one-nighter, but he wasn't my type at all. He was shorter than I liked my men, which was a deal breaker for me. Granted it was only by an inch or two, but he was still shorter than six feet. It might seem trivial to some, but I liked what I like.

I unbuttoned another button on my blouse and pulled the collars out toward my shoulders to reveal a little more cleavage. Georgia looked at Tristan still licking his lips, then shifted her eyes to me. She's a huge advocate of an office love affair between us.

I had my sights set on a target, a very tall, gorgeous target. Set to display my assets like bait to catch a fish, I took one more drink of my wine, tousled my hair one last time, and looked at Georgia. I was ready to begin my mission. "Walk with me to the restroom."

"I don't need to pee."

"We're just going to walk by the two guys that are on the other side of this wall." I pointed my finger in case she wasn't sure I meant the only wall near us.

"I think I'll pass," she said.

"Okay, but I just hate walking back there by myself." I gave her my pouty face.

"*Fine*, come on." *Way to take one for the team.*

I walked slowly, well aware of the embarrassment I'd feel if I tripped or twisted my ankle in my five-inch heels while walking past them trying to be cute. I tried very hard to keep my gaze forward and not look down at the two of them when I was close to their table, but I couldn't help it. I shifted my glance downward, trying not to move my head too much. They both had their hands up on the table. I saw the ring on Mr. Personality's finger, and no ring on Mr. Serious'. Neither man made any attempt to look in my direction. *What the fuck?*

Once I entered the restroom, I stared in the large mirror and took inventory of myself, making sure nothing was untucked or out of place. I'd never been ignored like that before and felt slighted by it. The thought of not garnering at least a quick glance flummoxed me.

"Did you see them? Both are really good-looking, don't you think?" I pulled my hair up into a loose bun on top of my head. Before Georgia could answer, I continued, "But they didn't even look in our direction."

"There's always the walk back. Maybe they're on a business meeting and are wrapped up in the conversation."

"Whatever! It's after five on Friday, and happy hour." Again, I fussed over my blouse making sure as much of my thirty-six barely-B cleavage was visible. One day, I'd get enough money for a boob job.

"You know you're driving Tristan crazy; he really likes you."

"We've had this conversation before; I can't do an office fling, Georgia. What if we don't work out? Then what? We have to work together, see each other every day, and be miserable? No, thank you. And seriously, I'm not even attracted to Tristan." If only she knew about the secret that was between us. No one knew, and I hoped it stayed that way forever.

****

I had broken the cardinal rule a few months after Sky and I separated. I had known Tristan had a thing for me; his eyes always seemed to follow me, staring, lusting in silence. One Friday night, things started out as innocent flirting back and forth. After everyone else from work left, the flirting had taken a more serious turn. It began as little touchy-feely strokes on the arm and pats on the hand. That led to his fingertips creeping up and down my back with feather light strokes. A few too many glasses of wine had me leaning into him, purring like a kitten in heat while he petted me.

We were led down the path to the improbable. My mind kept screaming at me, 'Don't do it; don't sleep with him!' But I needed someone to relieve the ache between my legs, and I couldn't stop myself. At the time, I didn't want to stop myself.

We were waiting for the bartender to deliver our final drink when Tristan leaned in with his hand placed strategically behind me, his thumb right at the crack of my ass, lightly moving across my clothes, whispering in my ear, "I would love to take you home with me." I felt my sex contract and spasm with need, sending a shiver through me. I knew I shouldn't, but I agreed to go to his house for one final drink.

Once we arrived and Tristan opened the front door, I stepped into his cozy bungalow. He fetched us both a beer. When he handed mine to me, he clasped my hand and pulled me off the couch into his thick, muscular chest, holding me tight to him at the waist. His compliments rolled off his tongue as smoothly as water going over a fall. Without warning, he took the liberty to kiss me. I didn't open myself for him right away, but within seconds, I relaxed into his embrace and let him devour my mouth. My response to his kiss was the green light he had been hoping for.

He walked me backwards with his lips locked tight on my mouth, holding me close to make sure I didn't trip. He slipped my top off over her head, exposing my hardened nipples. His hands cupped them as his mouth suckled and licked them both, rolling them between his thumb and index fingers like a true tit-master before lowering me to sit on his bed.

The sex was super-hot, but I knew it was a mistake the next morning. A huge mistake. At the time I was so glad I hadn't stopped myself. Now, not so much. He had been my first after Sky and I separated. I was fortunate he'd kept his mouth shut.

****

I shuddered at the memory.

Giving myself a wink and smile, I prepared to return to the group so I could finish my glass of wine.

As we walked back toward our table, I couldn't help but shift my eyes down at their table again when I sauntered by, swaying my hips with more emphasis this time. Mr. Personality looked up; his eyes met mine, and his mouth curved into a crooked smile. Mr. Serious kept his eyes and conversation focused in the direction of his buddy -- off me. I didn't even exist to him.

When we made it back to our table, I reached up and ripped the ponytail holder, in disgust, from my hair, releasing my tresses to flow freely down my back once again. I glanced over and noticed Georgia looking at me with a smirk on her face.

"What?"

"Nothing, Nikki, relax. Maybe he doesn't like women, maybe he's engaged, or maybe he's married and doesn't wear a ring. Maybe he just doesn't think you're his type. Who knows what's going on with him, but you look fine -- it's not you."

I chose to go with he doesn't like women. Damn shame, too. I'd had plenty of single and married men at least glance at me and acknowledge me. He didn't budge. *Fuck him.*

I retrieved my cellphone from my purse to check the time and to make sure I hadn't missed a call. It was getting close to nine thirty. I wanted to sneak a peek at this guy one more time before I left because I knew I may not ever see him again. Maybe I wasn't his type, but I could swoon, right? I couldn't stay out more than another half hour. I had promised my mom that I'd come by no later than ten thirty.

With all the fiddling with my phone, I came close to missing Robert and Carla saying good-bye. I called out to them both to let them know I'd see them on Monday. About fifteen minutes after they left, Georgia decided it was time to call it a night, and we all said goodbye to her.

There were three of us remaining: Tristan, Candace, and me, which was perfect for the three available seats at the bar now that those who previously occupied the seats were gone. We moved our party, and ordered a final drink.

A hand grazed my left shoulder, startling me. I jerked around so fast that I almost toppled the stool. There he was, his smiling face.

"Hi." He extended his hand out to shake mine. "What's your name, beautiful?" At least one of them had noticed, but not the one I wanted.

"I'm Nikki," I said, looking past him. Just as I was about to look back, I saw him out the corner of my eye, rounding the divider. Holy fucking smoldering sexiness, he was hotter than an August day in Florida, and my panties had just combusted.

"Nikki, beautiful name; I'm Connor," We shook hands, and I gave him a quick smile. Connor was good-looking, and he had a beautiful smile. He wasn't on his friend's level, but good-looking.

I looked over at his friend, who was about five feet from us. Before I could stop myself, I all but jumped off the bar stool and took a couple steps to meet him. I extended my hand to shake his and introduced myself, "Hi, I'm Nikki."

Our gazes crossed for the first time. His dark, piercing eyes sang the seductive tune, come-hither-and-let-me-fuck-you-senseless. The woodsy, citrus smell of his cologne immobilized me. Everything about him was hypnotic.

"Jeff." His outstretched hand met mine. Tingles cruised through me, and butterflies danced in my stomach. My heart pounded against my chest, feeling like it was going to burst through my rib cage.

"It's… it's nice to meet …you." Spoken like a true stammering jackass, yet he was calm and cool. I felt my face heat and flush. He was so tall, I'm six feet one in my heels, and he was easily four or five inches taller than me.

"Nice to meet you." Jeff shifted his eyes down at me with a smirk that screamed, 'oh, God, not another one.' Conceited bastard probably thinks I'm a stupid groupie. He turned away from me, while my roaming eyes glanced down again to make sure there wasn't a ring on his finger. I wondered if he'd felt the same thing I had when he touched me.

He pulled his hand back, then slid them both in the pockets of his slacks pulling the fabric taut across the front. *Good mother of God, is that the outline of his …?* My breath hitched. I snapped my eyes back up to his face to avoid being caught checking out his junk.

We exchanged the 'do you come here often' banter and other forced small talk before I peeked at my phone, seeing it was almost ten o'clock. Connor was doing most of the talking. I got the feeling he was never at a loss for words. It felt weird talking to them, watching Jeff's eyes roam the restaurant. I couldn't help but speculate that he was looking for someone and I was curious what was going on in that beautiful head of his.

"I hate to meet and run, but I need to get home. You know, like Cinderella." I joked. Jesus fucking hell, I was standing there in my H&M special, and they were dressed to the hilt. I was already a ragamuffin to them.

"I always thought midnight was the bewitching hour," Tristan chimed in.

"Not tonight." I turned to Candace and Tristan to tell them good-bye. Tristan reached forward and wrapped his arms around me. *Really? Are you trying to stake claim to me?* I wanted to grab his fingers, bend them back one at a time, and pry his freaking hands off me; instead, I shrugged myself free and then told him and Candace bye.

Turning back to Connor and Jeff, I flashed a quick smile. "Maybe I'll see you guys around sometime."

As I reached for my purse and grabbed my cellphone off the bar, Connor reached across and slid a business card into my hand. "Stay in touch," he said with a wink. "We're going to have to get going, too. It's late; we can walk you to your car if you want."

"I'm fine, but thanks for the offer." I smiled at Connor. "I'm parked right out front." I smiled again at both of them, gave a quick hand wave, and headed toward the front door.

Once in my car, I looked at the business card. It was Jeff's card, not Connor's. Connor must be the wingman.

He'd acted so aloof; maybe he wasn't interested. *Well, I am, and I have his business card.*

One nagging thought was for certain; I felt like an ass for throwing myself at him. I slipped the card in the outside zipper pocket of my purse.

Chapter 2

My mother had become an invaluable part of reviving my social life, which had hovered around the need for life support, but I was limited on Friday nights by her patience after watching two-year old Abby during the week. She loved her grandchild, but being older and watching a toddler was proving to be a challenge. In addition to chasing after a non-stop, into-everything, talk-your-head-off baby, my stepfather needed her assistance and attention, though he would say otherwise.

My Friday night had to be cut short in order to pick up Abby.

Later that night, I lay in bed, my mind racing, I was still awestruck by how tall and handsome Jeff was, confused by his standoffish response to me, and even more puzzled by Connor giving me his card. Why had it been Connor who had given it to me? Why hadn't Jeff asked for my phone number? Why didn't Jeff give me his card? Damn him for being so fucking good-looking.

****

I would be lying if I said Jeff was the farthest person from my mind the next morning. He was in my waking thoughts as I lay on my back, eyes focused on the ceiling, seemingly under a spell named Jeff. I was trying to put together the puzzle pieces that had been tossed onto the table before me over the past twelve hours. What should I make of last night, and what should I do next? Everything happens for a reason; that's what they say. So was the thing that happened for a reason meeting Jeff or being forced to leave early?

Well I couldn't call him over the weekend; all I had was a business card with a work number. Who does that anyway? Gives out a work number? Oh, right, Connor gave it to me. Jeff didn't give me his number. He didn't ask me for my number. He barely even said ten words to me. If I saw him again and he didn't ask for my phone number, I'd know for sure he wasn't interested. No, I wouldn't call. I refused to call.

After dragging myself out of bed, I rifled through my dresser, looking for some sexy underwear. I yanked my pastel pink mini sundress off a hanger and trudged down the hallway to the shower. My thoughts kept going back to Jeff. *Reality, Nikki; reel it back in,* I kept telling myself over and over that he was an untouchable, that's why he acted that way last night. *He won't give me the time of day because I'm not on his level.*

Sky, my ex-husband, needed me to bring Abby to his house that morning because his car was in the shop, again. He drove what I called patchwork orange. His rust-bucket jalopy car from hell was a hideous orange color and was in the shop more than it was out. I didn't understand how it passed inspections.

Once I had myself dressed and ready, I rushed Abby up from her deep sleep, got her dressed then she was hoisted up onto my hip for the trip downstairs to make her second favorite food, French Toast.

While she sat quietly picking at her food, I began the searching and digging in my purse for my car keys. Then, as I was rummaging in the outside pocket, there it was, Jeff's card, teasing me, goading me, beckoning me. The butterflies in my stomach resurfaced, while I stood staring at it like the card had magical powers. Finally, I stuffed it back into the zipper pocket, zipping it in, and trapping the devil that was tempting me.

"How're you doing over there, baby?" I asked Abby.

"I done, Mommy."

"Okay, let's go brush your teeth and wash your face. Then we can go find Daddy."

"Yay!" Abby's excitement was a breath of fresh air. She loved her daddy. I was looking forward to seeing him too.

He was my reality. No matter how fucked up it sounds, I was still holding on to him, even after two years apart. Saturday mornings had become our time. I had been on plenty of dates in the past two years yet our sex life remained intact, more than intact; we were still like super magnets whenever we were close to each other. We saw each other almost every week. I still had a strong physical attraction to him and probably always would.

He had tried so hard to convince me not to follow through on the divorce, but my tolerance of his irresponsible work habits had been pushed to the brink. His promises to change were of no consequence. I'd heard it all so many times, but there was no follow through or even the slightest attempt to really change. Despite the overwhelming sexual chemistry, I had outgrown his uninspired laziness. I couldn't take it anymore. I was tired of shouldering the responsibility of supporting our family while he played video games and dabbled in meager jobs with no hope of becoming a reliable income source.

I drove over to Sky's house with Abby, like I'd promised him I would. I didn't have anything planned for the day. Sky was seeing some woman he'd met in a restaurant, but it wasn't serious; at least, that's what he told me. I wasn't sure if she'd be at his house or not, but was hoping she wasn't. It was awkward for me if he had a girlfriend over when I was there.

I often wondered if any of them asked him what happened between us. We looked so right together, we got along great, and our senses of humor were so similar. We were still like best friends. Many times, I looked at the women he dated and wondered why her, but it's not my business to interfere in anymore. As long as they didn't do anything stupid where Abby was concerned, I didn't care. I can't care. *Oh, who am I fooling? I do care.*

I rang Sky's doorbell, and he answered in his blue silk boxers that I had bought him on one of my shopping sprees. He looked very delectable standing in front of me. I could feel the spasms and dampness beginning to rage against the cloth down there.

"Hey, baby girl!" He grabbed Abby and gave her a big hug and kiss on the cheek like he hadn't seen her in months.

She wrapped her little arms around his neck and squeezed tight. "Daddy!"

Turning to me, he said, "Nik, you look beautiful as ever. Pink is my favorite color on you." He winked. "You want to come in for some coffee?"

"Sure." Who in their right mind can resist a cup of coffee from a sexy guy in silk boxers?

He set Abby down in the living room next to her toys he kept in his apartment, and we walked into the adjoining kitchen.

"What do you have planned for today?" he asked me.

"Nothing special; maybe I'll go find Jackie and head to the mall." Jackie was my best friend. We had known each other since kindergarten. We learned to ride bikes together, we were in Girl Scouts together, and we got our first job modeling together. We hit a rough patch in high school that separated us for some years, but fate brought us back together when we were in college.

"How about you? What's on your agenda?" I sat at the small table with my eyes drinking him in from his beautiful face to his sexy toes as he fumbled with the coffee maker. My tongue licked across my bottom lip, then I bit down gently.

"I'm hoping to get back to sleep for an hour before I take Abby to the park. I bought her a new movie; hopefully that does the trick to keep her occupied."

"That's terrible, Sky," I said, my brow furrowing. "She's a baby. You can't just leave her sitting there alone for an hour while you sleep."

"I didn't plan to leave her alone for that long; I'll lie on the couch near her. I'm pretty sure I won't go back to sleep. It's just wishful thinking."

He walked over to the table and set both mugs down. My eyes were drawn to his tight, muscular abdomen that rippled all the way down then disappeared underneath his waistband. My heart skipped a beat thinking about the last time we had been together, two long weeks ago. He turned to get the cream and sugar, and my eyes followed him, admiring his perfect round ass. His arms were muscular and strong, and his shoulders were broad, tapering into a slim waist. Now *this* was a fine ass man! He was sexy as hell; I squeezed my thighs together and felt the tingle run through my heat. He knew he was tantalizing me.

"I'll tell you what I'd really like to do." He peered over his shoulder with those wicked blue-gray eyes. Our eyes met. I knew that look all too well.

"There's no time. Abby will get restless."

"Not even for a quickie? Can you really say no to me?" He grabbed at the front of his boxers, pulling the soft, supple thin material tightly around his growing erection as he closed the distance between us. The wink sealed my fate. All he had to do was say the word.

My sex-o-meter went from six, because I'd wanted him when he first opened the door, to ten just like that, and now I had to have him in me. "Fifteen minutes. It has to be quick."

He ran his fingers along my jaw, toward the back of my head through my hair, then pulled his fingers lightly back to the front of my neck and down my chest. "That's my girl. Go get ready while I put the movie in for Abby." He sent shivers up my spine with his touch. This was definitely not the reason for the divorce.

Sky came in his room and saw me lying on my side, arm bent and propping up my head, my hair pushed back, leaving my shoulder and breasts exposed, facing him in the matching panty and bra set he liked the most; red satin, with little hearts and bows. "You vixen; you want this just as much as I do." He walked over to me, pulling down his boxers and revealing his full erection as he climbed on the bed near me.

Once he was within hands reach, I encircled him gently with my fingers. I coaxed him in closer to me, then licked the dripping dew from the tip before I wrapped my waiting lips around his engorged helmet. I loved sucking him, especially when we didn't have a lot of time. I controlled him. It was a way for me to get him to the brink of exploding, then I'd pull him out of my mouth before bringing him to the edge again.

As I continued to work his length in and out of my mouth, he removed my panties just before sliding his fingers over my mound, then in and out of me.

"You're so wet," he growled out. "It never fails, baby. I love it when you want me."

I wanted to feel him in me so bad I was bucking and grinding into his hand.

"You're so fucking beautiful, Nik."

I managed to get one word out of my mouth past his erection that I had sucked deep into my throat; "Thanks." My sucking became more intense as my desire grew.

"Slow down, baby, or it'll be over before we get started. It's been a while for me, too," Sky said as he rubbed his fingers through my hair. *Nikki, don't even ask; it's not your business.*

He pulled back out of my mouth, rolled me onto my back, then grabbed my legs behind my knees, pushing them forward. He leaned in and ran his tongue across my clit, through the slick folds, and to my waiting hole.

"I need to feel you inside me, Sky."

"You will, baby; trust me, you will." He plunged his tongue deep inside of me over and over, causing me to groan and wiggle my hips up against his mouth. He was so skilled. He flicked and sucked my clit until he forced me to orgasm.

"Holy fuck!" My hands fisted his hair, then dropped to grasp the sheets.

"Yeah, enjoy that, baby. This is just the beginning."

"Now, please! I'm begging you, now."

He plunged his fingers deep into me, finger fucking me as I moaned his name through clenched teeth and raised my hips to meet his thrusts. He withdrew his hand and licked my juices off of each digit. Watching him do that sent a feverish ripple from my sex up to my scalp. My lower back arched as I closed my eyes, thinking how good it would feel to have him sink into me. My sex spasmed over and over in anticipation of feeling him stretch me, fill me, fuck me.

I grabbed at him, hoping to pull him into me when he rubbed his swollen head against my slit, but he backed away -- *fucking tease*. Without warning, he plunged deep, filling me as I let out a throaty moan of satisfaction and appreciation. He continued to stroke me and grind into me deep, while thumbing my clit until he made me orgasm again.

"Oh, damn!" I moaned out into my forearm to try to silence myself. His intensity grew as he thrust into me, pounding flesh against flesh, sweat trickling down the sides of his face. I asked him, no, begged him, to find his release inside me. I wanted to feel his hot seed fill my cunt.

He slowed down to regain his composure before he continued to slam into me, then eased out, slammed again, eased out -- *oh God*. He simultaneously worked my hot bud like a guitar player plucking sweet notes on the strings. I covered my own mouth with my hands to muffle my screams as he brought me to orgasm after orgasm. Damn this fucking man; no one fucks me like he does.

He let out an animalistic moan as he lowered his head with his eyes closed tight, pressing tightly inside of me as far as he could, digging his fingers into my hips – overflowing me with his hot juices.

He collapsed on top of me, and we lay in each other's arms for a few minutes. It was just like old times. Hot, passionate sex, then melt into each other. No words were needed or wanted. Only today was different. Today, Jeff was on my mind as I lay next to Sky. I couldn't help but wonder what fucking him would be like.

I tried to get up but met resistance. Sky's arm was holding me in place across my waist.

"I have to go." I could feel his exhausted shaft throbbing inside me.

"Let me hold you just a few more minutes." His breath was warm against my neck. He pushed my hair out of the way and showered me with quick kisses, his warm, soft lips gently moving from my neck, up to my ear, where he whispered, "I wish you'd stay ... forever." He wrapped his arms around me tighter.

"We tried that already, babe; it didn't work, remember? We aren't on the same page."

I wished we were, but I refused to be broke. It was difficult to choke back the tears. I had grown to despise him as a husband, but I loved him as my fuck buddy.

I quickly slid out from underneath his loosening grip. I took a quick shower before dressing and returning to the living room, where Abby was playing with her dolls and watching the new movie.

For his wonderful and satisfying performance, I agreed to stay for an hour so he could take a quick nap. When he woke, I knew I needed to leave before we repeated. I was so addicted to him.

Chapter 3

By Monday afternoon, after an entire weekend of mulling over intriguing thoughts of Jeff, happy hour on Friday, and the card, I was wrestling with the idea of biting the bullet and calling him. The butterflies in my stomach had me so amped up. I was a bundle of nerves, and I barely got any work done all day. I sat holding his business card in one hand and my cellphone in the other, staring at his name and the numbers, drawn into the essence of the mysterious card owner.

"Just call him already," Georgia's voice called over my shoulder.

"What?"

"You've been pulling that card out of your purse and putting it back for hours. Just call him."

"I need to talk to you."

"C'mon, let's take a quick walk."

I dropped my phone into my purse and closed the bottom drawer, pushed my chair back from the desk and stood, then rounded my desk. We walked side by side down the hallway in silence until we reached the empty break area.

"So what's up?" Georgia said.

"I just wanted to bounce something off of you; tell me what you think." I looked down at my hand, still holding the card tight. "After you left Friday night, Connor, the shorter of those two guys from the restaurant came over with Jeff, and he introduced himself to me." I raised my eyes back to meet hers.

"That's kind of forward, but whatever; it's all good, right?"

"Yeah, that part was fine. Jeff, the taller, gorgeous one, walked over, but he didn't introduce himself. I introduced myself to him." With my eyebrows furrowed and shoulders hunched, I continued, "I practically threw myself at him." My head turned toward the raised hand holding the card. "And Jeff didn't give me this card. Connor gave it to me just before I left."

"Introducing yourself isn't a crime, Nikki; you'll be okay. That's kind of weird with the card, though. Maybe he's shy. Does it say what he does?"

"No, it only has the company logo, his name, and phone number. It's weird. He's weird, and his card is weird. That's what's been eating at me all weekend and today. Is he even interested? Why is Connor handing out his business cards for him? What if I call and he doesn't even remember me?"

"First of all, he has to remember you. It was just Friday, and you're gorgeous. There's no way he forgot you. Second, he may just have a hard time with that first introduction so Connor helped him out. Give him a call, and if he's a weirdo, chalk it up to something that was worth a try, and move on."

"You're right. Thanks. My friend Jackie tried to convince me to call while we were out shopping on Saturday, too. I will give him a call. Fuck it, what do I have to lose, right?"

"Exactly."

We walked back to our department, Georgia wished me luck, and I smiled my thanks before lowering myself into my seat at my desk. I set the card down on the desk in front of me, and, with my two index fingers, slid it up toward my monitor, then back to the edge of the desk. Inhaling deeply, I pulled open the bottom drawer of the desk that had my purse in it, reached in like it was a grab bag, and pulled out my phone. Inhaling, I leaned my head back, and closed my eyes briefly before lifting my head, exhaling, and opening my eyes. With resolve, I began pressing the numbers as they were listed on the card.

As the phone rang, my stomach churned like a man on a motorcycle was driving figure eights and popping wheelies in there. My heart raced, and my palms were damp. My fingernails tapped with rapid speed on the desktop as I waited. I would only allow four rings before hanging up. It was answered on the third ring by a pleasant-sounding woman, "Good afternoon; Jeffrey Carrington's office."

"Hello, may I speak with Jeff Carrington, please," I said.

"May I ask who's calling, please?"

"This is Nikki Carmichael."

"Do you have an account with us, Ms. Carmichael?"

"No ma'am, this isn't business related." *Fuck, I'm being screened. Maybe I'm not important enough to talk to him.*

"Mr. Carrington is on another call at the moment, may I transfer you to his voicemail so you can leave a message?"

"Yes, please. Thank you." *What the hell am I doing? This is crazy. I should hang up before his machine picks up ...*

"Hi Jeff, you may not remember me. It's Nikki; we met briefly Friday night. Connor gave me your card. If you have time, you can call me back on my cellphone." I left my phone number. It was on him now to either call me back or not.

I pressed end on the call, and a surge of regret washed over my body. I couldn't help but question if I should've even made the call in the first place. Why was I throwing myself at this guy? I picked up the card, slid it back into the outside pocket of my purse, and zipped it in. The message was on voicemail now, and I couldn't take it back no matter how much I regretted making it. All I could do now was hope his voicemail malfunctioned.

****

The next morning as I was scrambling in a mad rush to get ready for work, my cellphone rang. My heart sank. Calls early in the morning or late at night are known to be bad news. I ran into the bedroom and picked it up off my bed just in time to see an unfamiliar number.

"Hello?"

"May I speak with Nikki?" the deep voice asked.

"Who's calling?"

"Jeff, Jeff Carrington."

I was in shock, he actually called. But I was in a rush and couldn't believe he called so early. "Uh, hi, Jeff. This is Nikki." I stood there – excited, yet annoyed. I didn't have much time to spare in the mornings.

"I got your message. I have some time after my last meeting today. Would you like to meet after work?"

"Sure, I can meet you after work; just let me know where."

"Let's go to the bar where we met on Friday. Does five thirty sound good?"

"Yes; that's perfect. I'll see you then."

I hung up and stared at my phone as if it were responsible for what had just happened. I had been robbed of precious time by its ringing.

Mornings like these were the days I was most grateful for my mom. I didn't have to get Abby up out of bed and dressed because Mom had agreed to come to my house to watch her.

Change in outfit plans; now I had to think of something different to wear, something Jeff worthy. My clothes were all well organized and coordinated like Garanimals. I went to the closet and began flipping through hangers, pausing just long enough to give a quick yes or no. I was assessing each suit and dress as if it were being measured on a fuckability meter. I had no intention of having sex with this guy, but I wanted him to desire me, to want to have sex with me.

I found a nice low-cut red wraparound dress that gave my smallish boobs the enhancement they desperately needed to look enticing. Glancing at my less-than-satisfactory chest, I promised myself again that, one day, I was going to come into enough money to buy the tits of my dreams.

Instead of the sexy G-string, I grabbed a pair of nice beige cotton lace-edged panties from the drawer. I ripped the black blazer off its hanger, tucked it under my arm, slipped on my four-inch black patent leather pumps, scooped up my phone and purse, and headed down the stairs.

"Bye, Mom; thanks again for coming over and for everything." One day I'm going to surprise my mom and not be running late. Until then, I'd kiss her on the cheek as she stood by the front door and be thankful she had her own key and that she knew me so well.

"Have a nice day, sweetie."

"Oh, I'll be home late, is that okay? Can you stay later?"

"I'll take my precious little one with me to run a few errands. Come pick Abby up at the house on your way home."

"Thanks, again, Mom; you're the best. I love you."

"I love you too, sweetie."

I had more work sitting on my desk when I arrived that morning than I'd had all last week. Some of it was due to not accomplishing anything the previous day aside from twiddling that damn business card. My mind was all over the place.

"Did you talk to him yet?"

I glanced up to see Georgia standing near my desk. "Yeah, he called this morning."

"I didn't hear your phone."

"He called while I was getting ready for work."

"That's insane. I wonder why so early."

"Who knows. I'm telling you, he seems a little weird to me. But we're meeting tonight after work for a drink."

I was happy the place Jeff had picked for us to meet later was within walking distance so my car could stay in the parking garage.

"Don't stay out too late."

"I won't, Mother." We laughed together as Georgia walked away.

The day flew by. I needed a drink in the worst way. My head was pounding from crunching numbers all day. I worked in marketing. I never wanted to be an accountant, but it felt like I was part of a career change from hell. Before anyone had a chance to stop by and slow me down, I gathered my purse, phone, and jacket and headed to the restroom for one last vanity check. My fingers substituted for a comb, and I applied my sheer lip gloss. *If this guy doesn't want me, he's dead below the waist.* I grabbed my things and headed for the elevator.

Chapter 4

"How did it go yesterday?" Georgia was standing beside my desk waiting for me. She had her hand on her hip, one ankle crossed over the other and propped up on her toe, and a wry smile plastered on her face. She looked like she was ready for a lengthy conversation.

I took a couple steps closer before answering her question, "It was okay."

"That's it? Just okay?" She uncrossed her ankle and stood with her feet hip-width apart. Her hand lifted from her hip as she crossed her arms over her chest.

"Let's go get some coffee. I need it, and I'll fill you in."

"Sure."

I pulled open my lower desk drawer, dropped my purse and phone in and picked up my oversized mug from my desk. The two of us talked as we walked down the hall.

"So I got there on time, five thirty like we agreed, and sat and waited for him for twenty-five minutes. He set the place and time; he could have at least gotten there when he said."

"Did he at least call or text he was running late?"

"Nope, neither. So you can imagine how pissed I was getting. He didn't even apologize or give me a reason when he got there. He pretended like he was on time or like I should be happy he showed up. Arrogant bastard."

"Wow, that's…wow." Georgia reached for one of the Styrofoam cups stacked next to the coffee machine. "How was talking to him after he got there?"

"Perplexing. My questions were met with short answers at first. You know how hard it is to get a conversation going with someone like that?"

"Yeah, that would be aggravating."

"Aggravating is an understatement."

Georgia poured her coffee into her cup, then reached over to fill mine, leaving plenty of room for my creamer. "Did you cross him off your list yet?"

"Hell no, not yet. Sitting across from him was frustrating, but he's so damn good-looking. I could hardly take it, and I decided based on looks alone, he gets one final chance." I reached to get my favorite International Delight French Vanilla creamer and poured it into my cup until it nearly overflowed. "We're going to dinner on Saturday, then going to The Castle."

Georgia stopped on a dime, set her cup down, and her mouth dropping open as she stared at me. "Okay ...I'm shocked."

"If he blows it Saturday, though, it's over; done, no more."

"I never thought I'd say this, but I can't wait for Monday now."

The week seemed to drag on. I expected to hear from Jeff, but he never called until Saturday morning. He was obviously a morning person, which I found out when my phone rang at six thirty AM on Saturday. I, on the other hand, am not. He sounded chipper and wide awake, while I had the I-just-woke-the-fuck-up-thank-you-very-much voice echoing back at me.

Jeff confirmed our dinner plans and got my address so he could come pick me up. I couldn't help but wonder if he'd be on time, and whether we would make the reservation on time. I decided not to stress out over him. I had a few hours to tidy up the house and spend with Abby before Sky picked her up for the weekend. Once they left, I crammed all of her toys into the toy box in the closet. Then I was off to the salon to get my nails done before coming back home to get ready. *After all that effort, this guy better not disappoint me tonight.*

Jeff arrived early. I was still in my sweats when I let him in, and he had to wait a few minutes for me to finish getting ready. I had hesitated to let him come pick me up, but figured if we were going to spend the better part of the night together, why should I drive? At least if he was driving and ended up being a complete bore, I could have a few drinks and not worry about getting a ticket.

I felt like it was senior prom with him sitting downstairs waiting for me to make my grand entrance. My hair was done. I chose to wear it curly, more curly than normal. I had set it on hot curlers after blowing it dry then back combed it to add more volume. I was looking forward to going out and wanted to look tempting to every man in there in case Jeff failed to come through that night.

I slipped on my silky Lemon chiffon chemise dress that skimmed down my body. It was short; the hemline was a couple inches just below the curve of my ass. My nipples were visible; I couldn't wear a bra with this dress. I wanted him to want me. I wanted to be so irresistible that he wouldn't be able to keep from pawing and grabbing at me. I wanted him to want me so bad he'd push me up against a wall and take me in an alley. *I better stop; I can feel the wetness coming through my tiny G-string already.*

I loved that he was so tall and I could wear my tiger print six-inch sling-back pumps with black sequins covering the toe. They had a leopard spotted platform and gold piping that matched the heel. These were the most expensive shoes in my collection. I was six feet two inches tall in these heels; I'd be just a couple inches shorter than him. The finishing touch of face powder was dabbed on before I took one more look at myself in the mirror. *You're sexy, Nikki Carmichael.* I spritzed on my Be Enchanted body spray and was ready.

I pulled my door shut behind me and began the descent of the stairs into the foyer. Halfway down the stairs, I could smell his cologne. His scent was as sexy as he was. A musky, woodsy, spicy goodness … then I got a really good look at him, sitting there looking absolutely stunning as ever. It was so hard to believe I had such a gorgeous man sitting in my tiny two-bedroom house, waiting for me. I didn't go out with unattractive men, but Jeff was much nicer looking than all of them. I hated to admit it, but he was even better looking than Sky.

He wore a nice pale green dress shirt but no tie; the sleeves were rolled up midway on his forearm and he had chosen black slacks. He looked over, shifting his seizing brown eyes up the staircase at me, as I stepped down each rung like a wobbly-kneed new born deer. My knees shook at the sight of him staring up at me. His eyes were like heat-seeking missiles. *Guess where the heat is?* He stood and walked over to the bottom of the stairs. He held his hand out to steady me as I stepped down the last two steps. "You look fantastic."

"Thank you, you look quite amazing yourself." His fuckability scale was well beyond ten. "Let me just grab my purse and I'll be ready."

"No problem. I'm in your driveway."

I laughed. "It's actually the neighbor's driveway. It's okay, though; they're used to people who come over to my house pulling in there." I went into the kitchen to make sure the back door was locked, shut the door to the basement, grabbed my keys and gold clutch purse, and continued out to the living room. My eyes lapped him up from head to toe as I walked toward him. "I'm ready."

Never in my wildest imagination would I have suspected a Nissan GT-R to be sitting in my neighbor's driveway. It was the only car there, though, so it had to be his. This guy had money, but I already suspected that. He hit the key fob to unlock it, then opened the passenger door for me.

"Thank you."

He told me about the features of the car as we drove to the restaurant. Little did he know I loved cars and knew all about this one; he wasn't telling me anything new. The only difference between him and me was that I would never be able to afford one.

We made it to Bern's Steakhouse on time and were seated immediately. Walking through the restaurant to our table, I felt plenty of eyes on us.

I've never eaten there and one glance at the prices on the menu confirmed why. No man I had dated up to this point had the money to eat at a restaurant like this.

"Good evening, my name is Missy, and I'll be your server this evening." The stunning young brunette dug in her pocket, eventually extracting a pen. "May I start you with something to drink?"

"I'll have a glass of water, please," I quickly chimed in. I was taken aback by the price of a glass of wine. I'd be skipping drinking tonight, at least for now.

Jeff looked at me with his melt-me-in-my-seat sexy eyes, then placed his large, strong hand over mine. An electric current charged through my veins. "Care to join me with a glass of wine this evening?"

"Sure." I panted. I felt heat rush to my face while the butterflies began their revelry, and my eyes turned downward to look at his hand on mine. The riveting tingles took over my senses again, shooting into my hand and up my arm, melting me. I felt it all the way to my sex. How could I resist anything he was offering? I wanted that hand on my body.

"Great," he said, then turning to Missy, he said, "We'd like a bottle of the Burgundy, please. And a second glass of water, no lemon." My eyes snapped up to meet his as my eyebrows pulled tight. I couldn't believe he had just ordered a whole bottle. Maybe he'd misread the price list.

"Thank you. I'll be right back with your drinks."

"This place is so lovely." I looked around, wanting to pinch myself. I couldn't believe I was there.

"Have you been here before?"

"No, this is my first time; how about you?"

"I come here quite a bit. Business dinners and client meetings, you know."

No, I don't know. Do I ask him again today what he does? He had cleverly avoided the question when we'd met Tuesday night.

The infamous awkward silence cloaked us, and I found myself wanting to squirm in my chair. My mind was racing with things I'd love to ask, but having witnessed his ability to avoid and change the subject, I wasn't sure it would've proven fruitful.

Our young, cute, and perky waitress arrived with our water and wine. She adeptly opened the bottle and poured our first glass, requesting that Jeff make sure it was acceptable. My gaze was fixed on his lips as they touched the edge of the glass. I was trying to use mind power to have him lean in and kiss me, sharing the taste of wine. Fail. Jeff nodded his seal of approval.

We placed our dinner order before she left.

I lifted my glass to my lips taking a small sip of the ruby beverage into my mouth. The light earthiness and rich, delicious flavor invited me to sip again.

"What do you think?" Jeff asked, his eyes staring deep into my soul.

"Of the wine? Oh, it's very good." *Of you? I'd love to lick and taste you everywhere. I'm sure you're delicious and if you keep looking at me like that, you'll melt my G-string clean off.* I licked my lower lip slowly as I held my gaze on him.

"Good, I'm glad you like it."

We enjoyed the wine and continued with more small talk. I was hoping the wine would loosen Jeff up a little more so the rest of the night could be fun.

Before long, our meals were brought out. I had tried to order a salad; the steak ordering process seemed like a math chart that took special training to decipher and navigate. Jeff insisted I try the Filet Mignon and ordered for me. I ordered my sides of onion rings -- I have a love of onion rings that can't be explained -- and rice pilaf. He selected the Strip steak, baked potato with the works, and steamed broccoli.

The conversation got easier with each sip of wine -- funny how alcohol works. I noticed he refilled my glass, but not his. Probably a good thing since he's driving.

The evening was going really well so far. We finished our meal, and he let me know we were going to The Castle. Seemed like an odd club choice since neither of us visibly had a gothic or steam punk flair, but I'm always open to new stuff, so I wasn't complaining. He settled up the bill, and I gathered my purse.

As I stood, Jeff placed his hand on my lower back, which was the equivalent to pushing the floodgate button while touching me with an electric wand. I inhaled slow and deep. The tingles radiated through me. I could feel the wetness breaching the tiny silk barrier. After staring into his inviting eyes and listening to his deep, husky voice throughout dinner, I longed for him to kiss me.

We walked out to the car, where the perfect gentleman opened my door for me. Before I was able to lower myself into my seat, he stroked my face with his hands, our eyes fixed on each other. I tilted my head slightly into his hand as he caressed me with the gentlest touch. *Is he reading my mind?* I was waiting for him to lean in and kiss me. I leaned forward and held my gaze on him, wanting his mouth to consume mine, waiting to taste him. Instead, he pulled back. I sighed and sat down, and once I was situated in my seat, he shut the door. Fuck, fuck, FUCK!

I wasn't familiar with where The Castle was located or how to get there from the restaurant, and my sense of direction had been tampered with by the wine. To be honest, half the time, if it wasn't for the navigator app on my phone, I'd be lost. As Jeff drove down the street, I realized each house was getting vaster than the previous one. I was mesmerized, sitting in the passenger seat as stiff as a statue. I thought he was driving through a very wealthy section of town to get to our destination, until he clicked on his turn signal and turned into a gated driveway. He slid a card into the card reader at the gate to open it, then drove through and up the driveway, stopping right outside the garage.

"We're here. Come on in." I pulled the door open and got out, looking in astonishment, and taking in the entire surreal sprawling landscaped scene. There was a four-car garage. I drew in a deep breath as I realized *this* was the castle he had been talking about, this was the fucking castle.

It was when I looked back down the driveway that I noticed the gate in front of the driveway had the look of one that would possibly be found in front of a castle. This home was really nice; he obviously used a play on words.

"Nik, come on." I quickly walked over to join him at the bottom of the steps before walking up to the front entrance door.

He unlocked the front door and pushed it open. "After you," he said, gesturing politely. I walked over the threshold and stopped. *Are you shitting me? Am I on an episode of Cribs?* This house was amazing.

It was beautiful, endless square feet of meticulously decorated opulence. As we stepped through the double entry doors, we walked onto a large white marble-floored foyer that opened all the way up to the second floor, where there were two huge skylights. Two hardwood curved staircases stood about twenty to thirty feet from the front door; large planters, each with a ten to twelve-foot plant, were positioned at the bottom. At the top of the stairs, there was a walkway balcony that extended all the way from the leftmost corner, around the walls of the living room to the rightmost corner. There were four columns stretching to the ceiling. Looking between the staircases on the main floor, I could see the back room.

"Oh my god, do you live here?" Mystery man had just become even more arcane. I had known he was strange, but now I found myself hoping he wasn't dangerous. I had no idea why he had brought me here.

"Yes, this is mine."

The living room was right off to the right of the foyer. It had an open ceiling that reached up to the second floor as well.

"This is amazing."

"I'll show you around; we can start in the kitchen."

I bent to take my shoes off. "Do you cook?"

"Only if I absolutely have to; and leave those on."

I pulled the straps back over my heels. Jeff took me through the house, making sure to show me the huge kitchen that had a ten-foot section of wall made of accordion glass panels that opened, extending the living space out to a beautiful, lit covered patio with a full stainless steel outdoor kitchen, patio furniture, and a well-lit walking path.

"What's out at the other end of the lights?"

"The path leads to the pool and pool house." Of course; because why wouldn't he have a pool and a pool house?

Back inside the house, the kitchen opened up to the right, into the gathering room, as he called it. How rich do you have to be to have a gathering room? I'd never even heard of such a thing. The gathering room was decorated with white leather furniture and had a floor-to-ceiling fireplace. "Part of this space was supposed to be an office, but I don't work from home or have a desire for an office. I told them to knock down the wall that would've been here and add a door on both ends of the room to lead into the conservatory." He used his finger to point out where the wall would have been between the gathering room and the area that should have been an office.

"What do you use this for?" We stepped through the door and into the conservatory. The room looked so comfortable, and it had French doors that led out to the back patio.

"If I'm having a party, I can set up another table in this area for guests." The conservatory had a wet bar and additional seating as well. We stepped back into the space that was supposed to have been the office and crossed the room back into the foyer. "Under each of the staircases is a half bath." *Kind of excessive.* We walked back through the staircases and into the kitchen.

Off to the other side of the kitchen was a butler pantry that seemed like it was the size of Abby's bedroom. So … do people have a butler if they have a butler pantry? Walking through the butler pantry led us into the dining room. There was a table large enough to seat sixteen people. There was a wide pillar, probably two-feet wide with a four-way fireplace that separated the dining room and the smaller, more intimate living room.

The living room had a television, and the fireplace wall on this side had a stone surround. It seemed more livable than any other space in the house so far, besides the kitchen.

"Your house is amazing." What do you say to someone who has seen my shack of a house earlier then brings me to his emperor's castle? I was completely in awe; I'd never been inside a house like this. The closest I'd been were the few times when my mom had taken me to open houses when I was younger.

We climbed the stairs so he could show me the second floor. None of the doors to the bedrooms were visible from the foyer; each had a small hallway off the balcony. He told me the house has six bedrooms, six full and two half baths. We stepped just inside the first four bedrooms far enough to see the pristine staging without exploring the rooms. Each seemed like they were the size of my entire one-thousand-square-foot house and each had its own bathroom. I couldn't help but wonder why he'd really brought me here. And why had he skipped that fifth hall?

Next, we went down the stairs to the full finished basement, which had a beautifully appointed movie theater with seating for twenty, a bar, and a fitness space that was like a mini Planet Fitness, a basement master suite, and kitchenette. Nothing was missed in this house as far as I could tell, but I also lived in a two-bedroom house that only has a living room, kitchen, and a make-shift dining area downstairs with two bedrooms and two bathrooms upstairs, so what did I know?

He then led me to a corner of the basement and pressed a button on the wall. Within seconds, a door slid open and revealed an elevator. *Really? A fucking elevator? Again, why did he bring me here?*

He pressed the button and the doors closed.

"Now you will see where I spend the majority of my time when I'm not at work or by the pool."

The doors closed. His heated eyes met mine. My mind wandered, and I tried the telepathy thing again. I wanted him to kiss me, take me. Press me into the wall of the elevator, his mouth consuming mine, his hands grabbing my hair, his strong fingers pulling me and lifting me to wrap my legs around his waist as our lips are locked. Feel his strong fingers slide inside my wet heat. Nope, it still wasn't working.

When the elevator opened, we stepped into a hallway with a set of double doors right in front of us.

"This is my bedroom."

He opened the doors to reveal the second-floor ridiculous master suite, as if the elevator to the basement wasn't outlandish enough. He ushered me into a very spacious bedroom, yet there was no bed. *Maybe he has one of those Murphy beds or a sofa pull-out,* I thought.

"How high is this ceiling?"

"It's ten feet in here."

The room had furniture arranged for seating and there was a three-sided gas fireplace. There was a couch, two chairs, and a coffee table. A laptop was sitting on the coffee table. There was a double door on the wall between the two chairs.

I wasn't sure how much more of this house I could take. I felt like a pauper who had escaped and sneaked into a mansion. I was waiting for security to come get my broke ass and throw me out. He placed his electrically charged fingertips on my lower back and escorted me through the double doors into a room that actually looked like a regular bedroom, that is if by regular you mean super-sized-regular.

The bedroom had a huge king-size poster bed with a canopy attached. It sat against a wall in the middle of two floor-to-ceiling windows that made it look breathtakingly grand. On the wall opposite from the bed was a very large flat screen TV.

"So, wait, if this is the bedroom –"

"That was the sitting area; it's part of the bedroom."

I giggled at the absurdity of having a sitting room. My eyes drank in the furnishings, which were top line.

"That TV is huge. And how nice is that to watch TV while lying in bed?"

"It makes me not want to get up on Sunday mornings."

"I'll bet."

The en suite bathroom had marble sink countertops, a double or triple-sized shower, a huge sunken soaker tub, heated marble floor, and stainless steel fixtures. As we walked out of the bathroom, Jeff swung open the doors on each side of the small hallway that opened to two very large walk-in closets, each almost the size of small bedrooms.

I felt like I had stepped into a magazine photo. He told me his assistant had helped him find the decorator when he purchased the home. I stood in amazement, taking in the entire room, my mind boggled by his home. One day, I wanted this. I wanted a huge house just like this.

"You'll never guess what I like the most in the house right now," Jeff said as he held my hands. Our eyes met. If my eyes could talk, I knew they were saying 'kiss me, damn it.' His lips were perfect and slightly tinted from the wine.

"I will guess…the master bedroom or that amazing movie theater."

"Right now, it's you."

Corny; he's got no real swag. He pulled me into him, holding me by my shoulders and kissed me with the utmost delicacy. He pulled back and stared into my eyes. Swag or not, he was fine as hell and kissed like an angel.

"You don't mind being here, do you? We can go out if you'd prefer."

"No, no, it's been great." I was still shocked he'd said I was his favorite thing and still feeling confused about the reason he had decided to bring me here. We had only been out one other time, and it hadn't been what I'd call a successful date. He really didn't know me. I figured that wine must have been working overtime on him. *Light weight.* Whatever it was, though, I found myself hoping that it wouldn't stop. I wanted him so bad; I needed him to put out the fire burning between my legs.

"Good." He stared at me. "I have a feeling it will get even better." I could feel his zeal and lust burning into me, penetrating me, as he glanced down my body and back up, my sex contracting as his nonverbal cues propelled his intentions to me.

He pressed his soft lips into mine again, and this time, his tongue slipped inside. Our tongues whisked and swiped while his hands moved from my shoulders to my waist, then down, cupping my butt cheeks. He squeezed me firmly into him, pressing me tight against his bulge. His hands slowly raised my mini dress up so he was able to slide his hands across my exposed butt cheeks.

"What a nice, soft ass," he whispered into my mouth. The thong I had on was the skimpiest one I could find. His hands were so soft against my skin, making me crave more of his exquisite touch, shivering with longing.

"Thank you." You're not the only one who can work magic, my gorgeous man. My hands caressed his back and shoulders, using my fingertips over his shirt to make him squirm into me closer as he held me tight. His hands were working at pulling my dress over my head to reveal my breasts.

"You are beautiful," he proclaimed as he took a step back to look at me thoroughly. He turned me around so my backside was facing him, "Mmm, Mmm! What a great-looking ass."

He turned me back around into him and ran his fingers through the length of my hair, kissing down my neck to my eagerly waiting hard nipples. I let out a low moan.

He led me over by his bed, where he sat down and pulled me up onto him, my thighs straddling the erection that was still trapped in his pants as he lay back flat on the comforter. I rubbed my hungry sex up and down over him, feeling my mound and his length pressing together. My breath hitched, anticipating how good it would feel to have him inside me.

He quickly rolled me over so I was beneath him. He hovered over me before standing to remove his clothes, never moving his eyes from mine. "You're sexy as hell."

"I like what I see, too," I replied, my voice now husky with need. I scooted back farther on the bed, and moved onto my elbows to take him in, but I couldn't sit still. Once his pants were removed, he joined me on the bed, his erection readily available to me, coming closer and closer to my face. *Another non-verbal cue, I get it, you want me to suck your cock.* I took his thick head in my mouth. He reached his hands to the crown of my head, signaling me to take all of him into my throat as he moaned his approval of my fine-tuned craft. "Oh, damn, Nikki."

I could feel his erection getting even harder and deeper into my throat. I tried to pull back, but he held my head tight in place, almost gagging me. I wanted to feel him inside my hot sex; I was so hungry for him to fill me. He rubbed his hands down my stomach to my mound and brushed feather-light strokes across my heat. His fingers slid under the waistband of the tiny sheath that was protecting me from full exposure. He parted my wet, swollen lips, stroking twice before sliding into my eager hole.

He withdrew from my mouth and bent down to kiss me. His breathing was ragged, his impatience to sink deep into my sex was evident. He lay on the bed next to me, kissing me, caressing and kneading my breasts, then running his fingers back down to my molten wet slit.

His smile was the sign that he was more than ready to give me what I wanted. He reached for a condom that was in his top nightstand drawer, removing it from the packet and rolling it on in what seemed like one fluid motion. He stroked himself a couple times, then earnestly he pressed into me, just allowing the hard, bulbous crest to part my lips and sink in to just beneath the mushroom-shaped top.

After teasing me for a few minutes with just the tip while massaging my clit, he brought me to my first orgasm.

"Mmmm…give it to me." I'm not the shy, timid type. I knew what I wanted, and I wasn't ashamed to tell him. I might never see him again, so I planned to enjoy fucking him that night.

"Are you begging me for it?" His head continued to make shallow strokes at my entrance.

If that's the game he wanted to play, I'd play along. "Yes, I'm begging you; please, give it to me."

His eyes cut to mine with a stern, committed look. He was enjoying making me want and beg for more of him. He plunged into me deeply, causing me to arch my back and sigh as I felt him press into the innermost depths of my canal.

"Oh, shit," I moaned.

"Damn, you feel good." He intertwined his fingers with mine and held them to the bed up above my head, kissing me deep, his tongue lashing at my mouth, matching the full-length, deep strokes that were inducing me into an orgasmic high.

He pulled out. "Get up on your hands and knees, and spread your legs." He spent time worshiping my ass, caressing, kissing, and tonguing me. He licked down my ass and around to my wet slit, where he massaged my craving bullet until he made me shoot off into another wicked orgasm. "You're insatiable; I love it," he said fiercely.

He got on his knees behind me and thrust his throbbing erection back into me. "Mmm," I moaned out.

His stamina was incredible. As much as I liked looking at him and kissing him, I really enjoyed the fucking he was giving me from behind. I was able to let my imagination run wild as he varied the speed and intensity of ensuring my pussy was well fucked. He rubbed his fingers over my ass knot, applying slight pressure with his thumb pad. "Damn, you feel so fucking good, Nikki."

Two more orgasms and what seemed like an hour later, he removed the condom and stood on the bed over me. I felt his hot liquid shooting on my lower back and ass in several hot spurts as he moaned out, "Ah, shit!"

The more I thought about it, the hotter I thought it was. No one had ever done anything like that to me before. Not even Sky.

He wrapped me in his arms and held me tight while he kissed my back, between my shoulder blades. He rolled onto his side, pulling me over with him into a spooning position. "Damn, baby doll," he said.

"That was phenomenal; maybe I need to come to over more often." My comment was met with silence. *Or maybe not.* After several minutes, he helped me up off the bed and into the shower, where he joined me.

We dressed and went down to the kitchen. He offered me a choice of water or orange juice. His refrigerator was nearly empty, which was a surprise. We talked for a little while, I pried for a little more information out of him. I was surprised when he told me his age; he was older than me by ten years. I had just turned twenty-eight, and he was thirty-eight. I had never been with a man that much older than me before, but apparently, I had been made for it because sex with him that night was definitely in the top five best nights of sex ever.

I glanced at the clock and saw it was nearly one AM. We both decided it was time to call it a night, and he drove me back home.

Chapter 5

When I woke up the next morning, I found myself thinking about and lusting for more of Jeff. The thoughts of the night before had my sex quivering and contracting for more satisfaction. My mind was clouded by the memory of his eyes, his touch, and his kisses -- the way he'd taken me, the way he'd made me cum over and over, commanding me in his extraordinary bedroom. I couldn't resist touching myself, sliding my fingers in and out of my wetness while rubbing my clit, making myself cum while thinking of him.

Feeling satisfied for the time being, I clambered out of bed and searched to find something to wear before going to take a shower. I had to go pick up Abby, then head over to visit and have lunch with my mom.

My mom was a different person today than she had been years ago. She was so much happier than I'd seen her in a long time. I remembered all too well the pain she'd gone through when she and Daddy had split and finally divorced. She had apologized repeatedly for the fact that my brother and I had heard their end-of-the-relationship showdown. It wasn't her fault; neither of them had any way of knowing we were standing outside.

It was one of those things that you wish could be unheard. I can't think of anyone who would want to hear that last momentous argument, the proverbial straw that breaks the camel's back. The verbal exchange was so heated the final nail was securely pounded into the marriage coffin. It was so devastating.

Daddy was such an asshole.

****

My mom, Rebekka Hollister, was a very successful real estate broker. She was well known throughout Tampa and a beautiful person inside and out. She had a charming smile that could warm you like the sun. She never left the house looking less than perfect. She only wore mascara to accent her dark brown almond-shaped eyes. She had shoulder-length brown hair that she wore pulled back off of her face with a hair clip. She had to have a million of them because they seemed to match almost every suit she owned. She always wore tailored suits with skirts that fell somewhere between mid-thigh to just above the knee. She had a pair of pumps and a handbag to match every suit.

She was a flawless professional with a personality as large and wide as the ocean. She loved to laugh and have a good time when she wasn't working. I loved my mother dearly and wanted to be just like her as I was growing up.

My father, Calvin Hollister, was a tall, burly man. He wasn't obese, but he was carrying a few extra pounds and had a large presence. His voice boomed when he spoke. I remember he could be heard for blocks if he hollered out the back door to let my brother and I know it was time to come in.

He didn't physically look like he was a good match for Mom. He was nice-looking, just not the strikingly handsome man you would expect to be married to her. His style was more rugged-casual, and he was much more introverted. When he did speak, he had a tendency to come across as crude. He was a Marine veteran turned electrician and was most comfortable in a pair of worn jeans, a shirt that was a couple sizes too big, to cover his beer belly, and a pair of work boots. He was balding on top but refused to shave off the long graying hair he let grow around the sides and back; instead, he pulled it back into an uncombed ponytail. Whenever my parents went out together, he rarely dressed nice.

One Friday, in the early evening, as Gary and I were coming back from the mall and walking up the sidewalk to the front door of our house; we could hear our parents arguing. We'd never heard that degree of yelling and cursing by either of them -- especially not at each other.

"You act so prim and proper, but I know you're nothing more than a slut," we heard our dad scream.

"Motherfucker, you have no room to talk. You're the one out fucking every bitch you see."

"If you weren't so damn uptight, I wouldn't have to."

"Fuck you, Calvin; fuck you all the way to hell. You never respected me. I've had enough of your shit."

"You can't live without me. You're fucking pathetic; a fucking frigid, pathetic cunt."

"Am I a slut or am I frigid, asshole? I can't be both. You're such a dumbass."

Gary and I were in complete shock as we stood like statues on the sidewalk in disbelief. We glanced at each other; tears were running down my face.

We finally heard Mom yell, "Get the fuck out of my house, Calvin. Take your sorry ass to your dirty little bitch and get the fuck out of here now!"

"Good luck surviving on your sorry ass salary. The kids are grown; you won't get a fucking dime from me."

Gary grabbed my arm, yanking me loose from the position my feet felt cemented to, and told me to come on. We retreated to the car and left.

We returned to the house later that night to find Mom drunk and a tearful mess. She was so out of sorts. She had a half-empty Gin bottle sitting on the kitchen table in front of her as she sobbed into a tear-soaked dish towel. I knew the gin hadn't been full before she started, but she had still done a good amount of damage, and she didn't normally drink hard liquor.

Dad was nowhere to be found. We weren't sure if he would come back that night or the next day, or ever. But seeing Mom like that was so heartbreaking -- she couldn't have deserved any of this, not her. I picked up her glass and dumped the remaining drink down the sink and capped the gin bottle.

"It'll be okay, Mom." I said trying to comfort her. I rubbed my hand across her back and felt her shaking.

Gary and I helped her up and into her bedroom so she could sleep it off. Nothing else was said that night. She gave us each a hug, but continued to cry well after we left her room.

The next morning, I heard her stumbling out to the phone. She called her job and told them she was sick and wouldn't be in. I stayed in my bed not moving a muscle so I could hear what else she was doing. She banged around in the cupboards and dropped a few items, but it sounded like she was working on getting coffee. My suspicion was confirmed when the smell of the vanilla roast she loved so much wafted in the air.

My curiosity was eating at me; I had to go see what she was doing and how she'd fared after a night of drinking and crying. When I went to the kitchen, my jaw hung wide enough for my mouth to double as a fly trap.

"Mom?" She sat at the table, staring with a blank look on her face into the wall opposite her, tears streaming down her pale cheeks, with her coffee mug on the table in front of her. Tissues were balled up in her death-grip tight fist and her uncombed, disheveled hair looked like something out of a horror movie. I had never seen her look like this, and it concerned and saddened me.

"Are you going to be all right, Mom?"

She didn't reply right away; instead, her crying intensified. Her eyes stayed fixated on the wall.

After a few sniffs, the tears were wiped away by the tissue ball. "I'll be fine," she told me as her bloodshot eyes glanced up to meet mine. "Your dad's gone."

"I know."

"I doubt he'll be back, so don't expect to see him living here again."

"We'll be okay, Mom; right?"

"Yes, sweetie, we will." Her voice was calm and reassuring, but her face was anything but convincing.

I wanted to ask her what had happened, but I knew it wasn't my place to ask, and I didn't want to upset her any more than she already was.

After a few days of muddling through the daily rituals, Mom finally sat Gary and me down and told us what had happened, all the too-much-information and we-really-didn't-need-to-know that sordid details. It was a difficult story to listen to for more reasons than one, especially when she told us they hadn't gotten along for the past several years, but they made sure to give the impression that everything was just peachy between them. Gary and I heard way more information than children should ever hear about their parents' private lives.

"I hate to tell you this, but you both are old enough to understand and deserve an explanation," Mom began. "Your dad's been sleeping around, cheating on me over the years." *Gross, this is was way too much information.*

"Mom, you don't have to tell us this," Gary protested.

With a deep inhale followed by a long, labored exhale, she continued -- she was on autopilot. "I got used to it, you know, and accepted it as long as he was able to keep it hidden from you two and others, like our friends. And he had to always make sure his sluts stayed away from me."

Tears trickled down her face. "But the crux of this marriage-ending disastrous blow-up was when your dad's current, much younger girlfriend, posing as a potential home buyer, requested to work with me." Mom turned her head, staring out the kitchen window. "To tour a home with me."

She labored through a deep inhalation of breath and exhaled slowly before turning back to face us and continuing, "I had no idea who she was when we met at the house; she seemed like any other excited, eager homebuyer. As we neared the end of the home walk-through, she revealed her identity and proceeded to berate me. As if that weren't enough, the bitch let me know she's four months pregnant."

"What the fuck?" Gary's face reddened as he stood from his seat, feet just wider than shoulder width, shoving the chair one-handed with enough force to send it flying across the room and crashing into the wall. "How could he do that to you?"

"He did it to all of us, the selfish bastard. You'll have a younger brother or sister soon." Mom started to sob again.

"Fuck him and his bastard baby." Gary's face turned red as he paced the kitchen like a caged animal, huffing and puffing angrily.

"Oh, Mom." I walked over and wrapped my arms around her shoulders. I cried with her. Gary joined in, wrapping his long arms across our backs to hug us both into him. We stood there for a few minutes, wrapped in a group hug.

Mom pulled back slightly to break the circle. "I loved your dad so much, but we were going in different directions." Gary loosened his arms, and Mom walked over to the sink, looking out the window again. "I've got my flaws, you know. I'm not innocent. To be fair, I've had a couple flings over the years, too. What's good for the goose is good for the gander, right?" She cleared her throat. "Unlike your dad, I was careful, real careful. Your dad had suspected I was having an affair, but never could prove it or knew who with."

She slowly turned to face us. "I'm currently dating someone. It doesn't matter who knows now. Hell, this charade of a marriage is over." She clasped her hands in front of her. "We've fallen in love, and it feels great to be able to say it. I didn't think it was possible to love anyone as much as I had loved your dad." We were stunned by the revelations we'd just heard.

"What bothers me the most is that, despite all the problems we had, there was comfort in knowing he was still there... here," -- she raised her hands placing both palms flush across her heart -- "here with me."

We were dumbfounded. I felt like the world as I had known it was crumbling in around me. Everything I'd thought about my family was a lie.

On the weekend, Mom introduced us to Jim Lauren, the man she had been seeing secretly for the past year and had fallen in love with. Jim was a nice-looking older gentleman. He had a full head of thick salt-and-pepper hair. He had perfect white teeth that almost glowed when he smiled. His skin looked slightly wrinkled and leathery, like you get from too much sun over the years, but he was still very handsome. He was friendly, but also seemed cautious. I could see why Mom was attracted to him; he looked more like the type of man that should be with her. Jim shook our hands as he stood close to Mom, with one hand resting at her waist. She had a glow being near him; she seemed so relieved and happy to reveal her love secret.

Gary wasn't happy at all. We went out to the mall after meeting Jim.

"This is a really fucked situation, Sissy." Gary was so venomous about everything that had transpired. "First Dad being a complete douche-bag, getting some bitch pregnant while still married. Now Mom springs her boyfriend bullshit on us. We went from the happy-assed Cleavers last month to a cluster-fuck of a family now."

"I don't want to be an older sister to anyone."

"Fuck the baby; that's Dad's problem, not ours."

We both felt betrayed by our own father. As far as Dad's other family, we wanted nothing to do with the baby or the baby's momma.

"Mom seems happy with Jim. Don't you want her to be happy?"

"Of course I do, but goddamn it, how much shit are we supposed to have dumped on us at once? I mean, seriously."

"I know; I just want Mom to be happy. I can't take seeing her sad and crying like that again."

"Or drinking; Jesus Christ, that was awful."

We walked around window shopping and talking for another hour or so before going back home.

After a few months, Gary came around and was more accepting of Jim. Seeing how he treated Mom, how much he loved her and would do anything for her, made it difficult to harbor any thoughts of ill will toward him. He was a really good man. He and Mom sold the old house and found a beautiful, larger new one to start their life together in Tampa right on the Bay with a boat slip and dock at their yard. Mom asked for a smaller home, but Jim insisted there always would be two extra bedrooms in whatever house they owned, he wanted to make sure there was always room if we, or his own children, came to visit.

Mom and Jim got married a few years later. Gary came home from college and walked Mom down the aisle - - who better than her son to give her away? Gretchen, a coworker of my mom's and her best friend, and I, were the maids-of-honor. She chose both of us because Gretchen was like a sister to her, and she didn't want to upset her by asking her to have been a bridesmaid. I didn't mind sharing the honor with Gretchen, I knew how much she meant to my mom.

The happily married couple honeymooned for two weeks in Hawaii before returning home. Mom was the happiest we could ever remember seeing her.

Dad lost touch with both of us after he left home. I'd seen him around town. He wasn't with that baby's mother anymore. He had a new flame -- an older woman, maybe even a little older than him. He seemed sad. I couldn't help wondering if he ever thought of us.

Gary refused to have any more contact with him since he didn't try to make an effort to see or talk to us after the split. That was a lot easier for Gary, since he was out of town for college. I was still in town at the time, finishing my senior year of high school. Dad lived on the other side of town, so chances of seeing him were slim, but it was still difficult for me.

My prom and graduation were overshadowed by mixed emotions. I was so happy to finish high school and ecstatic that Mom and Jim – well, Jim, anyway -- bought me a new car. But my true wish for graduation was to have Dad show up and surprise me. He didn't need to get me anything, just be there and say he was proud of me. It had been three years since I'd seen or talked to him. I was leaving for college in a couple months and was torn trying to figure out if I should make an effort to go see him before leaving or just let sleeping dogs lie. I felt so wracked with confusion about why he'd pretended we no longer existed.

For the sake of my own sanity, with all that was going on, I chose to focus on getting ready for college.

****

My mom and I are very close, and I don't know what I'd ever do without her, but I still wonder to this day what is going on with Daddy. Maybe one day I'll try to find him…maybe.

Chapter 6

Sky called me before I left the house to let me know he wanted to keep Abby longer. I assured him I could come get her later in the evening, after spending time with Mom. Actually, I welcomed the peaceful visit without Abby's interruptions.

Jim was home and feeling feisty as ever. We all decided to go for a drive to Picnic Island Park, where we could enjoy the bay and walk along the beach. Jim didn't want to drive, so I offered to drive his car, his black Mercedes ML63 AMG SUV.

Mom and I gathered drinks and snacks to take with us. We usually stayed for a while, and dehydration doesn't look good on any of us. After getting everything together, we went to the garage, where I climbed in the driver's seat, bouncing up and down like a kid at an amusement park.

"Be careful when you press on the gas," Jim said. "This car has a lot more power than yours."

"Okay." I smiled like the Cheshire Cat in *Alice in Wonderland* when I turned the key to start it. I pressed the garage door opener to let me out. I'd tried on several occasions to get behind the wheel of his car, and Mom was always quick on the 'No' reply. This time, I asked Jim when she stepped out of the room, and he was more than willing to let me drive.

"And no speeding," old party-pooper Mom chimed in.

"Okay." Looking back, making sure the driveway was clear, I backed down to the sidewalk, checked again, closed the garage door, then backed into the street.

"Watch that —" Jim started, just as I shifted into drive and pressed down on the accelerator, throwing us all back into our seats. Jim, who hadn't buckled into his seat belt, grasped the backs of the front seats to hold on for dear life. "You did that on purpose, Nikki." Jim laughed.

Mom clutched the passenger door and the console. The corners of her mouth turned down as she glared at me with tightness in her eyes and forced my name out through her pursed lips. "Nicolette." *Yikes, she's pissed.*

I'm so glad Jim has a good sense of humor. He knew I was going to punch the gas on takeoff. After a few minutes of driving, we arrived at the park. Parking was a little difficult, but that was normal for a nice day. I found a spot, and we all got out. I had opened the trunk and begun digging in the insulated bag to get us each a bottle of water when the dreaded question was asked.

"Sweetie, are you dating anyone yet?" Leave it to Mom to jump right in with the question I was hoping to avoid.

"No one special." How could I tell her the man I had just been with the night before was ten years older than me? And I had no real idea how to categorize what we were, regardless.

"Don't rush her, Rebekka; she's still young." Jim placed his arm around Mom's shoulder and pulled her in close to him, kissing her on the forehead.

"I know. I guess I just want you to be happy, Nikki, dear."

"I know, Mom, and I appreciate your concern." We walked down to the beach as we continued to talk. "I'm not unhappy or lonely, though; Abby keeps me company."

"That isn't the same." Mom frowned at me. "How is Sky? I haven't seen him in a few weeks."

I swallowed hard. "He's fine." I guess they'd be surprised to know I was still having sex with Sky, but that wasn't their business.

"Give him our love when you see him. I really like him."

"I will. I'll see him when I leave and go pick up Abby."

"What a beautiful day out, and I get to spend it with the two most beautiful women in the world. Am I a lucky son of a bitch or what?" Jim blurted into the conversation. He must have seen the pained look on my face. Jim was more in tune to physical cues than most women.

"Oh, Jim, thanks, but that's a bit of an exaggeration." Mom blushed.

"My perception is my reality; how dare you piss on my parade, woman." We all laughed.

It was so fun being out with them, talking and enjoying the day. They walked hand in hand nearly the entire time. We stayed in the park for a little over an hour before we decided to go get something to eat.

Mom and I decided to make Chicken Parmesan over angel hair pasta with garlic toast instead of going to a restaurant. Jim walked straight into the family room plopping down in his favorite massaging recliner. It didn't take long before we heard him snoring.

"Is everything going okay with him?" I whispered to Mom.

"Sure, he's fine. He tires easily with the heat and physical exertion, but he's fine."

"Did they find out what's going on yet?"

"They keep running tests, but no clue what's causing him to be so tired all the time." She looked into the family room, her face aglow as she continue in a low, soft tone, "My tiger is just fine, though."

"Earth to Mom, Earth to Mom, come in, Mom." We both laughed. It was great to see her so happy. Jim was the best thing to come into her life. He wasn't demanding or crude or impatient. He just loved her.

"I want you to find your true love and be happy, sweetie. I do worry about you." She reached out, stroking down my shoulder and arm.

"What if Sky was my true love? What if he was the one?"

"If he was, you'd still be together. Someone else is out there waiting for you. That perfect someone is still out there. He's going to be a lost soul until he finds you."

"I don't know, Mom."

"You have to date to find your Mr. Right, sweetie."

"I know, and I am, just nothing serious. Trust me, if I find him, you'll be the first to know." We finished cooking and preparing the plates. I set each of them on the table that looked out over the back-yard. What a beautiful view. From the kitchen, you could see the bay, their boat slip, and the dock.

"What do you want to drink, dear?"

"Want to share a bottle of wine?" Wine brought back memories of the previous night.

"Sure, I'll go find us a nice bottle."

"Do you have a red burgundy?"

"I thought your preference was Zinfandel. What do you know about burgundy?" Mom chuckled.

"I'm learning things." I winked at her.

"There's some in the cellar; I'll be right back."

She returned and popped the cork, then retrieved three wineglasses from the cupboard, filled each halfway, and set them on the table. Mom rousted Jim with a kiss on the lips and a whisper in his ear.

By the time we finished eating, it was nearing six o'clock. I helped clean up the kitchen and washed the dishes before saying goodbye. I knew it had been a long day for Jim, and I was ready to go get my daughter and get home.

I knocked on Sky's door. No answer. I knocked again, and a few seconds later, Hope opened the door. "Hi, Nikki." *Fuck.* I was hoping she wouldn't be there. I'd met her before; she and Sky had an on-again off-again relationship.

"Hey, is my little monkey butt ready?"

"Not quite yet; come on in. She's finishing watching a movie, but it's almost over." She stepped to the side, unblocking the doorway so I could enter the apartment, then closed the door behind me. "Hon, Nikki's here," she hollered as she walked back down the hall to the bedroom. I noticed she was wearing a pair of Sky's boxers and his T-shirt. A pang of jealousy pierced my heart.

Sky appeared with his hair a mess, wearing a pair of sweatpants, a T-shirt and bare feet. He looked sexy even at his worst. "Hey."

"Is she almost ready?" I snapped through clenched teeth. I felt restless, pacing slowly to keep my feet moving. I wanted my kid and out of that apartment, now.

"Give her another five minutes or so." Sky took a step toward me. "Are you okay?"

"Yep, fine. Just tired and want to go home."

Sky took a couple steps closer. "Don't forget, baby, I know you."

"Don't, Sky; leave it alone." My eyes were prickling with tears; I could feel them burning inside my eyes, on the brink of tumbling down my cheeks. I needed to maintain my composure, and talking to him right now was going to send me down an emotional freefall I didn't want to ride. Why did he call me baby? *Damn him.* I don't know what it was about seeing Hope at his place that always made me lose my shit. Maybe it was the fact that she was fucking drop-dead gorgeous.

"Mommy!" Abby came running down the hall and jumped up at me. I picked her up in my arms and hugged her tight, losing myself in the scent of baby lotion.

"Are you ready to go, baby girl?" I shifted her onto my hip, supporting her weight with my arm across her lower back.

"Yep."

"Tell Daddy and Hope bye."

She turned and waved as she hollered, "Bye."

Hope came and kissed her on the cheek. "Bye, Angel." She even smelled gorgeous -- ugh.

As Sky stepped closer, I could smell the Dove soap. I loved that smell on him, fresh and clean as a whistle. He leaned in, my breath hitched, his eyes focused on mine, and I licked, then bit my lower lip in desperation as my throat pulsed. He leaned in farther still holding his gaze on me, and my lips pursed as he kissed Abby on the cheek. "Bye, Princess. I love you." His eyes never left mine.

"I wuv you." Abby's arms stretched to wrap around Sky's neck, pulling me toward him with her. She gave him a long, wet kiss on the neck. Sky smiled while Hope and I laughed. I hated sharing that moment with her. When Hope looked at me, our eyes met, and the smile on her face turned to a grimace while her eyes narrowed and her arms crossed over her chest.

I walked over to the door where she was standing, and she took a step to make sure to open it for me. She probably wanted to put her foot in the middle of my back and literally kick me out. *I'm such a fool*, I thought as my face flushed. "I'll see you guys next week." I stepped out, and the door closed quickly, behind me.

After getting Abby buckled into her car seat, I sulked behind the steering wheel, both hands on it in the ten and two position, resting my head between them. I couldn't believe I was fretting over Sky. We were divorced. He was going to move on; I had.

I raised my head, and in autopilot mode, eyes barely focused, started the car and began driving down the road. Shaking my head from side to side, I sighed out, relaxing my shoulders. I felt silly, school girl crush silly. I had to shake this and move on.

After getting in the house, I got Abby bathed and gave her a snack before tucking her into bed.

My mind still refused to shift from Sky. Was he my Mr. Right? I climbed in bed, pulling the covers up to my chest, and relaxed back into my pillows. I rubbed my heart as I replayed in my mind that day on campus when I had seen him for the first time, me stalking him, and the first time we were alone.

****

When I returned to college for my junior year, it didn't take long for me to find the most handsome freshman on campus. I wasn't looking for a freshman to date; he just happened to be a freshman. He had the females on campus buzzing as soon as he stepped out of his mom's Jaguar. Mandy and I were moving into our new dorm room when I saw him. My mouth gaped as I said, "Oh my God."

"Fuck me," Mandy stammered out when her head spun in the direction I was staring in.

"He's mine," I declared as I swallowed hard. "I love his parents, and I don't even know them. What wonderful people they must be to have created perfect him, though."

We stood in awe, Mandy holding a microwave as I clutched my jewelry box. He was walking toward us.

He was six feet tall, and had shoulder-length brown hair.

"Need a hand?" he asked. He had long eyelashes and killer bluish-gray eyes. He was clean-shaven, showing off his strong jawline.

"Sure, thanks," Mandy said as he took the microwave from her arms. There were dents across her skin where the microwave had been resting.

"I'm Skylar Carmichael. Just call me Sky, everyone else does, except my mother." He had such beautiful, kissable full lips.

"I'm Mandy, and this is Nikki." All I could do was smile. Sky smiled back at me. His smile was a little crooked and so irresistible, with a hint of dimpled cheeks.

"I'll follow you," he said to Mandy. My tongue was tied in knots and working overtime to make sure I didn't drool. My mind was working like a steam engine -- so young, so chivalrous, so damn gorgeous, and so soon to be all mine.

Watching him walk allowed me to be appreciative of whatever workout plan he had because he had a perfectly round, tight ass. His shoulders were broad. He was fit and trim -- perfect and sexy. His body language screamed confidence and sex appeal; he had an intriguing swagger in his simplest movements. My goal was to get to know him before any of the other females got to him.

We walked down the hall about twenty feet before reaching the room. Mandy opened and held the door for Sky.

"Thanks so much; I really appreciate your help." Mandy stretched out her arm to shake his hand after he set the appliance down on the counter, revealing the raised reddened marks from the microwave.

"You're welcome."

"Now that you know where we live, maybe you can stop by. That is, if Nikki here can take herself off mute."

They laughed at my expense. I shot them both a snarky fake smile. "Yeah, come by any time," I managed to squeak out.

"Maybe I will." He winked. "Later."

Once he left and I shut the door, I blurted out, "I'm going to rub one out while thinking about him tonight. Did you see his eyes? Oh my god!"

"He is ridiculously good-looking. You two would look so good together," Mandy gushed.

From that moment, I was obsessed and turned into the campus stalker. I got his schedule from one of my friends who worked in the registrar's office. He lived in an adjacent building from mine, and I made sure our paths crossed as much as we crossed campus for class.

A few weeks after moving in, Mandy was out with Creighton, and I was sitting in our room clad in a pair of running shorts and a tank top with no bra, engrossed in my smut book, when a knock on the door startled me. We had gotten used to the other girls on the floor just dropping in without knocking. It was like a floor-wide slumber party on most nights.

I sauntered over to open the door, and to my surprise, there stood Sky. Stunning as ever, his black T-shirt was molded to his body like a second skin. His physique was truly impressive. The muscles in his chest and arms were proof that he spent plenty of time in the gym. His body fat had to be close to zero percent. He looked amazing.

"Hey," I said.

"Did I catch you at a bad time?"

"No, not at all. Come in." I poked my head out slightly and saw three of my floor-mates staring in my direction, whispering furiously to each other. *Eat your hearts out, bitches.* I closed the door and locked it. "So what brings you to my neck of the woods?"

"I figured I'd take you guys up on the offer to stop by. Is Mandy here too?"

"Nope, she's out with her boyfriend." I sat on my bed scooting my ass back so the pillow was between my back and the headboard. "You can sit down." I patted the bed where I wanted his perfect ass.

"Where's your boyfriend tonight?" Sky took his assigned position on the bed, making sure not to pull his feet up onto the bedspread.

"I don't have one, not yet." I was hunched over slightly, in a feeble attempt to make my hardened nipples less obvious. I pulled my legs up and crossed them in front of me. The way I was sitting with the shorts so short, it was a good thing I had shaved or my hairs down there might have shown.

"Got anyone in mind?"

"Yep, I definitely have my eye on someone." *I'll give your fine ass one guess who.*

"Lucky guy."

"Thanks. So how about you? Do you have a girlfriend?"

"No, we broke up before I came here."

"Too bad." I flipped my hair back over my shoulder. Good riddance to bad rubbish -- out with the old and in with the new.

"It was only a matter of time. She started getting clingy and annoying. Then things really went south the closer it got to me leaving."

"Well, hopefully you can get over her soon and move on." *With me.* "You're a freshman, right?"

"I'm hoping the same, and yeah, I'm a freshman. Enough about me; tell me more about you. I seem to see you all the time."

"I'm a junior and normally keep pretty busy. Tonight is a slow night, not much homework, so I'm just hanging out, reading."

"What do you read?"

"Erotica is my favorite. I love a good hot, sexy bedtime story." *I'd love to make you part of a good hot, sexy bedtime story.*

"I can't say I've ever read Erotica, but I've heard about it. It's like porn, right?"

"No, it's erotic romance; you know, it has a romantic story. But … seriously, what's up? It seems so random that you came by tonight."

"I was coming by to see if you wanted to come over for a bit since my roommate isn't around tonight, but neither is yours."

What's cooking in that mind of yours, Sky? "Were you going to lure me to your place and take advantage of me?" *Oh, wait, that's what's in my mind. Why are we still wasting time talking?*

His face flushed. "Nah, nothing like that."

"Then what?"

"I don't know. I guess I never really thought how I'd –" He stopped mid-sentence as I went into seductress mode. I leaned my back against the headboard and closed my eyes. I inhaled deeply while slinking my hands with sensual movements down my sides, across my hips, caressing down my knees and back up toward my hips again. My hips rocked while my breasts invited him closer. I rolled my head up, slowly opening my eyes. I was beckoning him to me without saying a word.

"Holy fuck." Did he really just say that out loud?

"What?" I replied coyly.

"I think we both know 'what.' You know why I came by, and now you're teasing me."

"I don't tease, darling. I please." My glance shifted downward to the crotch of his jeans. I let my hands glide up my sides slowly as I rocked my hips forward, emphasizing my small waist. My hands caressed over the outside of my sensitive, pleading breasts, continuing up my neck and into my hair from the nape. "Some of us women aren't into game playing." I slid the ponytail holder that had been on my wrist off, and pulled my hair back off my face and neck. "Just tell me why you came by, because we're probably thinking the same thing anyway."

Sky looked like he was going to explode. His hooded eyes were massaging my breasts, kneading them with his gaze. Yeah, he wanted me. I wanted him too, and he knew it. He studied me as I slid my legs out of the crossed position and over toward the floor. My feet touched the floor, and my ass rose up just enough for him to catch a glimpse of my round butt peeking out of my shorts. He was falling under my spell. I took two steps to walk past him, and he reached out, grabbing my wrist, pulling me down into his lap.

"So now you have me; what are you going to do with me?" I batted my eyes part joking, part flirting, and one hundred percent begging for his touch.

Sky wrapped one hand around the back of my neck and guided me down onto his warm lips while sliding the other arm around my waist, pulling me into him nice and snug.

To make sure there was no mistaking what I wanted, I gave him a slight nudge to topple him back so he was flush on his back, but my lips never left his. I climbed on top of him, straddling his hips so I could feel his hardness while I rocked my hips ever so slightly. Rocking forward, I shivered as his thickness pressed against my swelling clit, then rocked back to remove the pressure. I needed to feel him in me so bad. I was sure he would feel how wet he was making me through my shorts. *Jeez; fuck me!*

"Would it be safe to say we've solved the mystery?" I asked, with my lips lightly touching his – teasing, taunting, and flirting.

Sky flicked his warm, moist tongue across my pink satin lips. "Mystery solved. Mission not accomplished … yet." He slid his hands under the bottom of my tank top; his fingers danced lightly against my skin as they made their way up to my eager breasts. Goose bumps rose on my skin as he continued stroking my hardened nipples with the pads of his thumbs. I melted into his hands as our eyes locked on each other.

"You want this off?" I tugged at the tank top shoulder strap.

"Not yet; I like it." He pulled me back into him, crushing my mouth on his, sinking his tongue deep in my mouth, tasting me, and I lost myself in him. Without warning, he held me tight and rolled me onto my back, so he was now in the top position. "Now, it comes off." He sat me up briefly, yanked the tank top off in one clean swoop, then laid me back down flat on the bed.

He positioned himself between my legs, kneeling on the floor. "These too." He tugged at my shorts as I pressed my feet into the bed frame for leverage to lift my ass. The shorts joined the tank on the floor. My wet, slippery sex was exposed to him, waiting and wanting him.

This was really happening; it had been a few weeks, and I needed this so bad -- God, I wanted him. He pulled his T-shirt off exposing his muscular, hairless chest. He was so damn sexy. I perched up on my elbows so I could observe and admire my prize. Once he tossed the shirt in the same direction as my shorts, he unbuttoned his jeans and unzipped them, sliding them down his narrow hips, exposing his dripping length. My eyes widening in delight, I thought, *if he knows what to do with that thing, this is going to be a really good night.* He sat down to pull his pants off over his feet, removed a condom from his pocket, which he laid on the floor, then tossed them to join the other garments.

He returned to his kneeling position, facing me, and let the soft touch of his fingers glide up the inside of my thighs, up and out over my hips, then up to my waist. Once he reached my waist, I rocked my hips forward, grinding into the mattress before returning to the original position. Then, with slow precision, he let his tongue follow the trail made with his left hand up my inner thigh. The heat from my sex got warmer as he closed in on my sweet spot.

His tongue explored my wet slit, delving into the folds. "Sweet Nikki," he murmured. His hands slid across my stomach, down over my mound, and his thumb stroked and rubbed my engorged clit while his tongue probed and plunged into my heat as I came unhinged. My eyes squeezed tight, and the tingling feeling rippled throughout my quaking body as I screamed out his name. "Sky, oh, damn!"

He rose up over me, rolled on the condom, and took his time entering me, stretching me, taking me. Once our skin was pressed together, he withdrew and again filled me with slow precision. "Damn, you feel so good, just like I thought you would," he whispered to me.

"You can go faster if you want."

Ignoring me, he continued his slow, rhythmic pulsing in and out of my wet hole. The pad of his thumb still fondled my clit. He leaned back slightly, changing the position and place he was touching deep in me, then picked up speed with both his stroke and thumb. My breathing became ragged, and I was moaning as he got me closer to the edge. He continued until I exploded, bound to him in rapture. "Oh, damn! Harder, Sky; do it harder." He obliged, his thrusts hard and powerful, until he found his release. "Oh, damn, girl!"

We were inseparable by November and talked about marriage in December. Then Sky came back to meet my mom and Jim over Christmas break.

Chapter 7

Waking up feeling just as tired as when you went to sleep sucks! I decided I should have taken a sleeping pill.

Monday's are day care days for Abby, so I had to pick up the pace. My normal Sunday-night routine had been interrupted by my own ridiculous actions at Sky's apartment. Every time I saw Hope, I had the same reaction. She was beautiful, a twenty-something version of Sofia Vergara, only, to me, Hope was so much more beautiful. She modeled part-time and worked part-time in a bar somewhere near his job.

Maybe the reason she bothered me so much was because she wasn't like the other women he'd dated since we split. The others didn't compare to me looks-wise. Maybe it was because she was tall and slim, had a perfect body, beautiful olive skin and was flat-out drop-dead gorgeous. Maybe because she made me feel like I was no longer good enough to be with Sky, because why would he ever want me again after her? Maybe because, deep down, I thought he had stronger feelings for her that he wasn't ready to admit.

Whatever it was, I didn't have time to worry about it. I needed to get to work, and the last thing I needed was to be late today because I was throwing a pity party for myself. *Fuck it. I'm moving on, and Sky is moving on.*

After showering and getting dressed, I ran in and woke Abby. She gave me her breakfast order of toast and candy as I dressed her in her overalls, with the butterfly top that matched, that Sky had given her. *Why the hell did I just put my kid in overalls when I know she would rather wear a skirt? Fuck it, I have to keep it moving or I'll be late. I can't be late today.*

Hoisting my precious cargo onto my hip, I ran down the stairs in bare feet and walked fast into the kitchen, setting Abby on the chair at the table.

"You can have toast, but no candy."

"Candy."

"Not right now, later. Would you like an egg with your toast?"

"No!"

"Would you like a pancake?"

"No!"

"A waffle?"

"No!"

"This is your last chance, a peanut butter and jelly?"

"Yes!" I knew that would be it. I should just start there every morning and save myself the hassle.

I made the peanut butter and jelly, cut it diagonally into four pieces, and poured a glass of milk. "Don't make a mess."

"I won't, Mommy."

"I'll be right back down; don't get off that chair." I snapped as I turned and took off running back up the stairs into my bedroom. I pulled the dress I had laid out on my bed over my head and shimmied into it, then went in the bathroom to put on my mascara and lip gloss. I rushed back down the stairs to check on Abby, praying I wouldn't slip on the slick, worn-out carpet. I wished I had set my alarm thirty minutes earlier, then maybe I wouldn't have felt like I needed another shower already.

"All done?"

"Yes, Mommy."

"Let's go upstairs and get your teeth brushed." Fuck, I should have put her lunch together while she ate, then I could be getting ready while she was upstairs with me. Where was my head today?

I walked up the stairs behind Abby. She refused to let me carry her because this morning was as perfect of a time to throw a mini I-can-do-it-all-by-myself tantrum as any. When we reached the top step, after what seemed like five thousand hours, I convinced her I needed to pick her up to brush her teeth, which stopped the repeat performance she was winding up for. As soon as she was ready, she rode my hip back down the stairs. I sat her on the couch with her Velcro-close shoes and let her try to figure that out while I made her lunch.

"I did it."

I looked at her feet and stifled my laugh. The shoes were not on all the way, and they were on the wrong feet. "You sure did, baby; can I make them tighter for you so they don't come off?"

"Okay."

I quickly switched them and pulled the Velcro tight. "Are you ready to go see Ms. Jane?"

"Yeah, I like Ms. Jane."

"Okay, hold your lunch, and I'll get my keys." *Damn it, my fucking shoes.* "I'll be right back." I ran back up the stairs, grabbed my slide wedge sandals, and ran back down the stairs, where I dropped them and slid my feet in. "I'm ready." *Fuck, my keys.* I darted into the kitchen and grabbed the keys off the table, and scooped up my purse by the strap.

We raced out the door, locking it behind us, and I was ready for what was starting out to be moron Monday.

I dropped Abby off at day care and made it to work with two minutes to spare. My first meeting was with my manager and it took the entire one hundred twenty seconds I had to get to his office on time. No coffee, scatter-brained, and heart racing a mile a minute, I walked over to his assistant to let her know I was there.

I walked out fifteen minutes later feeling battered and bruised. My ego was resting in the palm of my hand, in need of some serious CPR and TLC. He called it constructive criticism, but I called it a warning that a written warning was coming if I didn't get my shit together. How in the hell had I managed to screw up so bad last week? I'd never made such careless mistakes before, and I had been doing this job for years.

"Pick up your face, darling," Tristan said and smiled at me as I passed.

"I'm not in the mood today."

"Need a strong shoulder to lean on, or cry on?"

"No, I need a drink already."

"It's only nine thirty. Kind of early, don't you think?"

"No, and if you don't stop asking me questions, I'm going to scream." I looked up with glassy eyes. "I'm sorry. I'm having a shitty day already. I screwed up something last week, leading to a Monday morning ass-ripping session."

"I'm sorry to hear. I'll let you get back to work. If you need anything or are interested in a drink after work, let me know. I'll go with you."

"Thanks."

I pulled up the account that had all the mistakes and reviewed my work. *Idiot, you know better than to add those two numbers.* I made the change, but something still didn't seem quite right. I looked and looked until my eyes crossed. I needed caffeine.

I locked my computer, grabbed my mug, and headed down to the break room. I was happy no one was in there. I couldn't take any more distractions or idle chatter. I needed to get this screw up fixed and resubmitted by lunchtime. I poured my coffee, added the cream, and stirred. I fell into a trance looking at the coffee as I swirled it. This day was officially shit. It had to get better, though, because it couldn't get worse.

I walked back down to my desk in time to hear my cellphone ringing. I yanked it out of my purse and saw it was Sky. Great; I didn't really want to talk to him. I let the call go to voicemail and unlocked my computer. I thought I had figured out what I'd done wrong. I made a couple more changes and came up with the result Jack fuck-my-life-today Granger told me I should have gotten. One crisis averted. I sent the attachment via email to him and got busy on the next task of the day.

My cellphone rang again – it was Sky again. This time, I answered it, against my better judgment. "Hey." Butterflies began taking over my insides, and my chest felt hollowed out.

"Hey Nik. Is everything cool today? You know, I really want to talk to you about yesterday."

"I'm fine, Sky. I don't want to talk about it, really."

"Something is going on, and I want to know. Did I do something to upset you?"

"Look, I'm sorry, okay? I don't know what you want me to say."

"What are you apologizing for? What's going on? What got you so upset?"

"You're not going to let up, are you?"

"Nik, I know you better than that and I could see it in your eyes. Something is going on and we need to talk, period."

"Fine, I'll tell you. I got jealous seeing Hope there. Are you satisfied? I always get jealous when I see her." I sniffled as tears prickled in my eyes. "I have to go; I can't talk about this now."

After I hung up, I sat there horrified. *I can't believe I just hung up on Sky. I can't believe I just told him I'm jealous of Hope. Fuck, can this day get worse?*

With my phone out, I decided a call to Jeff might cheer me up. I needed to shift this bad juju away from me. I pressed the numbers on the card, and it hit me, I still didn't have a number for Jeff other than his work number.

His phone was answered on the third ring by the same pleasant-sounding woman. "Jeffrey Carrington's office, how may I help you?"

"Jeff Carrington, please."

"May I ask who's calling?"

"This is Nikki Carmichael."

Is this business-related?"

"No, this is a personal call."

"If you'd like, I can transfer you to his voicemail. Is that okay?"

"Sure, thank you."

Right about this time I felt like I should go home, crawl back in bed until the next morning, and try all over again. And look, it was only ten fucking thirty. Only five and a half hours left of this torture before I could get some alcohol in me. Just one glass of wine; that was all I needed. I would figure out how to hit the reset button. I was surprised Georgia hadn't come by yet. Maybe I needed to go find her.

"Nikki." Jack's voice caused the hairs on my body to bristle and shoulders to hunch. I could hear his clopping footsteps getting closer to my desk. I raised my eyes just as I heard him gasping for breath over the wall of my cubicle. "The numbers look much better now. Good job."

"Thank you."

"Pay closer attention next time, and don't make silly mistakes. You know it always takes more time to redo work than it does to do it right in the first place."

"I'm really sorry. I'll be more careful in the future." *Perhaps you can just take me out back and shoot me next time.*

"All right. I'll let you know if I need anything else." He turned and walked away.

I dropped my forehead onto my desk, arms dangling, with my fingertips skimming the ground. A few seconds later, I heard Georgia's voice laughing at me. I turned my head slowly, never breaking the connection my forehead had to the wood desktop, to see her doubled over, arms clenching her stomach, laughing.

"Sweets, we need to do lunch. Do you have anything on your schedule?"

"No, please, take me far away."

"We can go to the mall food court, if that's far enough."

"It'll do. What time do you want to leave?" I lifted my head and raised my eyebrows, hoping she would say now, knowing that was impossible.

"We can leave at noon. I'll be back when I'm ready. Try to hold it together until then." She chuckled as she walked away.

Georgia was right; I needed to pull it together.

I heard my phone chime, signaling a text message. I unlocked the screen and saw Sky had sent me a message.

Sky: We are not done talking. Let's meet later.

Me: Meet me at the bar across the street from my job. We can talk, if you insist.

Sky: I'll be there at 6.

I finally got back on my computer and checked my emails. I replied to those that needed my attention, and the others got moved to the archive folder. I switched applications and opened my marketing tool to review the other accounts I had worked on the week before. I needed to make sure that if I had messed up anything else, it got corrected before submissions at the end of the night.

"Are you ready?" I was so busy studying my files, I didn't hear Georgia tap on my desk.

"Yes, let me save this real quick and we can go." I grabbed my purse and phone, and we made our way through the door to the elevator leading down into the parking garage.

"You have a lot to catch me up on."

"I know. The weekend was bonkers."

"Just tell me this right now; did you cut Jeff after Saturday night?"

"No. He came through with flying colors, slam dunked it, knocked it out of the park, and whatever other metaphor you can think of."

"I'm right over here." She pointed to her silver Pontiac G6. She unlocked it, and we got in, quickly fastening our seatbelts.

"Where did you guys go for dinner?"

"Bern's."

She stopped the car in the middle of the ramp. "Seriously? That place is five-star and really expensive." She accelerated again.

"I know. I saw the menu. He also ordered a bottle of Burgundy."

She stopped again. "A whole bottle?"

"Georgia, if you don't drive, we'll never get out of the parking garage." I laughed. "And yes, he ordered the whole bottle. We shared it."

"How was The Castle? That club is mostly gothic, steam-punk type crowds. I was thinking about you in there and how much you *wouldn't* fit in."

"The castle I went to wasn't a club. You're not going to believe this, but it was a sideways reference for his house."

Georgia slammed on the brakes again, and the car behind her laid on the horn. "Shut the front door!"

"Georgia, stop doing that! You're going to get hit, and it'll be your own fault." I sighed. "I'll tell you the rest at the mall so we get there in one piece."

We parked the car and walked in through the entrance next to the food court. I was craving Chick-fil-A and planned to get the largest fries possible. Georgia headed over to get pizza. We met at a small table near the soft-serve ice cream kiosk.

"So tell me everything, and start from the beginning." Georgia leaned in, eager to hear, as she sprinkled the crushed red pepper flakes out of the packet on her slice of pepperoni. "Did he pick you up, or did you guys meet somewhere?"

"He came by and picked me up; I gave him my address Saturday morning when we talked." I shoved my hot waffle fries into a peeled-back ketchup container. "We had a reservation for seven at Bern's Steakhouse. When we walked out to his car, I was floored; he drives a Nissan GT-R."

"Nissan's are common, no big deal. I'm more impressed that he took you to Bern's."

I pulled my phone out of my purse and googled the car. Once I had a picture and the retail price available, I shoved my arm across the table with my phone facing her, displaying the information. "See, that's what he drives."

"Damn. I didn't know Nissan made anything that expensive." She took a bite and chewed before continuing to talk with food in the side of her mouth, looking like a chipmunk. "So tell me what you were wearing and about Bern's."

"I wore my flimsy super-short yellowish gold dress with thin spaghetti straps and my animal sling-backs." I crammed a few more ketchup-covered fries into my mouth and chewed. After swallowing, I continued, "Bern's was really nice. I've never eaten somewhere so high-class. The steak was so tender it was like cutting through soft butter, and the flavor was unbelievable. I was shocked when he ordered the bottle of wine. I think that helped loosen him up. We had a nice conversation with dinner." I took a bite of my sandwich.

"We left Bern's, and I thought we were going to the club, The Castle. I had looked it up to see what it was and wasn't crazy about it, but hell, you only live once, right?"

"Right, so about the house … please continue."

"I thought I was on that show *Cribs*. His place is huge, ridiculously huge, ten-thousand-square-feet huge. Needless to say, he's loaded." I chewed and swallowed another bite of my sandwich.

"He gave me the grand tour. He has an elevator and a movie theater that seats twenty. His master bedroom is absolutely huge. The house is sick. Do you remember that movie *The Big Lebowski,* when John Goodman said 'those rich fucks'? That's what I was thinking walking through there. He even has a pool and pool house, but I didn't see them; it was too dark."

"What did you guys do? Did you end up going out somewhere?"

"No, we stayed in. I did what any other red-blooded woman would do who was out with such a good-looking guy, had been treated to a dinner at Bern's, and seeing he's very wealthy -- I fucked him."

"Seriously? That was like the second time you went out. You don't even know him."

"I know more about him now than I did, and I know I'd like to see him again, but let's keep it real. Honestly, I may not see him again, Georgia, and I don't care. I couldn't pass up the opportunity knowing I may never hear from him again."

"Most men don't keep the easy ones, though, Nikki."

"Yeah, I know. I still don't regret it, though. I called and left a voicemail for him this morning."

"Why call so soon? You should have given him a couple days to see if he'd call you."

"My day has been so fucked up, I thought talking to him might help."

"Yeah, what's going on? Tristan said you snapped at him and that you got scolded in your one-on-one this morning."

"I messed up on an account last week. My mind has been all over the place since I saw Jeff in that restaurant. And on top of that, I saw *Hope* again Sunday night."

"They aren't getting serious, are they? But, I mean, Sky has a right to move on; you divorced him. One woman's trash is another woman's treasure."

"I'd hardly call Sky trash -- maybe uninspired and broke, but definitely not trash. Anyway, I got jealous seeing her -- damn near crumbled right in front of him and then felt like a complete ass after I left his apartment."

"Shit happens; don't sweat it. You've got bigger fish to fry now anyway."

"I agreed to meet Sky after work to talk about this; he's not letting up, and he's going to put me on the spot again about getting together. I just can't do it. I love him, but I just can't. I hate when he has me cornered." I took a bite of my sandwich and held my ketchup-covered lukewarm fries in my hand, waiting to shove them in my mouth.

"Any idea when you'll see Jeff again?"

"No clue, and I still don't have his cellphone number. I'm telling you, there's still a weird vibe with him."

"Was it worth it? Sleeping with him?"

"Right now; yeah, yeah it was."

"We have to get back. Grab your food, and you can eat in the car; just don't make a mess."

I wrapped up the rest of my sandwich and jammed it back in the bag. The fries had to go; they were cold and gross. I hefted my purse onto my shoulder, and we headed back out and across the parking lot to the car. I felt just a tiny bit better after talking to Georgia about my near collapse over Hope and Sky, and not being judged by her. Now I just had to deal with Sky later.

We walked back in the building and saw Tristan in the hallway; maybe he was just returning from lunch. Georgia leaned over to whisper in my ear, "Did you know he's secretly dating someone in Customer Service?"

"No way! Really? Who? For how long?"

"Christy. They've been a thing for a couple of weeks. I'm not supposed to say anything so don't you dare tell anyone."

"I won't say a word." My heart sank a little. I felt a knot form in my gut. A part of me wondered if I had made the right choice by not giving Tristan a chance. Maybe we could have -- *Just stop already; he isn't my type, and there was no desire to give him a chance at anything other than being a quick fling.*

"I'll talk to you later, Georgia. I have to go get some work done."

"See you."

I made it back to my desk and got my belongings put away, unlocked my computer, and brought back up the accounts I was working on before lunch. Another day of number crunching, only this time I had to be hyper-paranoid because I couldn't afford to mess up again.

An hour and a half later, I closed my eyes and took a deep breath. The relentless mind-numbing staring at numbers was turning my brain to mush. Before I opened my eyes, my cellphone rang. Thinking it might be Jeff, I pulled it out of my drawer. My heart raced and I held my breath momentarily when I saw the number for Abby's day dare.

"Hello?"

"May I speak with Mrs. Carmichael?"

"Yes, this is Mrs. Carmichael."

"I'm sorry to bother you at work, but Abby isn't feeling well. She doesn't have a fever, but is complaining her tummy hurts."

"I'll be right there."

I hit the end button on my cell and clicked the save button on my computer. I jumped up from my chair so fast it nearly toppled over backwards. I walked down to Jack's assistant. "Is Jack available? I need to talk to him. My daughter's sick, and I have to go pick her up."

"Just go; take care of what you need to. I'll give him the message when his meeting's over. If you need to be out tomorrow, just give us a call."

"Thank you so much."

I ran back to my desk, logged off, grabbed my purse, and rushed out to the elevator.

After getting Abby home and settled in her bed, I called Sky to let him know I wouldn't be able to meet him later.

"Hey Sky, I hope I'm not interrupting anything."

"Hey. No, I can talk."

"I wanted to let you know, I won't be able to meet you later. I had to pick Abby up, she wasn't feeling well."

"What's wrong with her? Is she okay? I'm coming over; I need to see my little princess."

"You don't have to come over; she'll be okay. They said she was complaining of a tummy ache."

"I'll be at your place at six. Please don't tell me I can't check on my daughter, Nik."

"I'd never keep you from seeing her, you know that. I'll see you later then." *Damn it!* I thought I had an excuse to get out of this wretched conversation. He'd be by in a couple of hours, just time enough to clean up the kitchen and vacuum the floors. One of the benefits of a small house is that cleaning is quick.

The doorbell rang just as I was stuffing the vacuum back into the closet under the staircase. Six o'clock, it was show time.

Chapter 8

If there's a bigger sucker walking the face of the earth, I wanted someone to show me. He was stunning when he slept, and he had taken care of Abby through the night, but having Sky in my bed this morning was not the way to move forward after telling him it just wouldn't work between us. I guess I shouldn't complain now that it was the light of day, though; I hadn't been complaining last night when he was making me scream in ecstasy. And what was I supposed to say when he walked out past my mom? Jeez, she was going to be floored. It wasn't really her business; I'm a grown woman and he was the father of my child, but still. I left him lying there asleep while I dragged myself into the shower.

I couldn't believe he'd told me he would break up with Hope if it would make me happy. That's not what I wanted. I didn't know what I wanted, but I knew that wasn't it. He said no one would ever replace me in his heart. He said he'd do anything for me. *Anything except get and keep a job. Why does my life have to be so difficult?* I stepped out of the shower, standing on the plush brown rug, my eyes covered by the towel. As I wiped the towel over my face and opened my eyes, there he was.

"Jesus! Are you trying to give me a heart attack?"

"No, I just noticed you were up, and I missed you."

"Sky, look, I appreciate everything you did last night -- *everything* -- but my mom is coming by this morning to watch Abby, and I'd rather you not be here when she shows up. I just don't want to have to deal with that or try to explain anything to her."

"No problem. I have to get out of here anyway. I have an interview this morning at ten o'clock."

"That's great. I hope it works out for you."

"Before I leave, I just want to say that I meant everything I said last night. No one can replace you. I love you so much." His eyes were a flashback to our wedding day. Beautiful bluish-grey pools of lust, and full of love.

"I know you do, and I love you too. But we both need to move on; it's best that way. I don't want to give you false hope that we can or will reconcile."

"A man can dream, can't he?" His eyes were laser focused on mine, and his hand stroked over my slippery wet shoulder, down my arm, grasping my fingers. "I'll see you on the weekend."

"Yep, we can finalize Abby's birthday party plans, too."

"Absolutely."

As soon as he cleared the doorway, I exhaled and slumped down, sitting on the closed toilet seat, my shoulders rounded and head dropped, and my arms hung limp in my lap. I felt weak. What was I doing to him? To us? Tears welled up in my closed eyes. It wasn't supposed to be this hard. I sat there for several minutes, thinking about how selfish I had been not to make a clean break from him. I didn't care about getting ready or getting to work on time.

Once I heard him leave through the front door, it was my signal to find the strength to trudge through another day. I was happy my mom was coming by because it took some of the morning pressure off. But I was probably going to be late, with no reasonable excuse.

I arrived in the office fifteen minutes late and was greeted by Jack standing next to my desk.

"Good morning," I said, trying to seem like nothing was wrong.

"Good morning. How's the kid feeling?"

"She kept me up all night," I lied; I was up all night but not because of Abby, "but she's feeling better today. My mom is watching her for me."

"That's good. Glad to hear it." He slapped an open hand on the top of my cubicle wall and walked away. That's it? No fussing because I was late? I'd take it; I definitely wasn't in the mood to hear a bunch of blather.

Candace walked by just as I put my purse in my drawer. "How's Abby?"

"She's feeling much better today, thanks."

"Great. Have you talked to that guy from the bar? What was his name again?"

"Jeff. Let's go get some coffee, and I'll bring you up to speed on him." I grabbed my mug, and we talked as we walked to the break room, where we were met with Tristan and Georgia. After getting my coffee, and sharing my life story with them, I made my way back to my desk with a happy hour date for Friday after work. At least I had something to look forward to.

Before I started work, I called Jeff and was once again sent to his voicemail. After hanging up, I let out a long, low sigh. *Forget him; you have other things to worry about, like getting caught up with your work and not making any more mistakes. He used you, and you used him; it's over, so move on.*

All week, my mind raced between Sky and Jeff, with work getting done in between my daydreams. Friday night happy hour quenched my long overdue need for a drink, but despite my attempts to stay engaged in the conversations and have a good time, my mind continued to wander back to the men at the root of my angst. By seven o'clock, I told everyone I'd see them on Monday and left for home.

Saturday morning, I was startled out of my sleeping-pill-induced coma by my cellphone ringing before six thirty. I reached over, and through hazy vision, made out the displayed name, Jeff. I had saved his office number under his name; I couldn't believe he was working on a Saturday morning. I needed to let him know not to call me before ten o'clock on Saturdays. We had a nice conversation once the brain fog cleared. He said he'd been out of town all week but wanted to take me out again. I had never heard of the restaurant he mentioned, but he assured me it was very good and told me to be ready by six o'clock, and that he'd come get me.

I was cleaning the house when Sky came by to get Abby. Her overnight bag was sitting by the front door, and she was jumping on the couch like it was her personal trampoline. I was relieved he didn't rehash our conversation from Tuesday morning. He and Abby left, and I quickly finished squeezing her toys into the toy box in the closet, put the finishing touches on the kitchen, then went to the salon to get my hair done. I wanted to wear it in a nice up-do, but my attempts at doing it myself in the past had failed miserably.

My stomach fluttered, and my heartbeat raced as I flipped through my wardrobe to find something breathtaking to wear. The perfect dress practically jumped out of the closet at me. When in doubt, go for the little black dress. My Rachel Roy form-fitting dress that reached mid-thigh was perfect. The high neckline would give the classy look, and the lace zip back was the sexy, flirty look. My black patent leather pumps were the perfect shoes.

Jeff arrived a few minutes before six, and I was ready when he rang the bell. He stepped in for a few minutes, wrapping me in his strong arms and lowering his soft lips on mine, kissing me like a sailor just returning from six months at sea.

We arrived at Mise En Place just before seven o'clock and enjoyed a glass of wine at the bar while we waited for our table to be ready. Jeff's touch on my arm and lower back had me squirming on the stool. He stood close enough behind me that I could feel his body heat.

"I can't wait to get this dress off of you," he whispered in my ear.

"I'm looking forward to it, too. We can leave now, if you prefer."

"Be patient, kitten; we have all night, and I plan to use you for each minute of it." My back arched at his fingers running up my spine.

"What's good to eat here?"

"You, pussycat, but you aren't on their menu." His warm breath was teasing my sex with the impending pleasure sure to come. "I think we should share the Get Blitzed Tasting Menu so you can try more than one thing."

We were called and walked over to our table. *White tablecloths and real cloth napkins, I can get used to this lifestyle.* Jeff ordered for us, including the wine. We enjoyed our meal, Jeff settled the check, and we left to go back to his place.

Chapter 9

I jumped up and realized I wasn't at home. How long had I slept? What time was it? I glanced at the clock on the nightstand past Jeff's still form -- one seventeen. It was so dark in the room, it was hard to tell it was daylight out, but knowing we hadn't gone to sleep until after two AM, I knew it was afternoon. Sky was supposed to come by at two thirty. I needed to get back home or call him or something. I wrapped myself in Jeff's robe that was lying across the bench at the foot of the bed, slid my cellphone from my clutch purse, and tiptoed through the room and down the stairs to get out of his earshot. I couldn't deal with talking to Sky, so I quickly sent a text message instead.

Me: Can you keep Abby until 5?

Sky: Yeah, where are you?

Me: Having lunch with a friend. I'll be there by 5 though. I really appreciate it.

Sky: No problem.

I walked back upstairs, tucked my phone back in my purse, slipped off the robe, and crawled back in bed.

"Is everything okay?" Jeff mumbled out.

"Yes, I just needed to let my mom know I would be late getting to her house." *Way to go; telling lies already.*

"Good. I have plans for you for the next hour." Jeff rolled over toward me, his erection skimming across my thigh. His soft touch sent a craving rippling through my body that caused my legs to involuntarily spread for him. I was ready for him to consume and fill me with his eager manhood. He reached for a condom out of the nightstand before taking his position between my legs and pressing deep into me, thrusting hard, deep rhythmic strokes for what seemed like hours until he found his release. I had needed this last Sunday. I really could get used to this … and him.

He washed me in the shower, until his attention was sidetracked to licking my still-hard nipples and rubbing my clit, coercing another orgasm from me. "Damn, you're insatiable," he said appreciatively.

"You make me that way." I pressed him back against the shower wall and climbed up on my tiptoes, barely able to cover his mouth with mine. I could stay there and fuck him all day and night. We finally separated and finished washing up before exiting the shower and getting dressed. I was slipping my shoes on and saw it was almost three o'clock.

"Do you have time to grab something to eat?"

"Sure, but something quick, if you don't mind."

"No problem; your choice."

"Do you eat fast food?"

"It depends on the place."

We went through the drive-thru at Wendy's -- they have the second-best fries ever, behind Chick-fil-A, and the Spicy Chicken sandwich is my favorite -- then Jeff dropped me off at home. He told me before I got out of the car to save the number he rattled off because that was his cellphone. I reached for my phone and typed in what I remembered, asked for the rest, and saved it.

I was sitting at the kitchen table, taking sips of my water, and immersed in thought when the doorbell rang and Sky entered with Abby.

"Hey, Nik," Sky called to me.

"Hey, Sky, thanks again." Abby jumped into my arms, wrapping her little arms around my neck and squeezing tight.

"Hey, baby girl. Did you have fun at Daddy's?"

"Yep, I got a new toy."

"Let me see it."

"Abby, let Daddy talk to Mommy for a minute, then you can show her." She skipped to the living room, where Sky had set her bag.

"So who's the guy?" Sky asked as soon as she was out of sight, his eyes tightening, jaw clenching, and lips thinning.

"No one you would know." I swallowed hard, averting my eyes from his prying glare. "I met up with him earlier today. It's nothing serious; we were getting something to eat, and I knew we wouldn't get back in time." My heart was pounding so rapidly I thought it was going to burst out of my chest cavity. *Great, now I'm lying to Sky. I've never done that.* "How'd your interview go?"

"It went fine. I'll know more this coming week." His gaze was probing me, scanning my face, seeking cracks in the story I'd just fed him.

"Sky, I have to apologize again for last weekend. I was so irrational. I feel really bad."

"Don't sweat it; you're moving on, and so am I, right?" The snippy tone he used sliced through my heart.

"That's right. How is Hope?"

"I wouldn't know; if I see her again, I'll ask her."

I looked at him; his eyes had become cold, empty, and full of hurt. "I've got to go."

"You can –"

"No, my empty apartment is waiting for me." He turned his back to me, facing the front door, and raised his hand above his shoulder, signaling he was leaving, "See you next weekend." He kept walking without even stopping to say goodbye to Abby, pulling the door firmly behind him.

Fuck! I walked into the living room and leaned my head against the door. I had never meant to hurt him like this. He had to have known; this guy wasn't the first one.

I turned to Abby, who was staring at me from the floor with the corners of her little mouth turned down. "Where's that new toy?" I asked her. Her expression changed to a smile, and her eyes became bright as she ran over to me holding up a new doll.

"See her."

"I do; did you give her a name yet?"

"No."

"Well, let's go get some juice, and we can think of a name for your new baby." We had juice and crackers while going through every female name I could think of before she decided to settle on Sissy. I was surprised she said my nickname Gary had given me when we were younger.

We played with her other dolls and Sissy until it was time for her to get her bath and go to bed. Tomorrow was day care, and I wasn't planning to have a repeat of last Monday.

After getting Abby settled in bed and assured she was asleep, I went into my bedroom and lay in bed, thinking of Jeff. I reached for my cellphone on the nightstand and called him. I had to talk to him before I went to sleep.

After thirty minutes of talking, I confirmed our plans for the upcoming Saturday. This time, no restaurant, I was going to drive over and we'd cook at his house.

He finally told me more about his career. He was the director of product management and sales with a technology company. He traveled between two to four days a week making sure clients and businesses were well-trained and happy with their purchases, and he handled whatever else they might need.

He gave me strict instructions for calling him during the week now that I had his cell number. No phone calls between eight o'clock in the morning and six in the evening. He said he wouldn't be able to answer the phone during meetings or in the evening if he was at dinner with a client anyway. I couldn't help but think it made better sense for him to call, since he knew when he'd be available.

I wanted more time from him, but I knew he was working to get promoted, and there was no way I could demand more. Plus, he traveled a lot, so what could I do.

****

We dated for the next two months, seeing each other mostly on Saturday nights and talking as much as his schedule allowed during the week. I had gotten comfortable with him, and we both enjoyed the time we spent together.

He was coming over the following day, after he got back in town. It was time for me to reveal my one little secret I had kept hidden from him.

Chapter 10

My palms were sweating. The lump in my throat made it difficult to swallow, and to top it all off, I felt dizzy and lightheaded. Anxiety sucks. I couldn't sit still; I paced like a caged lion as my stomach roiled. I shook my head, let out a lengthy sigh, and cracked my knuckles while fighting the bile rising in my throat. What if he didn't take the news well? What if he got mad? What if he just left and never called again? I wanted him and a life with him so bad I would be devastated if he walked out on me. Somehow, I had to convince him not to leave when I told him the news.

The doorbell rang and caused me to jump and gasp at the same time. I walked over to open the door. "Hi, babe."

"Hi to you." He leaned in and slanted his eager lips onto my angst-filled mouth. He stood and looked at me. I averted my eyes, shifting my glance to the floor. He placed his fingers under my chin, lifting my gaze back to meet his, "Hey, are you all right, baby doll?"

"Oh, um, yeah, I'm fine," I said with a fake smile and forced chuckle. "Come in the kitchen. Can I get you anything to drink?"

"I'll just have some water." He pulled out a chair, spun it around, and straddled it, facing me, staring into me.

I reached out, handing his water to him. He took a couple of small sips as he watched me over the rim of his glass as I gulped mine down. My legs felt unsteady, but I couldn't sit down.

"What's going on? I've never seen you act like this. You look like you're going to either pass out or puke any minute."

"I have something to tell you. I've been, uh, kind of hiding a secret from you. But I want you to know now." I walked over to set my glass by the sink, then ran my fingers into my hair, scratching my non-itchy scalp. "I'm scared to tell you. I'm so scared you're going to run as fast as you can when I do."

"Are you going to tell me you used to be a dude?"

"No, nothing crazy like that."

"Then how bad can it be?" Jeff lowered his head, rubbed the back of his neck, then raised his eyes to meet mine. "Just tell me; we'll figure it out, whatever it is."

Hurry up and get it out, Nikki; Abby will be home in half an hour. I wrung my hands and felt the constricting tightness in my chest. I backed up to the sink countertop, leaning my back against it for support. Closing my eyes, I blurted it out; "I have a three-year-old daughter."

Hearing no reply, no movement, no footsteps running to the front door, I slowly peeled my eyelids up to see him still sitting on that chair, looking at me, void of emotion and unfazed.

"That's it? That's what's had you on the verge of a heart attack?"

"Yeah."

"Maybe I should tell you a little secret then …" He rose from the chair and walked toward me. He stopped within an inch from my face, then leaned down to speak into my ear. "I already knew." He straightened back up to look me in the eye. "Did you think I was going out with someone I knew nothing about, brought you to my home, and trusted you there without knowing anything about you?"

My mouth fell open. *He'd had me investigated. What else did he know?* I was at a complete loss for words.

He stood directly in front of me, towering over me with his arms folded across his chest. His fixed gaze narrowed, and his jaw clenched, "Baby doll, don't misjudge me again. I'm still here. I didn't run like you thought I would."

I released the breath I had been holding, quietly, slowly, as he continued to look down on me, making me feel like a fool for thinking I was hiding anything from him.

He uncrossed his arms. "I don't play games and prefer not to have people in my life who are into games. I'm always trying to stay one step ahead of everyone else." He held my face with a hand on each side of my head. "I'm prone to despise people who underestimate me. Don't lie or keep secrets from me, please." He planted a light, soft kiss on my lips then rose again to face me. His face softened back to the Jeff I had spent the past three months dating. "What's next on the surprise list, sugar plum?"

"I ..." I stammered and swallowed. "I'd like you to meet her ... tonight."

"You got me with that one; I sure as shit didn't expect that. I'm fine with that, but since the topic of kids has now been unleashed, we need to discuss views and attitudes about that. We can talk tomorrow at my house. Can you get someone to watch her?"

"She'll be with her dad tomorrow."

He pressed up against me, wrapped his strong arms around me, and kissed me on top of my head. The anxiety washed out of my body by way of tears streaming down my face. Jeff pulled back and looked at me, kissing my tears away, covering my face with kisses. He wiped his fingers to remove the remaining tears, then covered my mouth with his soft, sensual lips, kissing and licking at me, cupping my face. He wrapped me tighter in his arms. "Don't cry, baby." His gentle caring tone caused the tears to stream again.

The doorbell rang, and I jumped. "You need to relax, baby. Who all am I meeting?" he asked.

"It should be my mom, possibly my stepdad, and Abby, my daughter."

"Great; let them in. I can't wait to meet them all."

****

I rolled over and looked at the clock when the alarm went off. It was only nine. Sky was coming by at noon to get Abby, then I'd go by his place to get her when I left Jeff's later in the evening. Last night, Mom had looked like she had seen a ghost when I introduced her to Jeff; all the color washed from her face and her smile disappeared. She knew him or something about him, I could feel it. She would make a terrible poker player; her emotions and thoughts were very obvious in her facial expressions.

Other than that, everything had gone well. Jim liked Jeff. They shared a love of cars. Jeff took Jim out to see his car and let him drive it. I found myself thinking it was too bad my dad wasn't still in my life, because he would have loved the conversation and Jeff's car, too. He was the one who taught me about cars, we'd been to car show after car show when I was younger. He would quiz me on everything from engine size to horsepower to torque. Those were special times for me.

Abby had put on her shy act for about the first fifteen minutes, then the floodgate was lifted -- she talked non-stop. She took Jeff up to see all of her toys and introduced him to Sissy, her new doll. He handled it well, but seemed a little out of his comfort zone talking to a child. I admired his softer side. I found myself thinking he would make a great dad one day. I wondered if he had or wanted any. He was getting close to forty, after all.

I laid there for ten more minutes before deciding I may as well get up and get the day started. I gathered my clothes, walked into the bathroom and got in the shower. The water felt so good, I could've stayed in there all day. Sky had a key, so I didn't need to worry about letting him in. I didn't need to have a 'kid' talk. *Oh shit – the kid talk.* I wondered what this was going to be about.

When Sky arrived, I had Abby dressed and ready to go. Our conversation was brief. We were still friendly, but something between us had changed.

"Abby wants to go to Busch Gardens; I hope you don't mind taking her."

"That's cool. I wasn't sure what to do. I guess now I know. Thanks, Mom."

"I bought you three tickets from work. They were offering them for a discount."

"Why three?"

"One is for Hope."

"You don't pay attention to anything, do you? We aren't seeing each other anymore. I guess you're just so busy with Mr. Perfect that no one else matters to you."

"That's not true, Sky. I'm sorry."

"Yeah, just call when you're on your way over." He ripped the tickets from my hand, picked up Abby and her backpack, and closed the door behind him.

I refused to let Sky dampen my mood. His breakup was his problem, he was a good-looking guy, and I knew he'd find someone else. I was happy that fucking perfect bombshell Hope was out of the picture and I'd never have to see her again. I slung my purse over my shoulder, picked up the keys from the arm of the couch, sent a quick text letting him know I was on my way, and left to go see Jeff.

Jeff answered the door in nothing but a pair of drawstring silk pajama pants. He pulled me into a tight embrace. "Hey, beautiful." My stomach fluttered.

I wrapped my arms around his waist and held him tight. "Hey." I rested my head on his thick, muscular shirtless chest, relishing the feel of his bare skin. Being wrapped in his arms was a better feeling than being in the shower earlier.

"Let's go out by the pool. We can talk out there."

"Okay. I should have brought my swimsuit."

"Who needs a swimsuit? My backyard is like a fortress; it's clothing optional back there."

I looked at him with wide eyes, surprised that he had suggested skinny-dipping and intrigued at the idea of us both in the pool together totally butt-ass naked. We walked through the kitchen and out onto the patio.

"Want a beer?" he asked.

"Sure." He grabbed four cans of Bud Light Lime and motioned with his head for me to keep following him. That was no problem. I'd follow his fine ass right off a cliff.

His back-yard was fantastic, like a beautifully coiffed garden. There were so many flowers, trees, and bushes. The path leading to the pool was outlined on each side by red, white, pink, lavender, purple, yellow, and orange flowers neatly kept in a six-inch track of dirt just for them.

We arrived at the pool, and he motioned for me to sit where two chaise lounge chairs were separated by a small table. He opened my beer and handed it to me.

"This yard and pool are beyond words; it's so beautiful and bright. I'm glad the pool is finally fixed so we can come back here and enjoy this oasis." I leaned back in the lounge chair.

"I'll make sure to let the gardener know you think he's doing a bang-up job." He smiled and winked at me. "Let's cut to the chase today. I don't want to drag this out, but I have to say my piece."

I sat upright and turned to face him.

"I know you're younger than me," he started. "And if, at the end of this conversation, anything we discuss is a deal breaker for you, let me know, and we'll go our separate ways. But I have to be one hundred percent honest with you."

I leaned in. "Okay."

He looked me in the eyes. "I enjoyed meeting your daughter yesterday. I have plenty of friends that have kids too. But I've never wanted children of my own." He took a sip of his beer. "I'm thirty-eight and have successfully managed to avoid it this long and want to keep it that way."

"Maybe you'll change your mind in a couple of years; you're still young."

"People tell me to never say never, you know? Well, I'm ninety-nine point nine percent sure I can say never and mean it." Sweat was forming around his hairline as he took another sip from his can. It was hot as hell out here.

"I'm confused. Does this mean we aren't going to see each other anymore because I have a daughter?"

"No, what I'm trying to say is, I can accept your daughter, but if you want any more kids, I'm not the man for you. I don't want any children of my own now, or anytime in the foreseeable future. So that's it. You don't have to tell me today whether this is a deal breaker or if you can live with it, but you do have to know this is my decision, take it or leave it."

"Wow, that's something to think about."

"That's why I'm not rushing you for a decision. But know this, my mind isn't changing. If, after giving this some thought, you know that you want more kids, then I'll wish you well and make sure you get everything moved out."

"Okay."

"But I don't want this to dampen our day; I didn't ask you over so we could focus on this. I'd rather be focusing on you." He stood and untied the bow at his waist and slid his pants down to reveal his naked Adonis form. "Care for a swim?" He walked over and jumped into the pool.

I set my can on the table and pulled my sundress over my head. I slipped my thong panties down my legs and over my feet. I pulled my hair back with the ponytail holder that was around my wrist then walked over, stepping off the edge and dropping my thin body into the pool alongside him. He caught me as my head bobbed back up and pulled me into him. I could feel his erection caressing between my thighs, across my sex. My arms wrapped around his neck and I kissed, licked, and nipped at him. His hands slid down my back to my butt. He squeezed, pulled me into him tighter and made me quake with lust.

"I don't want an answer from you now, but I do expect one within the month; that will give you plenty of time to figure out what you want."

"I don't need a month, I already know. I want you. Whatever I have to sacrifice, I will. I just want you." I lowered my lips onto his again, our tongues thrashing and exploring each other. "I love you." My heart quickened. *Shit, can I rewind the last ten seconds? There is no way I meant to say that.*

His eyebrow raised, and he pulled back and gazed at me, studying my face. Without words, he pinned my back into the wall of the pool.

"Are you on the pill?"

"Hell yeah I am."

He reached down and grabbed my legs behind my knees, spread them wide, and pressed his swollen head against my slick, wet folds. He rubbed back and forth across me, teasing me, enticing me, then, without warning, he impaled me. As he pressed into me his lips consumed my mouth. The feel of him in me while my back scraped against the pool caused me to come undone, and my body quivered while my channel clenched in O-heaven around his hardness. His thrusts became hard and intense, and within a few minutes he found his release … inside me.

"I'm not done with you; that was an appetizer." He smirked at me. He held me in place as his lips explored my neck, my mouth, and my forehead, leaving a trail of kisses along the way. "God damn, baby doll."

He pulled himself up out of the pool and helped me out. We both went back to the chairs, lying there dripping wet and naked in the sun, drinking our beer. The silence was ominous. I glanced over to see Jeff lying there with his eyes closed. I closed my eyes as my mind raced. I tried to imagine what had made me slip out those words -- the three words that left me exposed and vulnerable. I was supposed to be protecting my heart like it was a bar of gold inside Fort Knox. He hadn't even said it back. Instead, he fucked me raw. He said he didn't want children, yet he fucked me without a condom, and shot his load in me. Did he change his mind about using a condom because I was on the pill or because I'd said I loved him, or did he just get caught up in the moment? I mean, if he wanted to make sure he didn't have kids, why put everything on me?

I woke to the feel of Jeff's hand massaging over my mound and lips. "Gorgeous, you need to put on more sunscreen, turn over onto your stomach, or go upstairs and shower."

"What time is it; how long have we been out here?"

"It's just past one thirty."

"I never put sunscreen on at all. Fuck, I'm probably burnt."

"Go take a shower, and I'll get the aloe." He stood, removing his hands from my snatch.

"Join me in the shower; we can get the aloe after."

I stood and grabbed for my dress and was handed a towel instead. "You'll need the dress later to go home. Go on. I'll be right up with your things."

The water in the shower was so refreshing. I lathered my body with the special request Dove body-wash he'd gotten for me. As I ran my hands over my soapy body, my thoughts went back to the pool. It may not have lasted long, but it felt so good. My hands slid down my stomach to my mound. He was skilled and satisfied me, but he always made me want more. I craved feeling him.

My fingers slid down farther, through my folds and to the slippery wetness of my heat. My fingers pushed up inside me as the water beat down on my back. Thrusting my own fingers in and out, I was getting close to the edge. Was it wrong to make myself orgasm without him? He'd never know, and surely he'd make me orgasm plenty more times when he got up here. My other hand massaged my clit at the same time my fingers continued to pump in and out of me. Within minutes, I muffled out a moan as the orgasm rippled through my body.

"I could watch you do that every day," Jeff said.

"I-I didn't know you were up here." My faced flushed and my skin warmed.

"I didn't want to interrupt you. I stood in the bedroom and watched. That was so damn hot." He brought me a fresh towel and set it on the edge of the Jacuzzi tub. His pants were once again slipped off, revealing his throbbing hardness as he entered the shower to join me. "I hope you were thinking of me."

"Of course."

"Good." His mouth covered mine as he pressed me flush against the shower tiles. "I don't want you in here; I want you out there."

"I'm showered and ready. I will wash you real quick." I squeezed body-wash onto my hands, rubbed them together, then pressed them into his well-toned torso. My hands caressed up over his shoulders, then across his strong chest. I pressed my breasts into him as I reached around to lather up his back. His hands lowered onto my back while his erection pressed into my stomach. My hands slid down his back to his tight, round ass, washing and feeling him, his cock throbbing against me. My hands slid around his hips, down his outer thighs to his knees, then back up his inner thighs to his heavy sack, the length of his shaft and his dripping head. *Get him rinsed off...now.* I pushed him back under the water to let the soap rinse off his magnificent body.

My hands made sure the soap was removed from everywhere before I lowered myself to my knees in front of him and licked at the delicious salty dew that had formed a string trail from his tip to the shower floor. I looked up at him as I took his crown into my mouth, water pounding down on me as I worked him in and out of my mouth. *I'd love for him to explode in my mouth. There you go again, using that fucking word.* My hands massaged his sack as my tongue lashed out around his cock to give my hands some assistance. "Oh, damn girl."

I used both hands, one to stroke his length as I licked and sucked on his head, and the other to provide the perfect technique to his balls. "You're going to make me cum if you don't stop." I wasn't going to stop. I wanted to feel his hot jizz in my mouth, sliding down my throat. I worked him even harder, pretending I didn't hear his warning. "I'm going to blow." He tried to pull back, but I wrapped my lips tight around the head, and held him tight with a hand around his ass. I took his entire length deep in my throat as my hand circled and twisted around the base. He thrust in and out of my mouth, and I knew it was coming. I bobbed up and down his length, sucking him, forcing the cum out of him. He exploded in my mouth, and I continued to move my mouth up and down, milking him as I swallowed every delicious drop. A little had escaped and ran down his length, which I quickly retrieved with my tongue. "Oh, shit!" he growled.

Chapter 11

Mom came by Monday morning instead of Tuesday to watch Abby that week. She had an open-house on Tuesday. Good thing my day care was flexible.

Once I got finished with my one-on-one meeting with Jack, I walked downstairs to the building lobby to call Mom. Her reaction to Jeff had been bothering me, and I needed to know what was behind it.

Just like I suspected, she eventually confessed that she knew of him. Her best friend, Gretchen, had dated him about two and a half to three years ago for six months. Things ended badly, when he was found in bed with an administrative assistant from his office. She wanted to make sure I didn't move too fast and always kept my guard up. I assured her I'd heed her warning. If she knew I'd told him I loved him she would freak out. I was still freaking out.

Jeff was out of town for the entire week, which gave me time to spend with Abby, get my nails done, and try to repair the damage between me and Sky. I hated that we seemed so distant.

Before returning to my desk, I called Sky and set up to have lunch with him on Wednesday.

****

The days flew by. Sky and I had a very good lunch date. We talked about everything except Jeff. He told me about the interviews and had gotten an offer for a job to start Monday. We talked about his mom and the progress he was having with their relationship. Things had gone straight to hell between the two of them when we decided to get married. She had stopped talking to him for over a year. Once the divorce was finalized, she reached out to him to console him for what *I* had done to him. She was paying his rent and other bills until he was able to get back on his feet. I told him Mom and Jim were there for him, too, if he needed any help with his job hunting.

I spoke with Jeff every night. We both pretended like the declaration of love never happened. I was haunted by it, but really couldn't beat myself up too bad. After all, I loved his house, his pool, his car, his generosity, and his dick. I could twist that into love of him if I was being creative.

My weeks were all scripted the same; work Monday through Friday, late night phone calls or the occasional Skype conversation with Jeff, talk to Sky once or twice, love Abby unconditionally, and spend Saturday and Sunday fucking Jeff. Sex had been taken to a new level since the first condom-free experience. That was the norm now.

It had been four weeks since the 'kid talk.' Jeff invited me over and I cooked dinner for us.

"The job I've been waiting for opens for resume submissions in a couple of weeks. I plan to submit my name," Jeff said.

"That's great news. Will it be a promotion?"

"Yes, more money, more responsibility, and probably a little more travel for another year or two."

I stabbed a piece of steamed broccoli onto my fork. He told me he would acquire direct reports overseas and would need to travel there twice a year for an extended amount of time, probably two or three weeks.

"Do they have a date they want the position filled?"

"Within a month after they open for submissions, they want the person they select hired and in the job."

There was a slight pause then he asked, "Have you had plenty of time to think over whether you want more kids or if you can live with my decision?"

I never raised my eyes from my plate. "I don't want to lose you. I'm fine with having just Abby; I don't need any more kids."

"I don't want you to feel like I'm forcing you to do something you don't want to. If you aren't comfortable with that, say it now."

"I'm comfortable with it, for real."

I could feel Jeff's blazing-hot eyes on me. I lifted my gaze to meet his. "Baby doll, move in with me. I have plenty of room for you and Abby here. I'd like to come home to your beautiful smile and magnificent body." This conversation had taken a serious and unexpected turn.

I was shocked speechless and sat slack-jawed. "I don't know what to say. This all seems so fast."

"There are no rules or timetables when things just feel right. Say yes, baby doll."

"Um, okay, then, yes." The smile on my face was so wide my muscles felt stretched. "What about my house?"

"Sell it. You live here now."

"When should I move my things? You'll be out of town, and I don't have a key."

"Here you go." He dug in his pocket and pulled out a set of keys he slid across the table to me. *Confident much?* "There's a key for every door. I know a moving company that can pack and move you during the week so you'll be here by Saturday."

This seemed fast. I felt overwhelmed, happy, excited, and scared. "I love you." *Really, I said it again?* It's becoming too easy to let those three words sneak past my lips. Jeff rose from his seat and walked to me, lowering his luscious lips onto mine. "You make me very happy, kitten," he whispered into my mouth before planting a light, closed-mouthed kiss on me. He left me breathless when he pulled back from me and returned to his seat. At least he'd acknowledged I said it, but what kind of fucking response was that? That's almost as fucked up as saying 'thank you.'

I was tired of not having anything nice or new. After struggling to survive week to week, paycheck to paycheck, being able to finally live without money concerns seemed like a dream come true.

I went to bed on cloud nine, but the next morning my feet were firmly rooted on the ground as I began seeing the reality in my decision. I had to let everyone know the news. This was not going to be an easy week. I couldn't afford to take time off. Who would take it worse, Mom or Sky? Was I really doing the right thing? Living in Jeff's house would be amazing. I couldn't second guess myself; my status was on the way up.

I walked through the doors at work with a confused, disturbed feeling nagging at me. My chest felt tight, like an elephant was sitting on it, and butterflies had made their home in my stomach. I was early enough to get a cup of coffee before my one-on-one, but I found out Jack had called out sick so it was canceled. I needed to talk to someone. I needed to talk to Candace. I didn't even know how or what to feel today.

I couldn't talk at work. I needed to focus and get things done. I sent a meeting invite for lunch to both Candace and Georgia. I could tell them both at the same time. I wasn't even sure if judgment was coming or if they'd be happy for me. Within a couple minutes, I received acceptance replies from both.

All morning, my head kept replaying the conversation with Jeff from the day before. My mind was so far from my work that four hours had passed and not one account was updated. And I'd have to double check what I'd done so far. My mind was everywhere except on work.

Candace and Georgia came by my desk to see me clutching my purse, raring to make an escape. "We can just go across the street to the pizza place, if you want." I stood and we walked out.

"That works for me." Candace was not particular, as long as the food was good.

"That's fine; pizza sounds good for a Monday," Georgia agreed as well.

"How are things with Prince Charming?" Candace asked and Georgia grimaced.

"Things are going well, really well. That's one of the reasons I wanted to talk to you guys today." I swallowed hard. As we waited for the street signal to change to walk, I divulged, "He asked me to move in with him."

"No gosh-darned way!" Georgia gasped. She saved pseudo-cursing for special occasions; I'm guessing this was one of them. Candace was rendered speechless; she just stared at me.

"He asked me yesterday."

"It seems way too sudden; what did you say?" Candace asked.

"Jeff said there's no timetable when things feel so right. I have to say, I agree."

"But does it really feel right, Nikki, does it?" Georgia asked with her eyebrows raised.

We walked into the pizza place. As we stood in line to order, I continued, "I already told him yes." We worked our way through the line to get our slices of pie, then took a seat by the window.

"You didn't answer my question; does it really feel that right?" Georgia leaned in, placing her elbows on the table with her fingers clasped together as if in prayer.

"Yesterday it did."

"Sky is going to have a shit fit," Candace chimed in. "Have you told him yet?"

"No, not yet. I haven't told my mother either. I haven't even told Abby. I wanted to start with you two to see what your reactions would be first."

"Well, brace yourself; the worst is yet to come." Candace took a bite out of her pizza.

I took a long drag on the straw, sucking a huge swallow of soda into my mouth. Georgia swallowed the bite she had been chewing to disintegration, then asked, "When are you moving?"

"He wants me there by Saturday."

"Something doesn't seem right to me. I don't know him, but –" Georgia quipped as Candace interrupted.

"If you're happy, and you think you're doing the right thing for you and Abby, I'm happy for you," Candace said, then added, "but I have to agree with Georgia that it seems too fast."

We sat in silence for a few minutes as Candace and Georgia finished their food. Mine was still sitting on my plate, the exact perfect triangular dough shape covered with greasy pepperoni that I'd paid for, untouched. My appetite had abandoned me.

"What are you going to do with your house?" Georgia broke the silence.

"Um, I guess I'll just sell it. I won't need it once I move in."

"Take my advice, and don't sell the house. What if things don't work out between you guys? What will you do if Abby hates it there or hates him? You'll need somewhere to go." Candace and Georgia were tag-teaming me with things I hadn't thought of.

"Those are good points. I'll talk to Mom about it, I guess. We better get heading back."

I finished the day more confused than I started. I only knew one thing: I had to talk to Mom. I called and made plans to stop over after picking Abby up from day care.

"Mom," I called as Abby and I walked in through the back door of her house later that evening.

"I'll be right there; I'm in the laundry room."

I paced around the house, looking at their knickknacks as if it were my first visit there. Abby mocked my movements, looking at and touching everything I did. My stomach fluttered and my mind blurred. I felt short of breath.

"Hi, sweetie." My breath hitched and I startled at my Mom's voice. "Sorry, I didn't mean to make you jump. Is everything going okay?"

"Nana!" Abby ran and gave her a big hug around her knee.

"How's Nana's precious baby today?"

"Good, Nana."

I turned to face her. "Everything is fine, just fine."

"What brings you by?"

"I just wanted to talk to you." I was wringing my hands furiously and my eyes darted around the room, avoiding eye contact.

"Tell me what's going on Nervous Nancy."

"Well," my stomach turned, leaving me feeling hollowed, "I was at Jeff's last night." I looked over toward their fireplace. "Is something different in this room?"

"Nothing is different today, except you. What happened at Jeff's?"

"You know we've been seeing each other for about four months now." Summarizing the short length of our relationship made things seem that much worse to me right now. "I'll just say it; he asked me to move in with him."

My mom gasped and placed her hand over her mouth. She took a deep breath, exhaled and talked through her widespread fingers splayed on her face like a hand-cage, "What did you say?"

"I told him … yes."

Her hand dropped from her mouth. "Nikki, you're a grown woman. I can't tell you what to do with your life any more than you could tell me. But I have to say, I'm a little surprised. No, I'm shocked that you said yes."

"I know you're skeptical about him, but I really like him. He has a fantastic house with plenty of room and a pool. Abby will enjoy that."

"Has he told you he loves you?"

"He told me I make him happy and that I mean a lot to him."

"Have you told him you loved him?"

My gaze dropped to my feet. "Yes, I told him."

"And he didn't say he loved you back?"

"No."

"Oh, Nikki, honey, what are you doing? Why are you settling for this? You could find someone to love you like you deserve to be loved."

"I think he loves me. I just think he has a hard time saying it."

"I hope that's it, sweetie. Have you told Sky yet?"

"No, I'll talk to him tomorrow."

My mom's eyebrows raised, and her mouth pursed into a scowl. We talked for another hour, including the Thanksgiving dinner plans that may or may not include Jeff coming to dinner. When I left, she was not any more convinced Jeff was the right person for me or that moving in with him was a good decision. We told Abby and she seemed happy, but she was three years old. She was sold on the pool and having a big room for all of her babies. Mom agreed with Candace and Georgia that I shouldn't sell the house. She suggested Sky renting it from me so he would have more room and to be out of the small apartment he'd been living in. I said I'd be okay with that if he was.

Chapter 12

"Have you lost your fucking mind? What are you thinking?" He raised out of his seat, standing above me, his nostrils flared and his eyes coldly boring a hole through my heart. "So I guess I'm supposed to be happy for you? You're moving my daughter into some strange douchebag's house that you barely even know!" His face reddened in splotches. "This is really fucked up, Nik."

"Please sit down, Sky; you're making a scene." I could feel my face heat up as I tried to shrink into an invisible spot on my chair.

"I'm not doing shit; you did this! Where's your head? You aren't thinking of anyone but yourself, you know. This is --." He eased back down, holding me tight in his gaze. "This is so damn selfish! You make me sick right now."

"You're really being an asshole about this."

"Me? Really? You have turned into a self-righteous bitch on top of it all, you know that?"

"Fuck you, Sky! I don't have to put up with your shit. I'm a grown woman. I have to make my own decisions for my fucking life."

"Yes, you are," he conceded. "But my daughter isn't. She's getting dragged into some strange place with a strange man she doesn't know."

"I don't want to argue with you. I just want to make sure you know what's going on."

"Look, I'm not coming over to that asshole's house to pick her up or drop her off. I don't want to see that fucker or his house. You can make plans to either bring her to me or we can meet at your mom's."

"That's not always going to work, Sky."

"It's going to have to or we'll go back to court." His eyes narrowed. "So on Saturday, before you're setting up to play house with this ass clown, you can bring her over in the morning."

I sighed deeply, "Fine."

"I swear I just don't get you." Sky stood and held onto the back of the chair tight, his knuckles turning white. He looked directly out the door. "If you're happy, I'm happy for you." His voiced cracked as he continued, "Just don't let this asshole take advantage of you, Nik." He released the chair and ran his fingers down through my hair before he walked away. I didn't even have a chance to reply. I set my elbows on the table and dropped my face into my open hands.

"Is there anything else I can bring you?" The waitress was so chipper that I wished I could buy some of that from her. I felt like I had been zapped of almost every ounce of life that was in my body.

"A sharp knife," I said and pulled my hands down my face and looked at her. "Just kidding. I'm ready for the check, please." I settled on the bill and returned to work.

"How did it go?" Georgia was standing at the edge of my desk. I raised my dead-pan gaze to meet her eyes. "Oh, never mind."

"It was terrible; major baby daddy drama. If there's one person I hate arguing with, it's Sky." I turned in my swivel chair to face her. "But it was worse than just an argument; he was devastated."

"Did he say that?"

"He didn't have to; I could see it in his face and hear it in his voice." I turned on my monitor. "Am I doing the right thing, Georgia?"

"Only you know that answer, Nikki; we're all on the outside looking in. We don't know what's between you and Jeff. We don't know or understand the connection you two have. If it feels right to you, then it's right. You're entitled to be happy … and to live in that big ass house."

She laughed and I forced a smile. "Everyone will get used to it eventually, and it'll be fine."

"I hope so."

"Let me know if you need anything. I'm not the best at packing glasses, but I can get pots and pans in a box."

"Thanks, but Jeff has a moving company coming by Friday to pack up the house -- everything. Then they'll deliver it to his place Saturday morning."

"Wow, that's a man who knows what he wants and makes sure he gets it."

"Yep. Hey, let's do happy hour on Thursday this week."

"I'm in. Tristan and Candace might be okay to come. I'll check with them. We'll find people, even if we have to grab strangers at the bar."

We both laughed, and Georgia went back to finish her work. I felt a little better after talking to her. She was right; I was entitled to be happy.

Friday night, by the time I stopped by my house after work, it was completely empty. The movers had packed and taken everything. Probably things I didn't even want. To my surprise, it was spotless, too. I had expected I'd at least get that wonderful task. I just stood in the small living room that had been mine for the past two years scratching my forearm, a nervous habit I'd had since I was a child. *What am I doing? Is this really what I want?*

None of our things were being delivered until Saturday, but Abby and I decided to spend Friday night at Jeff's house anyway. I let her sleep with me in his bed since it was a new place and he wasn't home. He was supposed to get home in the afternoon on Saturday, so my plan was to get Abby to Sky before he got there.

After returning to Jeff's house Saturday morning from dropping Abby off with Sky, I was in the kitchen looking through his cupboards and pantry to see what he had and what he needed. The list was easy; he needed everything and had barely anything.

Jeff came in the house with a dozen white roses, startling me. "Honey, I'm home." He walked into the kitchen and wrapped his arms around my waist, lowering his lips onto mine. His mouth was warm and inviting, and I melted into his embrace. "It feels so good having you here; you have no idea how much it meant to me for you to say yes. Did all of your things get delivered?"

"Yep, everything is here. And they told me my furniture's in storage."

"I wasn't sure what you wanted to do with it. I have plenty of furniture. Maybe you can sell it with the house."

"About that -- my mom suggested I rent it out."

"It's your choice, whatever works for you. Just be ready for pain in the ass landlord shit."

He reached his arm out, holding the beautiful bouquet for me. They were already in a clear vase, which was perfect. I set it on the countertop bar.

"Let's go out tonight. What do you think, dinner and a club for real tonight?"

"That sounds good. I'm up for anything with you."

"How about a shower? I need to wash work off me for the week and get into something more comfortable." He winked before his eyes took me in from head to toe, sending tingles of need raging through my veins. He grasped my fingers and led me up the stairs to the bedroom to join him.

After the shower and sex, we laid in the bed, naked in each other's arms. "We're throwing a party here in two weeks," he said.

"Is there any special reason?"

"You're the reason. I want to introduce you to some of my coworkers. My manager will be here, and some of the other people I work with."

"Should I invite some of my friends?"

"This one is specific to my job; we'll have another party soon, and we'll invite everyone."

"Do I need to do anything? I can cook or decorate."

"It' going to be catered, so you don't have to worry about that. All you need to do is shop for a dress and shoes, go to the spa to get your nails and hair done, and be your beautiful self."

"I think I can handle that."

"I'd like Abby to be here, if you don't mind."

"I'd love it. Thank you."

My mind raced. Sky wouldn't be happy, but he'd have to get over it. He could have her on Sunday. My life was changing for the better. My worries had been for nothing, this was so right. I snuggled in closer under his strong arm.

I woke up to fingers sliding through my slick folds, caressing, enticing, and teasing me. I could hear the noise my wet heat made as his fingers massaged me. I wanted him in me again so bad my sex was spasming at the thought of him filling me. Without words, he positioned himself between my legs, his swollen head pressing against my opening. He held his shaft and rubbed his helmet up and down my wet slit, then he slowly pressed into me. I let out a moan as I took all of him. His pulsing was slow and steady, reaching deep, stretching my walls around him. He lay on me as he wrapped his arms around me, cocooning me in his embrace. His lips lowered onto mine, consuming my mouth, owning all of me.

His thrusts increased in speed and intensity; faster, harder, whooshing, quenching our primal needs. Even as he filled me, my greedy pussy wanted more. He lifted himself off me, releasing my swollen lips from his. His hand moved to my mound and dropped his thumb pad onto my inflated clit, slowly massaging with torturous pressure. My body trembled as he pushed me over the edge and my orgasm shattered me. He slammed into me with a ferociousness that nearly made me black out. My eyes closed tight as I went over the edge again, screaming his name, "Fuck, Jeff … shit!" After a few more strokes, he found his release inside me, and he collapsed onto me. The weight and warmth of his body, the heavy breaths against my neck, and the swipes of his tongue caressing my skin was welcomed as my arms held him tight.

"I'm starving; how about you?" he asked suddenly.

"I'm famished."

"Back in the shower, sexy, then we'll go grab something to eat."

The huge shower was wonderful. Being in this house and being with Jeff was a dream come true. This was all I needed to be happy; a good-looking man with a nice job and a home bigger than a shoe box. Living in his beautiful house was the icing on the cake of our relationship. I was the queen of the castle, and he was the gorgeous, and sexy king. This had to be right; nothing wrong could feel this good. We showered and dressed, then headed out to his car.

"Have you ever been to the Tampa Bay Brewing Company?" Jeff asked as he held my door open for me.

"No, never."

"You, my darling, are in for a treat. They have the best meatloaf. And the beer is not your average Miller or Bud."

We talked on the drive, but my mind was drifting to the party he had planned in two weeks. I needed to find the perfect dress, and I was thinking that I needed to get Jackie or Mandy to help me. Oh, shit, I hadn't even told them about Jeff or that I'd moved in with him. Well, something for the to-do list next week.

Chapter 13

My excitement came to a screeching halt when I met Jackie and Mandy for lunch Monday and told them about Jeff.

"Who does that?" Jackie asked. "He moves you into his house after knowing you for only four months, why?"

"Not everyone moves slow, Jackie; you know, he's an older guy," Mandy came to my defense.

"See, and that's another thing, why is he still single and thirty-eight? I'm telling you, I smell a rat."

"I think you're being too hard on him, Jackie; he's a nice guy," I said defensively. "We're really happy together."

"Are you, Nikki? Or are you fooling yourself into believing you're happy because he's loaded?" Jackie was being relentless. "I've seen guys like him before; they're users."

"Give Nikki some credit, Jackie. She's not going to let herself get sucked in by some guy who's got money oozing out his pores. And what would he be using her for?" Mandy asked.

"Sex, hiding a secret life, who knows," Jackie continued. "Just be careful Nikki."

"I will. I am." I really needed my wonderful friend and protector, Jackie, to back off. She didn't understand how good Jeff made me feel.

We said our goodbyes, and I went back into the office to keep working. Having told everyone now, I felt as if a weight had been lifted from my shoulders. I felt more relaxed as I walked back around to the office lobby, but my mind was all over the place.

I didn't know what I wanted and wondered if I had gotten sidetracked by the big shiny objects like Jackie'd said. Sometimes the price you pay for what you want is exorbitant. I just hoped I wouldn't end up kicking myself in the ass in a couple years thinking about what I had given up to get him and the lavish life he could provide. But I wasn't really giving up anything, well, except having another kid. But I also couldn't say I wanted another kid. It was a small price to pay when I was gaining everything.

"Nikki, do you have time to meet this afternoon?" Jack startled me as he peered at me over the top of his black-framed glasses.

"Sure, what time?"

"How about three o'clock?"

"Perfect, I'll be there."

"Thanks."

We hadn't met the past couple of weeks for our one-on-ones. He had called in sick, then had to cancel the following week for an important last-minute meeting. This would be good to meet this afternoon since I'd been extra careful with my math.

I walked around to his office a few minutes early and let his admin know I was there. "Go ahead in; he just finished his call," she said.

"Hey, Nikki, it's good to see you. How is everything going? Have a seat."

I walked over to one of the chairs facing his desk and lowered myself, crossing my legs and pulling my skirt down to cover as much skin as possible. "Everything is fine. Work is going really well lately." I smiled as I provided my own appraisal.

"I agree; I'm very pleased with your work lately. We missed our last couple of meetings. I wanted to just take a few minutes to touch base with you this afternoon." He fidgeted with his pen. "Do you have anything you need to discuss with me?"

"No, not really. Work is going really well. I have plenty to keep me busy."

"You're not overworked, are you?"

"Not at all, I'm fine."

"Great, if you need anything at all, let me know."

What the fuck was going on? Jack was never this accommodating or concerned about workload. His motto had always been 'no matter how much gets dumped on you, find a way to get it done' … on time.

"I will. Did you have anything in particular you'd like to discuss with me this week?"

"No, I'm quite pleased with your attention to detail, as well as the work you've completed on the accounts. I wanted to follow up with you since our last meeting wasn't terribly pleasant."

"Thank you. I appreciate that."

He set his pen down on the desk, and with a matter-of-fact look, went completely off-topic, "Rumor has it you're dating Jeff Carrington."

"Yes, I am." He caught me off-guard with a question about my personal life that didn't involve my daughter. "Do you know him?"

"I don't know him directly, but my brother works at the same company as him." Jack's eyes wandered around the room, avoiding contact with mine.

"Are they in the same department?"

"No, my brother works in Finance. He tells me he'll be at the party Jeff is having."

"Great, what's his name?"

"Jason."

"I'm looking forward to meeting him."

"I'm sure he'll enjoy meeting you as well." Our eyes met. There was something about the look he gave me that gave me an eerie feeling. "Well, if you don't have anything else, I'll let you get back to work and talk to you next week."

I stood from my chair. "Thanks." I walked out of his office, pulling the door halfway closed behind me. *Why the hell did I just say thanks?*

The rest of the week went slow. I didn't go shopping. I was more concerned with getting someone in my house so it didn't just sit empty for too long. It took a lot of convincing, but Sky finally had agreed it would be better to live there than in the apartment. The house gave him more room and a separate room for Abby when she visited. It was also a familiar place for her. He would have to give the apartment complex notice before moving in, but he planned to be in the house within the next two months.

Sky told me he had just been hired for a full-time position in Accounts Receivable at a small furniture company. I was so excited for him. He'd finally be back to working in the field of his major -- now if he could just *keep* the job.

After a weekend of fulfilling sex, Jeff was back on the road for only two days this week. That was perfect for me to do my shopping and schedule my appointments for Saturday morning before he returned back home. I had to make sure to get Abby a cute dress for the event. I was so excited to share Saturday night with Jeff in his house, mingling with his friends and coworkers. Our relationship was so right.

****

"Baby, wake up," Jeff whispered in my ear.

"What time is it?"

"Nine thirty; isn't your appointment at ten?"

"Shit!" I flipped the sheet off my naked body and quickly got out of bed. I dug out underwear and clothes, dressed, and ran to get Abby. Any other day she would have woke up early, getting me out of the bed, and had me on the move much sooner. There was no way I was going to be on time. When I got to the stairs, Jeff watched me from the balcony near his bedroom, wearing nothing but his silk pajama pants hanging low on his hips, his arms folded across his bare, muscular chest and leaning against the wall. I'd give anything to be fucking him again instead of running out to get my nails done. I licked my lips as I admired his toned, tan body.

"Hurry back." He winked at me.

"I'll text you and let you know when we're done."

"Take my car; you might get there faster. The keys are on the counter." He chuckled. "Abby, take care of your mommy, and make sure you both get really pretty."

"Okay."

I scooped Abby onto my hip, and then ran down the stairs. If there were an Olympic event for running stairs with a child on your hip, I could win a gold medal. I set her down by the front door, then ran to pick up his keys from the kitchen counter and slid on my flip-flops. I turned in time to see Jeff still standing at the railing, looking down at me. I grabbed Abby's little hand in mine, blew him a kiss with the other hand, and pulled the door closed behind me.

We were late getting to the salon, but they made time for us. I decided I wanted the two of us to have similar hairdos. We also had very similar dresses. Instead of going with my first thought to find a sleek, form-fitting dress, I had decided to go with something a little less revealing, knowing his manager would be there.

My shopping had taken me into the bridal section of Macy's, where I'd found a beautiful fuchsia sleeveless pleated dress with an A-line skirt that was a couple inches above my knee. The dress had a wide sequined waistband. I normally wasn't one for over-the-top baubles and bling, but this dress was perfect, and I fell in love with it as soon as I saw it.

Abby's dress was also fuchsia, but with no belt. My shoes were white open-toed sandals with a white satin ruffle and four-and-a-half-inch heels. Abby had white patent leather flats. I refused to let Jeff see what I'd bought despite his nagging me to put it on. I wanted him to be surprised.

After five hours in the salon, a slice of pizza, and more candy than any child should eat when she can't run off the sugar rush, I sent a text to Jeff that we were on our way back. The party started at seven o'clock and it was almost four. If I hurried, I could get back by four thirty.

"I'm back, baby." I hollered through the house when Abby and I walked through the door. I could hear talking coming from the kitchen, so we walked that way. Jeff hung up his cellphone when we walked in.

"You two look beautiful."

"Thanks, but this isn't the finished product. Just wait until later." I walked around to get a drink of water and rubbed my ass across Jeff's crotch. His hands rubbed against my hips. He wrapped his arms around my waist tight and pulled me back into him so I could feel his growing bulge.

"Is this what you want?" he whispered in my ear. His lips caressed my nape, causing goose bumps to rise all over my skin. My sex responded to his touch with a twinge indicating yes.

I turned into him, and pulling his ear close to my mouth, I whispered back, "I think you already know I want you."

"We have a small problem," he whispered to me, then lifted his eyes, motioning in the direction of Abby.

"Abby, do you want to watch Cartoon Network before we have to get ready for the party?"

"Yeah," I was so happy she was able to sit in front of the TV and watch a show without getting up to wander around or get into anything.

Jeff took her in to get the TV turned on, while I made her a half of a peanut butter and jelly sandwich. We were a good team.

I followed them into the room with the sandwich wrapped up in a napkin in one hand and a juice box with the straw sticking out in the other. I told her I'd be back in a few minutes, then Jeff and I went up the stairs. We didn't have a lot of time. Not only were we risking Abby looking for us, we had to get ready for the party.

We went into the bathroom to brush our teeth. Jeff finished before me and slipped his silk pants off, standing at full attention behind me. I rinsed my mouth out, then I wiped it dry with the towel. He twirled and pulled me into him, lowering his mouth onto mine, his hands creeping up toward my hair.

"Don't you dare," I warned him.

"I won't now, but later, I intend to fuck you until you sweat all that hairspray out." I clenched at that riveting thought.

He held my shoulders and turned me so my back was to him. "Take those pants off and bend over." I did as I was instructed.

I bent at the hip, resting my hands on the edge of the tub surround. He spread my legs wider with his feet, opening me to him. "This has to be quick." His hands fondled my ass cheeks.

"I know."

He ran his fingers across me, between my moist lips. "Oh, Nikki, Nikki..." He pressed his swollen head inside me, balls deep, and we met skin to skin.

I moaned.

His fingers reached around, and he massaged my drenched bud while he stretched me with his slow, deep thrusts. I tried not to lose control of myself, but his magical fingers forced my release against my will. I pressed my mouth into my shoulder to muffle the sound while I bucked my hips, pressing back into him.

He wasn't as quick as I thought he would be. He took his time, caressing me, stroking me, filling me. He found his release shortly after my second orgasm, pumping me full of his hot cum.

"That will take the edge off; but I'm not done with you, baby doll."

"I sure hope you're not. I love your cock."

I jumped in the shower, washed, and was back out within minutes. I threw on my oversized shirt and shorts so I could run back down to check on Abby.

"Is everything okay in here?" I asked her.

"Yeah, I don't want more."

"That's fine. I'll put it up for later." I picked up the napkin and folded it around the remaining quarter of her sandwich, making sure not to drop any bread crumbs on the floor, and picked up the nearly half-full juice box. "It's time for us to get pretty. Come with me."

"Okay, let's get pwetty."

We went back upstairs to Abby's room. I left her sit on her bed for a few minutes while I went to get her dress out of my closet and was briefly diverted watching Jeff towel off. His back rippled, his chest muscles flexed, his arms were the strong limbs I loved having wrapped around me. He was my kryptonite. He made me wet, weak and unable to think straight.

Abby looked like a miniature princess. Her fuchsia dress was adorable, and I found a wide white ribbon to tie around her waist as a belt. It was long enough to make a large, looped bow at the small of her back. She wore white ankle socks and her white patent leather shoes with the strap across her foot. Now the trick would be to keep her clean. I touched up her hair, trying to secure the flyaway strands. She walked into my bedroom with me, and I set her up on the bed.

Jeff had rolled his sleeves up to mid-forearm and was buttoning his white dress shirt. He looked striking. His heated, dangerous-eyed glare rolled up to meet mine, sending a flood of lust thumping through me, seducing me,

194 * *Twisted By Desire*

immobilizing me with his sexual magnetism as he finished fastening his last button. He tucked his shirt neatly into his black slacks and fastened them. I forced my gaze away, breaking the hypnotic spell he had me under.

"Abby, you look beautiful." His features softened as he smiled at her. "The room's all yours, babe. I'll be downstairs."

"I won't be long."

"Take your time. There's no rush." He winked and pursed his mouth, kissing to me in the air. "I can manage everything until you come down."

Once he closed the door, I retrieved my own dress and shoes from the closet. I couldn't wait for him to see me in them. I rubbed Be Enchanted lotion from Bath and Body Works on my legs and arms. It smelled so good.

"Want some, Abby?"

"Yeah, I need some smell good."

I rubbed lotion on her little legs and arms.

I slid the dress on, then twisted and wriggled as I zipped it up. Next, the matching body spray was spritzed on my neck, exposed chest, back, and, with my back to Abby, a couple squirts up my dress to my cooch. I knew that Jeff liked this scent as much as I did, maybe more. If I was lucky, the party would end early, and he could fuck me every which way until tomorrow.

"You look pwetty, Mommy."

"Thank you, baby; you look pretty too."

"I know."

"And we have the same dress, that's why Mommy looks so pretty."

"I know."

It was after seven. I went into the bathroom and put on my make-up, then coated my lips with clear lip gloss over my light pink lipstick.

"Do you need some make-up too?" I asked.

"Yeah."

I used my translucent powder puff and dabbed it on her face, making her giggle uncontrollably. Then, I took my lip gloss and gave her a light coat.

"Let's go see how we look." I helped her down off the bed, put on my shoes, and we walked into the closet, where a full-length mirror hung on the inside of the closet door.

"We look pwetty."

"I agree, baby, and we smell pretty too. Are you ready to go to the party?"

"Yep."

Oddly enough, it was at that very moment that I realized I had not figured out the way Abby should address Jeff. For the past two weeks, she had just answered his questions, or interrupted him by tugging at him, but she had never actually called him anything to get his attention. "Baby, tonight, if you want to get Jeff's attention, you can call him Mr. Jeff."

"Okay." She'd never remember, who did I think I was kidding?

We stepped out onto the balcony overlooking the foyer, living room, and the formal waste of space room. There were about a dozen unfamiliar people downstairs with Jeff and Connor in the living room. Jeff had a bar set up in the living room and had hired a bartender to come in for the night.

I cleared my throat to get his attention before I took my first step down. I felt like the center of attention. All eyes were on me as I descended the stairs like a movie starlet. *If I trip or fall, I will be mortified.* Jeff came to the bottom of the steps and held his hand out to help steady me as I came off the last two stairs. He pulled me into him. "You look stunning. And that smell is going to drive me crazy all night. Way to make me want to fuck you, baby doll." He whispered in my ear, then kissed my neck. I flashed a devious smile at him. He knew I'd done it on purpose.

He took Abby's little hand in his and helped her twirl around. "You are so pretty, Abby."

"I know." Everyone laughed at her unintended arrogance.

Jeff held his strong hand splayed across the small of my back and walked us around introducing us to all of his guests. I met his boss, Michael, and his wife, Jennifer; Hunter, his personal trainer, and his girlfriend; Jorge, one of the men he traveled with frequently, and his wife; Sandy, another man he traveled with and his wife; Bridget, a co-worker, and her fiancé; and Carmen and her husband.

His attention to me was overwhelming. He made sure not to leave my side, and was also very attentive to Abby. Connor was at the party alone. Everyone except Connor was part of a couple. Jeff told me he was divorced and that the ring was a sham.

The doorbell rang, and Connor answered it. A beautiful, statuesque woman arrived and was whisked off to the kitchen by Connor. Maybe she was his date. Jeff pulled my attention back to the conversation with a squeeze around my waist. He was a phenomenal host. Jeff and

Michael's conversation quickly turned to work though. *Boring ... not party worthy.*

"Nikki, what do you do?" Jennifer asked.

"I work in marketing for a major retailer. I'm involved with print and online marketing strategies, and do a lot of trending."

"That sounds interesting."

"It is, most days." We both chuckled.

"How old is your daughter, five or six?"

"She's three, going on twenty-three."

"She's absolutely adorable, and tall. Is your ex-husband or ex-boyfriend tall?"

"Ex-husband." *Clever way to dig for information.* "Yes, he's tall, - not as tall as Jeff, but tall."

"I don't see a lot of resemblance between the two of you." She looked down at Abby.

"She looks a lot like her father."

"He must be quite the catch."

"For someone else, I'm sure he will be."

Jeff approached and placed his arm around my shoulder while blazing his prize-winning smile at her. "I'm sorry to interrupt, Jennifer, but I need to borrow Nikki for a few minutes."

"Sure, it was very nice talking to you, Nikki dear." She flashed a smile at us both and returned to Michael's side.

Jeff leaned in and kissed me as he inhaled. "You looked like you needed to be saved."

"I did. Thank you."

"No problem, darling," His heated gazed sent a chill up my spine. "The caterers are set up. I'm going to announce for everyone to come and eat."

"I'd like to go freshen up real quick first."

"You can clean up later, baby doll. I want you right here by my side." He leaned in and kissed my cheek, rubbing his low-cut bearded chin across my face.

His warm breath on my ear left me speechless. My mind drew a blank; I couldn't even think of a response to that.

He pulled me in tight to him, reaching his arm around my waist. "Everyone," his voice boomed through the rooms of the house and radiated through my body like a freight train. He commanded everyone's attention, every eye was on him. "Thank you all for coming out this evening. As you all know, Nikki has been brave enough to move in with me and bring her precious daughter." He kissed my cheek as some chuckled. "Baby, thank you."

I looked up to see Connor and the mystery woman standing in the walkway under the stairs. She was incredibly beautiful. She could be a model. With her heels on, she was taller than Connor, and he was almost six feet.

"And to let her know how much I cherish her…" Jeff lowered himself to the floor on one knee in front of me. *Oh my god -- no fucking way.* My heart raced, beating fast enough to burst clean out of my chest. He raised a small blue velvet box he pulled from his pants pocket up to me. I waved my hands by my face, fanning myself as my eyes prickled with impending tears. As he looked into my water-coated eyes, he flipped open the small lid to reveal a gleaming diamond ring. "I need you, Nikki. You mean more to me than you know. Marry me."

I heard a sigh, then noticed the leggy brunette beauty leave the room and go into the restroom. Connor stayed.

"This is so unexpected; I don't know what to say."

"Make me the happiest man on the planet. Say yes baby."

My walls clenched, and I was hypnotized by his intense stare. "Yes, baby."

He rose to both feet, placed his hands gently on each side of my face, and lowered his lips to mine. Everyone clapped and yelled congratulations.

The bartender made the rounds with filled champagne flutes for everyone. "The future Mrs. Carrington and I appreciate you all coming to our house and helping us celebrate getting engaged. The food is ready, so please, everyone eat."

Abby tugged at his pant leg. He bent down and picked her up, resting her small body in the bend of his strong arm.

Connor raised his glass to toast us. "To Jeff and his family."

The cheers of 'hear, hear' and 'congratulations' were echoing off each wall in the house. I was basking in the drunken glory of being engaged to this man - after four and a half short months. *I'm fucking engaged.*

Jeff balanced Abby in his arm as he placed his free hand at the nape of my neck and pulled me in for another kiss. She squirmed and wriggled, reaching to get into my arms.

I transferred Abby from Jeff's hands into mine and walked into the kitchen with her to get a drink. The stunning brunette was there and congratulated me. Her eyes looked wet -- she said it was an eyelash. She asked to see the ring. As she held my fingers, I felt a slight tremble. She congratulated me again and quickly walked away. I was so absorbed in the glow of Jeff's proposal, I never thought to ask her what her name was.

Chapter 14

I'd been caught up in a romantic twister. Sunday, I was thrown into the aftermath, back to reality day as Jeff went with me to drop off Abby. He drove while my mind ran through the events since meeting him. It seemed incomprehensible that I had been searching for a man just five short months ago and was now engaged. Sky was going to meet us at my mom's house to get Abby, and we planned to tell them all the news together. Mom was not going to be happy. Sky would be even more upset.

The crazy thing was, I knew I wasn't in love with Jeff. I loved what he could offer -- that house, this car, his power; I loved what he stood for and I loved how he indulged me, in the bed and out. Was that so wrong? Should I come clean and let him know how I felt? Should I risk breaking his heart if he really did love me, and be forced to move back into my small house? I'd be a damn fool to tell him. Maybe I'd learn to love him with more time.

"What's on your mind?" His hand reached over and rubbed my bare thigh.

"I was just thinking about how to tell them and anticipating their response."

"Don't worry about it. As long as we're happy, that's what matters, right?"

"Yeah, you're right, but …"

"You aren't changing your mind, are you?" He glanced in my direction. "After less than 24 hours, I'm going to have a runaway bride-to-be?"

"No, I'm not." Of course I was. I was struggling to reconcile my head and my heart. How could I marry someone I didn't love?

"Good." He stroked down my arm and redirected his gaze to the road.

My mind raced trying to imagine what the future had in store for me while trying to figure out how I had ended up where I was and if I should run. My mind would be put somewhat at ease if Mom surprised me and didn't freak out, but the chances of that were slim. I felt bile rise in my throat, and my stomach ached as Jeff turned the car into their driveway.

"We're at Nana's, Abby," Jeff cheerfully announced.

"Get me out!" she demanded, which was her version of 'Get me out of this damn car seat.' Can't say I blamed her; I'd want out of that thing too. Jeff had walked around to our side and opened my door, then opened the rear door so he could get Abby.

He set her on the ground, and she took off running to the front door.

"I feel sick." I bent over at the hip, leaning my ass back against the car. My head was down, and my hair fell forward, covering my face.

Jeff rubbed my back. "You'll be okay. It's not going to be as bad as you think."

No, it'll probably be worse. "I hope you're right. I need to sit down for a minute, though." I dropped down beside the car and bent my legs, pulling my feet in close to my butt. I crossed my arms over my knees and dropped my forehead to rest on them.

"Baby, fuck it, let's don't tell them. Jesus Christ, if it's got you all fucked up like this, we just won't say anything yet. Maybe you'd rather just elope, or, I don't know, end it all -- you go your way and I'll go mine. I don't know." I looked up at him, watching in horror as he ran his fingers through his hair while glaring down at me. "If they see you're happy, you mean to tell me they won't be happy for you? What kind of family do you have?" He crouched down to eye level with me. "Why don't you just fucking tell me what you want?"

"That's not what I want. I want to be with you." *I want to live in that amazing house, drive your car, and swim in your pool.* "Fuck it, let's go do this. I'll be okay."

He stood, then reached down and grasped my hand, helping me up to my feet. "I guess your first challenge will be to explain to your mom, who's in the doorway watching us, why you were on the ground." He winked at me and flashed that million-dollar smile.

After convincing Mom I wasn't pregnant again and that I wasn't dying of food poisoning, I flashed the ring and blurted out, "We're getting married." My gaze was met with her disapproving eyes, a subtle shake of her head and a scowl that screamed disappointment in my decision. Jeff held his arm around my shoulders tight to assure me I was going to be okay -- or to hold me up in case I passed out.

Jim broke into conversation with Jeff, while I was whisked away into the kitchen by my mother's nod of her head and scolding glare. I did *not* want to be in the kitchen with her. Abby trekked in behind us, yanking at Mom's shirt and asking for water.

"What the hell are you doing, Nicolette?" She pounded the counter top instead of raising her voice before getting a glass and half filling it, then handed it to Abby. *This is some serious shit, she called me by my full first name.*

"I know you don't approve of Jeff, and I know you probably think we're moving too fast. But I really want this. I want him."

"You have taken a complete loss of every bit of sense you've ever had. I'm not convinced you have any idea what you're doing. Have you told Sky?"

"No, he was supposed to have been here already."

"He's going to freak out." Her head shook so much, she looked like one of those bobbing head dogs that sits in a rear car window. "Are you thinking about anyone besides yourself?"

"Jesus, you sound like Sky. We're divorced, Mom. I'm not cheating on him. I'm thinking of me and Abby -- what kind of future we can have, you know, what Sky could never give us. And yeah, I guess I am thinking of myself too."

"Hey, hey, everyone," Sky called as he entered the house. Then within seconds, "Fuck."

"Well, clearly, he just saw your fiancé sitting in the living room." Mom pierced my heart with the stare she gave me. "You go tell him your *wonderful* news."

Just then Sky walked into the kitchen.

"Daddy," Abby screamed.

"Hey, princess." He rubbed his nose against her, giving her an Eskimo kiss.

His attention was quickly turned back to me. "What's that all about, Nik? I thought we discussed this?" He pointed into the living room in the direction of Jeff.

"We aren't at your house or his; this is my mom's house, so you can fucking get over it," I snapped. I didn't care at that moment that I was cursing in front of Abby. "I don't need you trying to run my life." I was so frustrated, I wanted to scream at the top of my lungs.

I took a deep breath then released it slowly to help bring my blood pressure back down, close to normal, before continuing, "Sky, I have something to tell you." I swallowed hard and felt a lump form in my throat. I struggled to breathe. "Jeff and I are getting married."

"Are you kidding me?" He turned his eyes toward my mom, "Is this for real?"

"Yep." She shrugged her shoulders and went back to shaking her head.

"You take a step closer to worse with every decision." Sky continued his rant and gave his deeper-dive opinion on me and my choices of late; it wasn't flattering.

"I didn't ask you for your blessing. I'm telling you -- fucking telling you; I don't need your permission."

Jeff came into the kitchen and was met with their four eyes, all scowling and shooting arrows into him. My eyes were glazed over and brimming with tears. He ignored them both and walked over to me, wrapping my hand and his, interlacing our fingers.

Jim walked in right behind him. "Hey, what's all the yelling about?"

"Did you hear, Nikki's getting married again." Mom spat the words out.

"Jeff just told me the good news -- happy news. I think it's great." Jim leaned in and gave me a hug, causing the tears to tumble down my cheeks. He pulled back and looked me in my tear-filled eyes. "Don't let anyone change your happiness, dear."

I heard Mom give her signature 'humph' in the background while Sky sighed.

Jeff interrupted, "We need to get going, baby doll; we have a reservation in thirty minutes." He glanced up at Mom and Sky. "It was nice to see you all again." He shook Jim's hand. "Always a pleasure, Jim." He pulled at my arm, loosening my feet from the imaginary cement they were mounted in. I picked up my purse, slung it on my shoulder, said good bye to Mom and Sky, kissed Abby, who was held in Sky's arms, then said good bye to Jim before we left.

"That was … interesting." Jeff scowled. "I guess I underestimated their response and actually thought they'd be happy for you."

"It's not over." I was shaking my head like my mom. "It's not even close to being over."

"It doesn't matter what they think; it's your life. They don't have to like or agree with every decision you make." Jeff opened my car door for me, then closed it behind me after I settled into my seat. He rounded the car to his door, and my eyes were fixated on his sexy body in that tight black T-shirt. He closed his door and started the car. "And who the hell is Sky to say anything? You guys are divorced. That pencil-necked fucker needs to worry about getting a job."

Screech! What? My head snapped in his direction. "He's working; he just got a job." I turned back to looking out the front window after realizing I was defending my ex-husband to my fiancé. We rode in silence for several minutes. My eyebrows pulled tight, my body tensed, and I could have sworn I could feel a wrinkle forming as my mind was working overtime.

"You know," Jeff interrupted my thoughts, "this should be a really good time for us. We need to come up with a date so you can start planning our wedding."

"I know; you're right." A smile cracked my face. "Do we really have a reservation somewhere?"

"Absolutely; I know this great place that's private, perfect for newly engaged couples who can't keep their hands off each other. It's just what you need after sharing important information with family that has left you stressed."

"That sounds good to me. Anything that relieves stress sounds like a winner right now."

"Oh baby, I have the perfect stress eliminator. You'll be so relaxed your legs will feel like Jell-O." He shot me that dangerous, carnal glance that sent heat coursing through me.

We arrived back at his house, and as soon as we entered the door, we shed our clothes and walked right out to the pool. Well, Jeff stopped and grabbed us some beers, then joined me. I challenged him to a chugging contest with our first can because I needed to get alcohol into my system quick to help my frazzled nerves to relax.

"You didn't really think you could drink faster than me, did you?" Jeff looked so sexy, I could have fucked him on the hot pool deck.

"Yeah, I did." I lay back on the chaise and closed my eyes. I felt his touch, skimming lightly on my inner thigh. One eye popped open to see him staring at me.

"Tired?"

"Not physically; I'm mentally exhausted."

"I have another beer for you."

"Thanks."

He leaned in and kissed my cheek, then worked his way up to my mouth, covering me with his warm lips. His tongue work was slow and seductive. He was casting a spell on me with his mouth. My hands reached up and fisted his hair, pulling him in tighter to me. He rose from his chair and joined me on mine, stretching out beside me, pulling me in close to him, wrapping his long strong body around mine. His erection was begging for attention as he rubbed against my hip.

I turned my body onto my side to face him then moved my hand down to feel his manhood, fully ready for me. The ache between my legs had me rocking my hips in toward him. I wanted him. I needed him. I was silently begging for him. He read my mind and slid his leg between mine, opening me to allow him to invade my space.

His bulbous head slid between my thighs and across my greedy, plump clit, forcing a moan to escape my mouth into his. His hand reached around and grasped a handful of my ass cheek, then slid down my outer thigh, pulling my leg up around his waist. He rocked with me, his length gliding through my wetness, teasing and torturing my slit.

"If you're too exhausted, I'll leave you alone."

"That would be just downright rude, Mr. Carrington."

He directed his eager head into my opening, giving me a small taste of what he was offering. I squeezed my walls around him. "I don't want to impose on you, or do anything you don't want." I rocked in toward him, trying to get him to sink into me deeper, but he withdrew just enough to spurn my attempt. "Not yet; you aren't ready for me yet. I need you totally relaxed, willing to completely forget about everything and everyone except me."

"I will, I promise."

"Not quite yet, baby doll." He massaged his head back and forth, careful not to go much beyond the ridge of his swollen cock.

"What are you doing to me?" He had me on the verge of an orgasm without really fucking me. His hand slid down between our stomachs, down to my sensitive clit.

He used his index and middle fingers to massage me. "You like that, baby?"

"Shit yeah. You're going to make me cum like this."

"That's what I want; I own your pussy right now." I was looking down at his fancy finger-work. "Look at me, baby." My gaze rose and met the eyes of my salacious predator. "I want you to just let yourself go and cum all over me, then I'm going to fuck the shit out of you." He placed his wet fingers on my lips, letting me lick myself off of them before he returned them to my clit.

His fingers picked up speed, massaging faster and faster, his thick head hitting me just inside my walls, in a spot I never knew existed but was damn happy he'd just found. Perhaps he should join the many famous discoverers as the great-mystery-spot-founder of my pussy, my very own Dicktopher Columbus. Within a few minutes, I couldn't take it anymore. "I feel like I need to pee; let me up please."

"You're fine; just relax and let me enjoy you."

"But I --" His mouth clamped down on mine with the most intense, breathtaking kiss.

"Shit, baby, damn!" My head fell back with my eyes closed tighter than ever before. My body curled in, my stomach muscles contracted to the point of pain, and the rest of me shook as the orgasm took ownership of me. My fingernails dug into the strong flesh on his shoulder. I smelled nothing, I heard nothing, and I saw nothing. I was lost. The lingering taste of me on my tongue was stronger than before. He continued to massage his tip inside me as he made the orgasm extend until I felt like I was going to pass out.

I lay there gasping, trying to catch my breath. Holy shit, what the fuck had he just done to me? My greedy pussy wanted more. I needed more. I needed to feel him against the back wall of my canal.

"Look at my leg." The smile on Jeff's face spread from ear to ear.

I looked down. My breath hitched and my eyes widened. "Oh shit, I peed on you?" I was horrified. "I told you --"

"No, baby, you squirted."

"I ..." my face flushed, "I didn't think that was real when people said it or when I saw it in porn."

"It's real, and you have proof right here." He swiped his fingers across his leg where it was wet, then licked them, moaning deep in his throat. He pulled his fingers from his mouth. "So fucking sweet, too." He leaned in to kiss me. I could taste the sweetness.

I couldn't help but have a fleeting thought, and a brief bout of jealousy, thinking of how many women he had made squirt before. His hand moved from his leg to my hip as he pulled me closer to him. He rolled on top of me finding his welcome mat between my legs, my drenched labia waiting for him to press through the entryway and let himself in. His arms were on either side of me on the lounge chair; his hips leaned in to me, sliding his large, hard cock across my slickness. I looked at him, hoping he could read my mind. *Get in me and fuck me.* No such luck; he slid himself over me, teasing me, my walls contracting with need with every swipe.

"So beautiful. So perfect."

"I think I'm ready, don't you?"

"How bad do you want me?" His hooded eyes sent waves of desire through my core. My sex clenched, trying to answer for me, trying to beg.

"Slide your fingers in and tell me what you think."

He slid two fingers all the way into me as I contracted my muscles around him. "Damn, baby. You feel so good." He pulled his fingers out of me and plunged them into my mouth. As I licked and sucked his fingers, he thrust deep into me, forcing me to gasp. His fingers slid from my mouth, and he lowered his mouth to take my hardened nipples, one after the other, into his mouth to suck and lick. His tongue licked up my chest, then up my neck to my mouth. His kiss was deep, and his breathing became ragged in my mouth as he pummeled me with powerful thrusts. My hands reached around, grabbing him tight around his waist, pulling him into me, wishing he could climb inside of me.

"Shit, baby." He buried his face into my neck, his hot breath annihilating me, melting me, molding me like putty.

He penetrated me with so much force the chaise wobbled. "Jeff, this chair is going to collapse."

"I don't care. I'll replace it. I can't stop; you feel so good wrapped around me." His thrusts continued with long, hard strokes.

"You like this, baby doll?"

"Hell yeah!" My eyes clung to his as his thrusts came faster and harder until we both found our release.

I have to admit, I thought the chaise would collapse and my head would get smashed into the concrete under his weight, but I'm not sure I would've cared as long as he kept stroking me.

Chapter 15

I had to keep telling myself that everyone didn't have to like my decisions. The problem was that *I* was even questioning the decisions I was making myself. I should have been excited to go to work and tell everyone that I was getting married; instead, I was dreading it. I couldn't think of one person who was going to be happy for me when they heard. Did they all know something that I didn't? Was I really doing the right thing? Finally, coming to the conclusion that I couldn't deal with the nay-saying, I decided I would tell them the next day.

The troublesome feeling deep in my gut was telling me I had to get things right with Mom and Sky, and quick. I could tolerate everyone else's negativity and cynicism, but not theirs. Thinking about the tension from yesterday had my stomach in knots.

Jeff was leaving that afternoon for three days, and I was thinking that maybe Mom needed to come over and see where I lived; or at the very least, we needed to talk through this. Maybe that would help her be more at ease with my decisions. With a sigh, I realized I was just kidding myself – she'd said she already knew of him through Gretchen. She hated him, and nothing was going to change that.

For my own sanity, I called Mom and asked her to meet me and Abby for dinner at a nearby restaurant after work. I wished Jim would be able to meet with us. He seemed to like Jeff, and he could be a strong ally for me.

By the time we got to dinner, I was exhausted. I hadn't expected it to be so difficult to hide my news from everyone. Candace and Georgia suspected I was keeping something from them all day and were hell bent to pry it out of me. I stuck to my guns and didn't say a word.

Abby and I sat in the entrance of T.G.I.Friday, waiting for Mom to arrive. My heart raced, and my stomach tumbled. I was fidgeting more than Abby. I looked up just in time to see her open the front door.

"Hi, sweetie," she said with a smile. "Hi, precious little Abby."

"Hi, Nana."

"I'm glad you met us, Mom." I stood and gave her a hug, biting my lower lip as I fought the nervousness from showing.

"Well, why wouldn't I, silly?"

The hostess took us to a booth in a nice, quiet area. It was perfect. Our waitress was prompt to arrive at our table. We ordered right away, and she disappeared to get our drinks.

"So is everything okay, Nikki? You sounded a little upset on the phone earlier."

How she could just pretend like I hadn't told her I was getting married was beyond belief. "I just feel," I tapped my fingers lightly on the tabletop, "I don't know. I need you to be okay with Jeff, you know? I need you to be okay with us getting married."

"Sweetie, it's your life; you're twenty-eight. You don't need my, or anyone else's, blessing to marry him. You said so yourself."

"It's not necessarily a blessing I'm looking for. I just need to know you can accept him as your son-in-law."

"If you remember, I wasn't crazy about Skylar when you told me you were marrying him, but I learned to love him just the same. Unless Jeff is a complete asshole, I'll learn to like him too."

"But that's part of the problem; you already think he's an asshole."

Mom glared at me, raised her eyebrows, and twisted her mouth into a shit-eating grin while shrugging her shoulders. Her expression and body language said it all; she wasn't going to change her mind about Jeff today or anytime soon.

We enjoyed our dinner and talked about everything except Jeff the rest of the time. When we finished, I settled the check and invited her over to the house, which she declined in her normal polite way and assured me she would come by another time. I wasn't offended. I knew it was getting late according to Jim's schedule. I still needed to call Jeff and get Abby ready for bed. Since I had moved in with him, Mom didn't come to the house to watch her anymore; I had to take her over there.

****

The nights were getting shorter, and the amount of sleep I was getting seemed less. As I walked from the parking garage to the building, I knew today was the day I would tell everyone that I was engaged. I had my ring on and had no reservations -- well, maybe just a few.

Georgia and Candace were standing near my desk talking to Robert when I walked in. Robert and I basically had the same job, but he hadn't been with the company for very long and he was quiet.

"Good morning, everyone," I said as I got a little closer to them.

They turned in my direction, and Georgia asked, "You need coffee?" Clear sign the interrogation was about to begin.

"I always need coffee." I chuckled. "Let me put my purse away and grab my cup." I felt an ambush coming in the break room, but I was ready for them.

Candace spoke up quickly, "You know what? It's still early; let's go to Starbucks in the lobby."

I looked at them both again and noticed Candace had her purse and Georgia had a ten dollar bill curled up in her hand.

"Okay," I grabbed a five out of my purse before closing the drawer. "I'm ready, then."

Before either of them had a chance to start with the inquisition, I blurted it out standing at the elevator. "So, I have some news."

"We knew you were hiding something from us," Candace said as she pressed the down arrow again.

I held my arm out straight so they could both see the ring on my finger.

"Holy shit!" Candace said as she grabbed my fingers and jerked my arm, dragging me closer to her. Her eyes rose up to meet mine with her mouth agape.

"You're en—en-- engaged?" Georgia stammered out.

"Yes, Jeff proposed Saturday night."

"I'm just … wow … I don't know what to say."

"It's congratulations, Georgia. Congratulations, Nikki; I hope this is what you really want. You know I want you to be happy."

The look on Candace's face wasn't as convincing as her tone. Her eyes met mine, and her lips pressed together and turned up at the corners into what could be described as a weak smile, at best. She looked away and kneaded my hand in hers.

"Congratulations, Nikki," Georgia chimed in. "I guess I'm just surprised at how fast you guys are moving. I mean, I want you to be happy too, you know?"

"Thanks, both of you. I'm happy. We're happy." The silence as we walked from the elevator to the Starbucks was deafening. We stood in line and each placed our order.

"Fancy meeting you all down here." Jack startled me. I hadn't realized he even came down here. That showed how much attention I paid to him. He showed up as our last latte was placed on the counter.

"Good morning." I lowered my eyes briefly before raising them to meet his.

"So what's the party about this morning? What brings you gals down here instead of the break room?"

We all looked at each other before Candace made a motion with her head as if encouraging me to let him in on the news. "Well, I was letting them know," I switched my coffee from my left to my right hand before extending my left hand out toward him, "I'm engaged."

"How nice for you. Congratulations." His strained tone of voice, not his half smile on his face, was more indicative of his true feelings. "Carrington didn't waste any time." He rubbed his forehead, then he walked away to step in line.

"We'll see you back upstairs, Jack." I spoke up for the others. He gave a slight wave and we left.

Once in the lobby, our conversation resumed. "That was weird," Georgia said.

"Jack is weird; that's why he's still single." Candace could never resist an opportunity to take a shot at Jack.

"He knows of Jeff through his brother. I guess they work together, not in the same department, just at the same company."

"Maybe you should find out what exactly Jack or his brother knows about him that seems to make him so uncomfortable," Georgia suggested.

"Whatever it is, it's in his past, where it belongs. Why would I stir up any problems for myself?"

"You are assuming it's in the past, but you don't *know* it's in the past." Georgia seemed determined to stir the pot.

"Georgia, stop it," Candace interrupted. Georgia's eyebrows rose and she threw her hands up, indicating her surrender ... for now, as Candace continued, "Just let her be. If there's anything to know, she'll surely find out before they walk down the aisle. I can't imagine they'll get married next week."

"God, no! I want to be on ... what's that show where they help brides find the perfect dress?"

"*Say Yes to the Dress*," we all screamed at the same time and laughed.

"Well, count me in for that," Candace immediately said.

Going up in the elevator and while walking back to my desk, we chattered about how much fun being on the show would be, but knew it would be difficult to get on there. I didn't even have a wedding date yet. Maybe Jeff and I could figure that out on the weekend so I could submit an application to the show. I didn't mind flying to New York, or maybe we could just go to the Atlanta store for the taping. The seven-hour drive would be a fun road trip for us, especially if I could convince Jackie and Mandy to come with us.

"I'll keep you guys posted on the date, and once I submit the form to be on the show."

We scurried to get to work before Jack made it back up and found us still gabbing. None of us wanted to get dragged into his office and given a stern talking to by him.

Chapter 16

Jackie: Bitch, when were you planning to tell me?

Me: Tell you what?

Jackie: I talked to your mom, don't play stupid with me.

Me: Sorry :(, I wanted to get you and Mandy together later and tell you.

Jackie: Meet us at Love's at six tonight.

Me: Okay, I'll be there.

Fuck me! This was not starting off as I'd hoped. I knew Jackie would be the hardest one to tell, after Mom and Sky. I couldn't even pretend like I was looking forward to telling her. Mandy was a wild card. I wasn't as worried about her or her reaction.

During lunch, I decided to go onto the *Say Yes to the Dress* Atlanta website and see what the requirements were for submitting to be a guest on the show. Jeff and I needed to figure out a wedding date, and I needed to ask him if he would have any interest in coming with me. Hmm, Hmm; Gown budget -- if I had to pay for it, then the cheaper the better. Everything else seemed pretty easy to answer and straightforward. I logged off that site and got back to work for the rest of the afternoon. I was so busy, the time flew. Before I knew it, it was time to go meet Jackie and Mandy.

I had a long-standing love-hate relationship with Love's Artifacts. I loved them because their chicken and catfish were so good, and I hated them because it was buffet style. I could sit in there and eat all night or until they kicked me the hell out for devouring my way into their profit margin. Maybe with a few drinks and the music, Jackie would mellow out and not rip me apart too bad.

I pulled into the parking lot at the same time as Mandy. She gave me her cute little wave, barely visible through the glare of the windshield. I had a special bond with Mandy. We kept a secret between us that we had promised to never talk about after she got engaged.

We both exited our cars and hugged briefly before going in to get a table while we waited for Jackie to join us. We were early, and Jackie rarely was. If she said six, she would be there at six, not one minute before or one minute after. I could never figure out how she did that.

We both ordered a beer from the bar.

"How are things with Creighton?"

"Don't get me started on him." She sighed and rolled her eyes before taking a drink. "He's annoying as hell lately."

"You don't have to put up with him, Mandy. You can do a lot better and you deserve so much more."

"Yeah, I know, but I'm just not ready to give up on him yet."

A familiar voice called out over our backs, "Hey, bitches, drinking without me?" It was Jackie. My heart beat picked up to a staggering speed, and my palms dampened.

"Hey, girl, what's up?" I said.

"Hey, Jackie." Mandy smiled.

"Hi, Mandy." She quickly turned her smiling face away from Mandy and transformed it into a glaring, demonic, squinty-eyed stare that soon felt like it was boring a hole through me. "And you, what in the everlasting fuck are you doing these days?"

"What's going on?" Mandy asked.

"You won't believe it when I tell you. I found out from Nikki's mom that our dear friend here is engaged."

"Oh, wow, that's some news," Mandy started. "Congratulations?"

"Thank you." I gave her a smile before Jackie continued on her rant.

"Look, Nik." She planted her hands firmly at her waist. Her gaze softened, but her penetrating eyes didn't lose contact with mine. "I can't tell you what to do, no one can. But I sure as hell, as your friend, can let you know when I think you're making a fucked-up decision."

I inhaled deeply before releasing the breath slow and steady. I tried to explain, "I appreciate your concern, I really do, but I know what I'm doing. I'm going to marry Jeff. We don't have a date set yet; we haven't even talked about a date yet. But rest assured, we're getting married. Oh, and we're happy." My jaw clenched as I crossed my arms across my chest. *There, damn it, I'm standing my ground.*

"Why?" Mandy questioned. "Why are you marrying him? I'm not saying I don't think you should, but I'm asking, do you think you know him well enough? And are you guys in love?"

"I thought you were on my side, Mandy." I huffed. "But to shut you both up, yes god damn it, yes, we're in love." I looked away unable to meet their eyes since I knew I was lying. I wasn't in love with Jeff, and he'd never even come close to telling me he loved me.

"Then I'm happy for you, Nikki. Rushed or not, I wish you both nothing but the best and a long, happy life together." Mandy smiled and stroked her hand down my arm. Her touch was calming.

"Well, I'll shut my mouth for now and buy the next round." Jackie waved her arm in the air to get the waiter's attention. "You know," she lowered her voice and looked at me, "I want you to be happy -- truly happy, Nik. I love you and would hate to see you do something for the wrong reason."

Our drinks arrived, and we spent the next couple hours talking and reliving some of our past. I couldn't help but wonder if Jackie was picking up some weird vibe from me.

****

She and I had known each other since kindergarten and had been through our share of ups and downs together. We were inseparable in grade school and junior high, but during high school, we each went our own way -- not my choice, it was Jackie's. She was able to live her dream as a model. She was beautiful and tall. And beautiful. I was so happy for her and I loved having her as a friend, but my friendship wasn't enough. She wanted to belong with the 'cool kids' group. I wasn't that cool in high school, not until senior year anyway. I wasn't allowed to hang with the cool kids, so she had to make a choice. I couldn't kiss her ass enough to keep her as a friend, so we parted ways, and I lost my best friend.

High school sucked without her. I'd watch her walk around the hallways and see her sitting in class. I was desperate to talk to her until I'd see one of her minions from the cheerleading squad or one of the hot guys from the football team come talk to her. I was jealous of the circle she was part of. I wanted to be like her so bad. Everyone loved her, including me. She was supposed to be my best friend forever.

We graduated high school without even saying a peep to each other that day. College was a welcome change of scenery and a new start for me. It gave me a chance to get over the loss of my best friend.

I came home in the summer after classes ended for my sophomore year of college. The summer months were filled with days of sunbathing on nearby Tampa, Clearwater, and St. Petersburg beaches. I rarely saw Mandy because of her summer internship and Creighton, but I did have a coincidental run-in on the beach one day with Jackie. That fateful day brought us back together. We saw each other from a distance, walked toward each other like two lost souls, and met in the sand, where we laid our towels out near each other to catch up. Our conversation was very strained and superficial.

"Nikki, darling, it's been far too long."

"Definitely too long; what have you been up to?"

"The usual, school has been a bore, but I'm going overseas to France for my senior year -- something to look forward to. You know, the study abroad program. My French classes will be put to use, finally, and I may find the love of my life, a stranger named Pierre." She giggled.

"That sounds interesting. Are you seeing anyone now?"

"Not at this time. I just broke up with my boyfriend. He was the football team captain and quarterback. I found out he had cheated on me. Me! Can you believe that?"

"That's terrible. I'm so sorry to hear."

"Don't be. I'm better off without him. He hasn't stopped calling me, begging me to get back with him. He swears he'll never do it again. But I don't know. I mean, he has good prospects of playing in the NFL and everything, and I would make an excellent trophy wife for him."
"You would look stunning on Sundays, when the camera finds you in the stands. But that rules out Pierre, and he might have been the perfect catch."

"Later for Pierre, the announcers could make sure everyone knows who I am -- Jacqoline Carter."

Jackie had changed her name to Jacqoline in high school, pronounced Jack-o-line, like gasoline -- not the name her parents had given her. Since they had both had passed away already, they would never know what a snob their daughter had become.

"That would be so marvelous for you."

We spent about another hour or so on the beach, talking, until I couldn't take her self-centered conversation any more. I considered throwing myself in the rough surf to get tangled in seaweed before being pulled out to sea to escape the train-wreck conversation. The sad part was, I knew my old friend was still trying to make herself seem better than she really was. She wasn't a bad person, and the Jackie I had known had never been this insecure. We exchanged numbers before I shook the sand off my towel, rolled it up, and packed it back into my beach tote.

A week later, Jackie called me. Not Jacqoline, whom I had endured on the beach, but my old childhood friend, Jackie. We both pretended like that day never happened. Maybe it didn't, maybe it was a bad dream, or nightmare. We spent quite a few nights together over the rest of the summer, reliving some of our favorite childhood memories. We never talked about high school.

Chapter 17

"Have you considered going to a therapist or psychologist, dear?"

"I'm not crazy, Mom."

"I'm not saying you are, but sometimes they can help you understand things and see things from a different perspective."

My life was a complete mess -- a cluster-fuck of confusion, secrets, lies, and betrayals. "I'll think about it; it may not be a bad idea."

"Let me know if you need a couple names. The gentleman I went to was really good. He helped me a lot after your dad and I split up."

"I had no idea ..." How did she keep that a secret from me?

"You didn't need to know. I'd told you and Gary way too much and really needed an adult to talk to." She paused. "Of course, you can always talk to me though, sweetie."

"Thanks, Mom." I rolled my eyes. No way would I tell her some of the things swirling in my head. My conversation with Jackie and Mandy last night had me doubting my own decision-making abilities again. Talking to Jeff after I got home helped reassure me slightly. But what kind of person would I be if I just backed out of everything right now because people questioned me? Did I want to back out?

"I better get back to work, Mom; thanks for listening."

"That's what I'm here for, darling. Have a nice day."

When I hung up, I wanted to just cry or scream or throw something across the room. Instead, I sent an email to Jack, requesting the rest of the week off after today. I needed to get away from everyone, all their questions, and clear my head.

After a nice lunch with Georgia, I returned to my desk to be met by Jack. The look of concern on his face made my heart skip a beat.

"Is everything okay, Nikki? It's not like you to make such a last-minute request for time off."

"Yes, everything's fine. I just need a few days to take care of some important personal matters." *There, now you can't pry into what I'm doing.*

"Well, you may take the time off. I was just a little worried that something terrible and last minute may have happened."

Way to keep digging. "I'm sorry; I should have said in the email it was for personal reasons." I flashed him a smile, mostly because I was elated I had the rest of the week off.

"Then enjoy your time off, and I'll see you next week – bright-eyed and bushy-tailed."

"Thanks again, Jack."

I was bouncing in my seat, figuratively, not literally. I spent the rest of the afternoon making sure to get all of the accounts I had been working on completed. I set up my out of office message in email and sent a quick email to Georgia, Candace, Tristan, and a few others who needed to know I wouldn't be in.

Before I made my great escape, Tristan and Georgia stopped by my desk to make sure everything was okay with me. Tristan offered his stress-relief massage, which I politely declined. I knew what that massage was, and I was all too familiar with the satisfying, orgasmic ending. I couldn't let that happen again. Georgia told me to call if I needed anything, which was nice.

When I walked out and got in my car, I took in a deep breath and released some of my anxiety when I exhaled. This would be so nice to have three days all to myself -- and with Abby after day care.

I picked up Abby, then stopped at the Publix to get the items on my grocery list. After I finished checking out and was on my way to my car across the parking lot, my phone rang. Much to my surprise, it was Jeff.

"Hey, babe," I said with a smile.

"Hey there to you, baby doll. What are you up to?"

"Just leaving Publix," I said. "It's nice to hear your voice."

"Is everything okay?"

Yes, everything is fine. I just miss you, that's all."

"I miss you, too, gorgeous. I'm sorry I can't talk longer, but I wanted to call you now to at least talk to you for a few minutes. I'll be out tonight; Blake and I are going out with clients for dinner and drinks."

"Have a good time tonight and don't drink too much." I hesitated briefly. "Oh, wait. Real quick, before you go, I'm off the rest of the week."

"So something is wrong. What's going on?" I guess taking time off from work was a red flag to Jeff that there was a crisis of some sort.

"I'm fine; I just need a break from everyone and everything right now. We'll talk tomorrow. Get going, so Blake isn't standing around waiting for you."

"I miss you so much, I'll talk to you tomorrow, baby."

"I can't wait. I'll dream of you tonight. Have a good time." I hung up the phone.

I quickly put my bags in the trunk, my baby girl in her car seat, and was on my way back to Jeff's house. I was pretty sure that, as I was driving home, the swimming pool was calling for me, and I was planning to go lay out for an hour after getting something to eat.

After Abby and I ate our sandwiches, we both put on our swimsuits and headed to the pool. She laid out in the chaise lounge near me, and within minutes had her eyes closed. It must be rough to be in day care.

I grabbed my laptop so I could do some googling on wedding planning. I wanted this one to be more elaborate than the first. I had money saved up and was sure Jeff would contribute some money toward it; after all, he had asked me to marry him. I guess that would be the second thing we needed figure out; the budget, right behind the date.

I started doing some reading on what all goes into planning a wedding and trying to figure out how to crunch their sixteen-month schedule into twelve, if we waited until next October to get married.

After I got Abby in bed, I took my laptop up to bed with me and continued searching and taking notes. It said to get my wedding party figured out, so I decided I would begin working on that tomorrow.

The alarm startled me. Much to my surprise, my laptop was still in bed with me. I went through my normal morning routine of getting Abby off to day care, then returned and decided who I wanted for my bridal party. I had to have Jackie and Mandy, for sure, and hopefully I could get Georgia at least, and Candace, too. I decided to call them all later to make sure they even wanted to be part of the wedding.

I decided on my color scheme while laying out back by the pool with my laptop on the table beside me: light mint green, light pink, and pale smoke gray. I created a Word document to keep track of everything and bookmarked the planning checklist I was using. I couldn't wait until the weekend to talk to Jeff about the date.

The hours flew by while scanning through all the images of gowns on the *Bridals by Lori* website.

It wasn't like this when I married Sky. We had both been dirt broke college students.

****

As reluctant as she was, my mom decided I should have a beautiful wedding in the back-yard by the water. She and I took a trip to Orlando to find the perfect dress at Minerva's during spring break. Jim and Sky went in search of a nice tuxedo.

Jim called in favors to make the arrangements and invited the closest of friends to celebrate. Jackie, Mandy, Creighton, and plenty of others from school came to join the celebration.

I looked beautiful in my southern belle princess ball-gown. The top was strapless, with a sweetheart neckline. It had a ruched figure-hugging bodice that fit snugly down across my hips before flaring out with a lace train that flowed behind me. It wasn't super expensive, but it was beautiful. More than I ever thought I'd have for a wedding gown. My headpiece was a whimsical feather instead of a veil. Sky had looked breathtaking in his white tuxedo, white vest, white shirt, white tie, and white shoes.

I was so happy to no longer be known as Nikki Hollister, but instead as Nikki Carmichael. Mrs. Skylar Carmichael. He was legally mine now.

The wedding was a huge gift. But Mom and Jim wanted us to have a honeymoon, if only for a long weekend. Jim knew a business acquaintance who was able to help make arrangements for us to spend four full days and four night's at the most magical place on earth, Walt Disney World. We were just in Orlando, but it seemed like a different world.

As a married couple, when Sky and I returned to campus for my final year of school, we were able to move into off-campus housing. The one-bedroom apartment was very simple, yet had all of the amenities we needed.

The living room was a large space with an adjoining small dining area. Both were carpeted and flowed perfectly into the kitchen, which had all the modern appliances to make life easier for a young married couple. I was most excited that we had a dishwasher. The bathroom was just standard with the shower/tub combo and was accessible from the bedroom and the hallway. The bedroom was large enough to hold any bedroom set. Fortunately for us, Jim and Mom supplied the furnishings for the apartment.

The complex had a recreation center with a fitness facility and a community pool. We were so happy starting our new life together.

****

A tear ran down my face as I thought about how happy and in love I had been. Sky had been everything to me.

I had to get things back to right between us. I couldn't live with myself if I didn't.

Chapter 18

Jeff was home by the time I returned from dropping Abby off at my mom's house Saturday morning. I walked in to see him sitting at the kitchen breakfast bar with his face buried in his hands. I walked up behind him and wrapped my arms around his broad, muscular back. God, I loved looking at his strong, sexy back.

"Are you okay?" I spoke softly in his ear before kissing him on his cheek.

"Yeah, I'm just tired. It's been a long week."

"Maybe you should go lie down and take a nap."

"Why don't you come up with me?" He turned his body halfway so his eyes met mine.

"I hardly think you'll get much sleep that way."

"That's the plan." He pulled me around in front of him, securing me snugly between his legs. His arms reached around and grabbed my butt cheeks, pulling me in tighter as I lowered my lips onto his. His kiss went from gentle to ravenous within a couple of seconds. His mouth tasted like peppermint gum. His scent was a mixture of him and hotel soap. I wanted and needed him; I'd missed him. I reached back and pried his hands from cupping my cheeks and held them in mine. Our lips still locked tight to each other while I guided him to stand. Once he was up on his feet, our lips broke free of one another.

"Come on." I tugged on his hand, but he didn't budge.

"Right here. We don't need to go upstairs if the munchkin is gone."

"She's gone."

He pulled me back, fisting my hair, pulling me tighter into him. His tongue thrashed and lapped in my mouth. My hands reached around his back and could feel the muscles along his spine flexed and rigid.

Without warning, Jeff slid his hands under my arms, picked me up, and set my ass on the breakfast bar. He resumed his seat in front of me. With quick movements, he slid my dress up, revealing my barely-there moist, white, lacy G-string.

"Breakfast of champions right here." He wrapped the thin material around his hand and ripped the G-string off. He grasped my thighs, pressing them back and apart, and nearly knocked me off balance as I scrambled to get my arms behind me to brace myself. He lowered his head into my waiting sex. He licked long and slow laps. "You taste so good, so sweet." His licks got faster, and his tongue separated my lips to allow him to sink deeper into me. He moved his tongue from my clit and slid it inside me, then back up. He licked and sucked on my clit as he slid his fingers inside me, massaging me, fingering me until I trembled and orgasmed.

Jeff raised his head. As he was getting ready to wipe his mouth, I grabbed his shoulders with my nails, digging in and pulling him up to me. Wrapping my mouth around his, I licked my juices from around his lips, nipping at them occasionally. As I consumed his mouth, he worked furiously to drop his pants and underwear down around his ankles.

He pulled his mouth back from mine and stood in front of me, stroking his length. I reached my fingers down and slid them between my slick lips, parting them, then pulling them together, trembling with need. He watched me intently as I rubbed my clit, then slid my fingers down and plunged them into my sex. I fingered myself as he watched, stroking himself faster. When I pulled my fingers back out, they went back to my clit, massaging until I orgasmed again.

"Damn, that was hot as fuck." He reached for my soaked fingers and took them into his mouth, licking and sucking them as he pressed his swollen head against my slit. I was so wet, he slid in with ease. He massaged me gently, using just the head inside me, and within minutes my body quaked with another orgasm as I screamed out his name over and over.

"Stop teasing me, baby, I want all of you," I complained.

"I wouldn't call it teasing; you seem to be enjoying yourself."

"I need to feel you in me all the way, god-damn it; fuck the shit out of me, please."

"How can I resist when you ask me like that?" He slammed into me hard and deep, making me gasp and hitch my breath. My arms were getting so tired holding myself up. I wasn't sure how much longer I could take this before I'd collapse. His thrusts grew harder, causing my ass to slide back. He reached down and grabbed my thighs, yanking me forward again. We both were startled when the doorbell rang.

"Fuck! That has to be the cleaning people." Jeff yanked me off the breakfast bar, "Go upstairs, I'll be right up." He pulled his pants up and fastened his belt.

I quickly grabbed all of our things off the floor and ran up the back stairs to the bedroom.

By the time he got upstairs, I had pulled my dress off and was lying with my head propped up on all four of our pillows, my legs spread wide open, and knees bent, exposing my wet flesh to him.

"Just the way I like you, ready and waiting for me." He pulled his shirt off, and his pants were shed and left on the floor. He climbed up onto the foot of the bed, crawling his way up me. A shiver ran through my body.

"Cold?"

"No, can't wait to feel you in me again."

"Wait no more, baby doll." He lowered his mouth onto mine, pressed his hips forward, and his shaft filled my desire. He wrapped his strong arms around me, holding me tight as he continued to slay my sex with his powerful plunges. I moaned and called his name as he drove me over the edge again. I felt like I was in a fairy tale, being taken by Prince Charming, with every moment more perfect than the last.

He rolled us, switching positions -- me on top of him as he lay on his back under me. I spread my legs wide and rose up off of him, not all the way, just until I could feel the ridge of his throbbing cock at my entry. Using my leg muscles, I controlled the thrusting and grinding, tilting my pelvis forward so my clit rubbed against his pubis. The power was euphoric, and the clit stimulation sent me over the edge again.

Jeff grabbed my hips, and as he held me up slightly off of him, his hips thrust up into me as he continued his onslaught. "I'm gonna cum, Nikki, god-damn-this-pussy-feels-so-good." He flipped me onto my back, and with hard thrusts, found his release.

We took a quick shower. He was going to lie down for an hour, and I was heading out to the pool so I didn't disturb him.

I was awakened by the sound of a strange voice, and noises I had never heard before.

"Sorry to disturb you, ma'am. I won't be long."

"Who are you?"

"I'm here for pool maintenance, ma'am."

I was swooning over how handsome this man was. "What exactly are you doing?"

"Pool maintenance. I try to get by once a quarter, per Mr. Carrington's service contract."

"No, I meant what all do you do to the pool?"

"I make sure the pool is clean, check the filters and pumps, test the water's pH and chemicals. And if Mr. Carrington has any special requests, I do them too."

"So what's your name?" He had the most beautiful shirtless, muscular body wrapped in sweat-covered bronze and tattooed skin, topped with green eyes.

"Carson, ma'am."

"Well, Carson, nice to meet you. Please call me Nikki, not ma'am." I couldn't help but stare. "Would you like some water?"

"Yes, ma -- sorry, I mean yes, Nikki, that would be great."

"I'll be right back." I stood from the chaise and walked into the house. I could feel his eyes on me. In a weird way, I was hoping his eyes were on me. I grabbed a bottle of water from the refrigerator and returned to the pool. "Here you go." I tilted my head coyly and pursed my lips into a smile as my eyes locked with his.

"Carson, good, you're here," I heard Jeff call out from behind me.

"Yes, Mr. Carrington; is there anything else you need me to take care of today?" He shifted his eyes back at me. "Thanks, Nikki."

The two of them walked toward the pool house, talking pool business. Jeff patted him on the back once they reached the door, then turned and walked back in my direction. This man had a lion-like stride. His legs were so long and his way of walking was powerful, forcing his calves and quadriceps to flex with each step.

"So you met Carson. He's a good kid, not like some kids these days. He's reliable, respectful, and hard working."

"How long has he been coming around?"

"He's been with this company for a couple years and got my account right away. He's working while going to college, so who knows how much longer until I get a replacement."

"So what's he doing now?"

"I heard some noise in the pool house that I want him to check out for me." Jeff took in a deep breath and held it for what seemed like minutes before releasing it. "Look, he's here to work on the pool only. Not here for chit-chat with you, not here to be given the fifth degree about his job, and not to be gawked at," he said using a pointed tone, his jaw clenched. "He's been made aware of who you are and he'll call you Ms. Carmichael or ma'am, and eventually Mrs. Carrington, but not Nikki. Do you understand?"

Jesus fucking Christ, why do I feel like a fucking five-year-old getting scolded by daddy? "I got it." I released a loud sigh as I leaned forward to get up.

"Where are you going?"

"In the house. I'll be back." *Fucking asshole.*

"Don't get mad at me because I called you out. If you're going to marry me and live in my house, you need to respect me." His eyes narrowed, and his voice was razor sharp. "I can't control your eyes, but that staring bullshit in front of me better stop or you will be back in your little house so fast it'll make your head spin."

I bit my tongue and kept from saying what I really wanted to. "I apologize if I disrespected you." Turning on my heels, I walked into the house. I hadn't come in the house for anything other than to get away from him. I was so furious that he'd just talked to me like I was a child. I paced back and forth for a minute and then heard him holler my name. *God damn it, what now?*

"What?" I hollered out the screen door.

"Bring us a couple beers when you come back."

Fuck you. "Okay."

I grabbed four cans of beer and walked back out to my chaise. "Here you go." I set them all on the table then kept walking and jumped in the pool to swim a few laps.

Before reaching the edge of the pool from my second lap, I felt his strong arm swoop me up, pulling me into him. "You can't be mad at me all night."

254 * Twisted By Desire

"I'm fine."

"Good, because I was thinking of going out later. Maybe we could go to The Rusty Pelican for dinner tonight."

"That works for me. I've never been there. I'm up for it, I guess."

"You're going to like it." He lowered his lips to mine and kissed me. "I have a reservation for six o'clock."

As we drove up to the Rusty Pelican, I fell in love with the rustic wood and glass building that sat pretty much all by itself on the waterfront. "What an awesome building."

"The food's pretty good too."

The sound of the waves and smell of food was so inviting as we strolled up the walkway to the entrance. Jeff stepped up to the hostess. "Carrington."

"Good evening, sir; party of two with a six o'clock reservation?"

"Yes."

"Give us a few minutes and your table will be ready."

"Thank you."

I stood looking out at the water. I was entranced by the stunning view.

"Carrington," the soft female voice called.

"Babe, come on, they're ready for us." Jeff touched my arm, and I jumped. I wasn't sure why.

We sat, and the waitress was at our table immediately with a glass of water for each of us. The hostess left the menus, and the waitress began telling us the daily specials. I was having a hard time focusing on what she was saying because the expression on Jeff's face and his fidgeting hinted at something being wrong. He rolled his right shoulder while twisting his neck to the right. His lips were twitching and curling in the corners. There was bad news coming, I could sense it. *Oh, shit, he's not going to tell me it's over, is he?*

"Can I start you with a drink from the bar?" the waitress asked.

"I'll have a Long Island Iced Tea, please." If I was getting dumped, I was going to get numb.

"A Jack and Coke for me, please."

"I'll be right back with your drinks."

My stomach was churning, and I began to feel nauseated. My chest felt tight when I took a sip of water to try to calm myself down, which wasn't working.

"What do you think of this place?" Jeff asked.

"I like it; it's very elegant. And the views are to die for."

"I was hoping you'd like it. They do weddings and receptions here. I wanted you to see it before your friends suggest renting a Fire Hall or some ridiculous shit like that."

My shoulders slumped as I gasped, closing my eyes briefly before opening them again. *Thank you whoever is out in the universe looking out for me.*

"I could see us being here." I glanced down at the menu. "But the prices are a bit much. But since you brought the wedding up, I'd like to talk to you about that."

"Talk away."

The waitress returned to take our order, then we talked about being on *Say Yes to the Dress*. He said he didn't mind if I was on the show, but added that there was absolutely nothing that could get him to appear on it. We also talked about what maximum wedding guest list count was appropriate. We decided no more than two hundred guests sounded about right. Neither of us had any idea how many people we should invite.

Our food was delivered to our table. I felt so good getting some of the planning details worked out, but we still hadn't talked about the two biggest things: the date and the budget.

"When we get done eating, I want you to go look at the Grand Ballroom."

"Okay, sounds good."

We finished eating, and Jeff settled the check. The hostess, Katy, was more than happy to take us back to see the room since it wasn't in use. They were setting up for a wedding that was to take place the following day, though, and it was breathtaking. As soon as we walked in, I knew our venue had been found. The room was huge and perfect. It would easily accommodate two hundred people. With the large windows, the view was available wherever you stood.

Katy took us to see the decorated gazebo area. I *had* to have my wedding here. I couldn't wait to tell everyone about this place. Katy retrieved a wedding planner guide and planner business card for me before walking us back out front.

We continued talking after we were home. I was so excited with how things were quickly getting checked off the list. The Rusty Pelican would be able to help with a lot of things on the overwhelming checklist.

"We still have two big things to talk about." I kicked off my shoes.

"Keep talking. You have about fifteen more minutes, because I do have other things on my mind." Jeff unbuttoned his shirt and sat back in the chair, looking delicious and fuckable. How was I supposed to concentrate on a wedding when fucking his magnificent ass was all that was on my mind?

"We need to figure out the budget and the wedding date."

"Well, let's see, today is October thirteenth." Jeff pulled his phone from his pocket, and continued to rattle off calendar information. "Valentine's Day falls on Thursday, so let's go with the Saturday before that."

"Two thousand fourteen, right? So I get sixteen months to plan the wedding?" This would be a piece of cake, according to the checklist.

"No, baby doll, you get four." He looked up from his phone to meet my shocked look.

"Are you serious?"

"Of course, why put it off for over a year? You can make that work, right?"

"Everyone says you need about a year to sixteen months to plan a wedding."

"Well, darling, you get four. Our wedding date is February ninth."

"Well, fuck me twice."

"Be careful what you wish for, you may just get it."
Jeff winked at me. He stood up and took his shirt off.
"Let's talk money tomorrow; enough of this wedding
planning crap for tonight."

This man was a living, breathing sex god. His body
deserved to be licked and worshiped from head to toe. His
six-pack was divine, leading to that tantalizing V. I could
feel myself getting wet just looking at him. I wanted to rip
those pants off him.

Jeff snapped his fingers in front of my face. "Are
you all right?"

"Yeah, I'm fine."

"I'll ask again, do you want a drink?" He walked
over to the bar.

"Sure, whatever you're having."

"Cool, a double shot of Fireball coming at you." He
peered at me with hooded eyes.

I licked across my bottom lip. "Sounds enticing."
My sex clenched watching him walk over holding a shot
glass in each hand full of the tasty cinnamon liquor.

"It's better than enticing; it's a promise." His arm
stretched over toward me with my drink in his hand. As I
reached for it, he raised the glass higher and stared into my

eyes. "About that request of yours, I plan to fulfill it tonight. I plan to leave such a lasting impression on you that you'll dream about me, feel me in you, and scream my name while you sleep."

My mouth fell open and my arms felt heavy at my sides. What were we wasting time drinking for? My words were stuck in my throat. He lowered his arm and my drink so I could take it.

As I reached for it, he leaned down to me and slanted his mouth on mine. His tongue plundered the depths of my mouth. The familiar butterflies that had danced in my stomach when we had first met resurfaced in grand fashion.

Chapter 19

I'm not sure if I actually screamed his name out loud, but in my dreams, I went hoarse reliving the night's incredible sexcapade. I'm pretty sure I had one of those night orgasm things because I was dripping wet down there when I woke up.

Jeff was still asleep, so I slipped out of the bed and out of the room. I went downstairs and got a pot of coffee brewing. While I waited, I retrieved my two packets of Stevia and my International Delight French Vanilla creamer. I reached up to get one of the larger cups on a high shelf and felt his warm, large body drape over my shoulder and reach up to get it for me.

"Good morning." I turned to him. He was standing at attention in his black silk boxers. My eyes crawled up his fine form to meet his eyes.

"Good morning to you; you weren't supposed to leave."

"Maybe next time you should tie me down."

"Don't tempt me, princess."

"Anyway, I needed some coffee."

"Bring it up with you; I've got some unfinished business to take care of." His eyes looked down at his erection.

"Why go upstairs? We have the house to ourselves." I dropped to my knees on the hard travertine tile floor in front of him and yanked his boxers down with one hand and wrapped my fingers around his shaft with the other before he could object. Peering up into his eyes, my tongue licked out around the swollen head and ridge. Our eyes remained locked on each other when I took him deep into my mouth, nearly gagging as he pressed against the back of my throat. I worked and twisted my hand at his base and used my mouth to lube and stroke him. He stood with his heated gaze fixed on me, watching me take him in and out of my mouth, getting deeper with each time. There was no way I could get all of him in my mouth, but I wanted to try.

I ran my tongue down and across the large vein on the underside of his shaft, down across his hanging sac, being gentle as I took it in my mouth, licking my tongue hungrily around him while holding the fullness of his nuts in my mouth. I released them to drop one at a time from my lips as my mouth ran up the length of his cock to the drips of salty pre-cum leaking from his head. I licked them off, then took him deep into my mouth, bobbing up and down faster and faster.

"Damn, are you trying to make me cum?"

I nodded my head yes, holding him tight in the grip of my mouth.

"I'm going to if you keep this up." His taste and feel in my mouth had my snatch wet and eager to be fucked, but this was about him right now, not me. I spit in my hand and used it as lube to massage him.

"Damn, baby, you are fucking hot. I can't take it."

I sucked with more intensity as I leaned into him, pulling him into my mouth. He stroked into me twice, and on the third stroke moaned, "Damn it, baby." He poured his hot fireball shot of cum down my throat as I lapped and swallowed it eagerly. I licked up and around his spent shaft, my eyes blazing with lust.

I stood and rinsed my mouth in the sink, poured my cup of coffee, added my fixings, and took a drink. Jeff wrapped me in his arms, holding me tight to him, kissing my neck. I knew he wasn't kissing me until I gargled and brushed my teeth.

"Well, that's one thing off the to-do list." I chuckled.

"For now, you beautiful wench. That wasn't exactly the plan, but we have the rest of the day, and I owe you now."

"I may have to take a rain check after last night. I'm kind of sore today."

"You can recover while I'm out of town."

"Okay, then." I opened the refrigerator to find something for breakfast. "What would you like; scrambled eggs, an omelet, or pancakes?"

"Four scrambled egg whites and toast, no butter."

"One boring breakfast coming up."

We finished eating our breakfast, and I cleaned the kitchen, then decided it was time to dive into the wedding budget conversation. It went well. When I told him I had about thirty-five hundred dollars saved up, he told me to use that for my dress. He would take care of everything else. I decided I would try to make sure it wasn't some ridiculous, exorbitant amount of money he had to fork over.

I thought we were done talking, but Jeff caught me by surprise. He left the kitchen, jogged up the stairs, and returned with some papers in his hand.

"We need to talk about this."

My heart sank. My chest tightened, and my stomach knotted. What had he done, spied on me again; dug up something from my past? I felt nervous just thinking what he might have in his hand. "What is that?" My voiced trembled.

"This, my dear, is a pre-nuptial agreement."

Erase my previous feelings; they were replaced by hurt and anger. I crossed my arms over my chest and took in a deep breath. "Okay, and...?" My reply came out every bit as snippy as I meant it to.

"And before we get married, I'd like you to read and sign it. You do know what a pre-nup is, right?" He raised his eyebrows and smirked.

"Of course I know what it is."

"Then you shouldn't be surprised that I'm asking you to sign it."

"I guess I'm surprised because you're not a mega millionaire or some shit like that. I don't want your fucking money, Jeff."

"Then that makes it easier to just sign the damn thing and be done with it."

"I think you've got a lot of nerve asking me to sign it."

"Why? Because I want to protect the fucking shit I've busted my ass working for?" His face reddened, and he put his hands on his hips as his chest puffed out. "I'd be a goddamn fool not to have you sign one. And you don't know what the fuck I have or own."

Well, now I was curious. What did he have that I didn't know about? "Having to sign that thing makes me feel like you don't trust me."

"Sweetheart," his lips thinned and his eyebrows tightened, "this isn't about your fucking feelings. I couldn't really give a rat's ass about how this makes you feel. You either sign it or go pack your shit." He threw the papers on the table and stood like a statue, staring at me.

My legs wobbled beneath me, and I squeezed my eyes shut to keep the tears from trickling down my face. I felt like I had been punched in the throat. I couldn't swallow. "Do I have to sign it now? Can I take some time to read it?"

"My attorney has been thorough," his jaw clenched tight, "and I'd expect you to read it."

"And if I don't sign?"

"It's a wrap between us; over, finished, finito." He flexed his chest muscles, and his arms tightened. "It's your call, but this is non-negotiable."

And to think the day *was* off to a good start.

"So, I'll give you the quick and dirty on this thing, then you can read it in more detail. It's good for ten years.

After that, it's a null and void document. Basically, it says if we divorce before the ten years, you leave with what you came with. If we make it to ten years and a day, the pre-nup is of no consequence anymore."

"Okay." I stepped back against the counter top and slumped against it. My eyes stayed fixed on the floor tiles.

"It's not the end of the world, Nikki. As long as we're married, it doesn't affect you. I didn't put shit in there like you'd only get a $50 a week allowance or you can only spend money you make. I've known assholes who have done that, but I didn't do that to you."

"Okay." I glanced up to meet his eyes before lowering them back to the floor.

"Jesus Christ, quit acting like a fucking baby about this." He slammed his fist on the table before he stormed to the bottom of the stairs. He stopped and turned back to face me. "You can't stomp and pout like a spoiled fucking brat and get your way. You either sign or you don't. We either get married or we don't. I told you, it's your call. And you may as well lose that pissy bitch attitude, too. I'm not dealing with that silly shit all day."

I sat at the table and gathered the pages of the agreement into a neat pile and set them off to the side. I heard his footsteps coming back down the stairs.

"I'll be back; I'm going over to see Connor."

"What time will you get back?"

"When I walk through that door, that's the time I'll be back. Look, we can get something else straight now, too. I've neglected seeing my friends on the weekends, but I'm not planning on that being the norm. And I don't answer to you. Don't think you have a leash on me or I need to check in. I'm a grown-ass man. If you need something while I'm out, I have a phone." He grabbed his keys from the countertop. "When I get back, I expect you to be in a better mood. Get over yourself and your self-righteous feelings."

My mouth hung open as I watched him walk out the door, slamming it shut behind him. My mom was right, he was a total asshole.

Chapter 20

I read that stupid fucking agreement so many times I could recite it in my sleep. I didn't see anything in there that warranted me getting so upset over it. I guess it was the principle that irked me. Then it was his smug berating that really pissed me off. Oh well, I was over it now. I knew one thing for sure; I was choosing *not* to move back into my house. I'd contact his lawyer and sign it by the weekend, before he got back home.

I needed to talk to someone but knew Jackie was the last person I wanted to talk to about this. She'd tell me to run. As much as Sky hated Jeff, I knew he wouldn't listen objectively. I had to talk to Mandy.

After work, Mandy and I met up for a drink, and I explained to her that Jeff wanted me to sign the pre-nup. She wasn't surprised and was taken aback that we'd gotten into an argument about it. She repeated what Jeff said, that he was protecting what he'd earned. By then I'd had time to cool down and think about it, and I got it, I really did. We had another drink, and I asked her if she'd be in my wedding as one of my bridesmaids. She was more than happy to be.

As we left the bar, I gave her a big hug. She held me tight and whispered in my ear that she missed what we'd had. I was stunned. That was the closest she had ever gotten to talking about our college secret.

****

In school, I'd had an inquisitive fascination with the sexuality of my good friend and college roommate, Mandy, because she dated both men and women. Although I'd only ever had sex with men, I couldn't help but wonder if I had any attraction to females or what it would be like to be with one. I never hesitated to say a woman was nice looking or comment on her very sexy ass or breasts. It was a niggling curiosity. Was there something more?

The thought of kissing a girl had been on my mind several times. How would it feel? Would it be different than kissing a man? Would I like it more than kissing a man? Would I find I really liked women? What happens after the kiss? The questions swirled in my mind like a tornado rushing through the open fields of Kansas.

One thing I did know without any doubt, if I ever decided to try it, it would have to be with a beautiful woman, and someone who made me feel comfortable and wouldn't do more than I wanted, someone I trusted, someone like Mandy. Even with that, I wasn't quite sure that could actually trigger me to try it.

During our sophomore year, we decided to remain roommates since we had become such good friends as freshmen.

One night, we were drinking, dancing around in the dorm, laughing and giggling -- nothing unusual for us. During the frolicking, I removed my shirt and bra then climbed on top of the small table in our room; still, nothing unusual. That table doubled as our stage most nights we were drinking. I encouraged Mandy to do the same, which she immediately did. Throwing her shirt off and revealing her perky, perfect-looking 36C breasts. I felt the nervous butterflies churning in my stomach. As we danced, I rubbed my hands across Mandy's waist as we laughed. What happened as the night progressed was very out of the ordinary for me.

The light touching became more sensual and our conversation went from light-hearted to testing my sexual boundaries.

I felt self-conscious and so out of my element, having never experienced this before. I couldn't help but think to myself that it was like being a virgin all over again. Mandy took the lead and planted a light kiss on my lips, then pulled back. After looking at me to make sure I wasn't freaking out, she kissed me again. This time, it was a deep kiss. Mandy's tongue probed my mouth. My tongue met hers. Her fingers continued to playfully tease my nipples. The arousal in my sex was surprising. I wasn't sure what to expect but hadn't expected that.

Mandy kissed down my neck, across my collarbone, and eventually down to my breasts, taking my hard nipple gently in her mouth and flicking it around with her tongue as she lightly circled and clasped the other nipple with her fingertips. Mandy was very gentle, yet confident in what she was doing. She had slid her fingers under the lace of my panties and tugged my shorts and panties down some, letting me know her desire.

I felt conflicted by the time I lay down in my own bed. I loved the feel of a man pleasing me. At the same time, I really enjoyed being with Mandy. She kissed better than most men; she was gentle, and her touch was soft. I also thought her oral skills rivaled most men's.

After the second time and less alcohol, I was convinced I enjoyed being with a woman but still preferred the feel of a man filling me. I became more in touch with my bi side when I wasn't dating. Over the next couple of months, I worked to resolve the unpredictable feelings that would creep up in my mind. I wanted Mandy; I craved the woman-on-woman experience again and again. I eventually stepped out of my comfort zone and took a turn licking Mandy down there. The first time I did it, I wasn't so sure I liked it and couldn't get to the mouthwash fast enough. We spent more weeknights and weekends exploring, touching and satisfying each other. Mandy introduced me to her Wand toy to enhance our encounters; however, the inability to feel penetration other than fingers left me still unsatisfied.

I eventually became more comfortable, warming up to and learning the art of cunnilingus nearly as well as Mandy. My only true gauge was the ability to make Mandy orgasm, which I was able to achieve with ease.

The frequency of our liaisons diminished once Mandy began dating Creighton, a man she knew from her Biology class.

Mandy was proposed to by Creighton after just six short months of dating, near the end of the school year, at which time she vowed to be completely faithful to him and discontinued all sexual contact with me. She also promised me to never reveal our exploits to anyone and vehemently requested I promise the same. Her intention was to not tell her fiancé -- she didn't think having an affair with a woman construed cheating. But she also didn't want to risk that relationship.

I was respectful of Mandy's wishes, but struggled on occasion to not embrace her, stroke her, kiss her, or feel her.

Chapter 21

I received confirmations from Georgia, Candace and, begrudgingly, Jackie that they would be my wedding party. I asked Jackie to be my maid of honor. She told me the thought of organizing parties to celebrate me marrying this guy made her stomach hurt, but she loved me and would bite the bullet.

I managed to sneak some time at work to fill out the online form for *Say Yes to the Dress* and got that submitted. My fingers and toes were crossed. I wanted to be on that show so bad.

My conversations with Jeff during the evenings were kept short. He seemed to be irritated with me still. As long as I signed the paper, that was what mattered. I figured once I signed he'd loosen back up. I hoped so anyway. He was coming in Saturday afternoon and would be home for four days this time. I didn't want four days of the cold shoulder; I wanted four nights of him taking me every way he could imagine.

The days of the week flew by. Before I knew it, it was Friday, the day I had my appointment with Jeff's attorney. I had no idea what to expect. I thought I'd go in, sign the paper with him as a witness, and leave, but that's not the way he did it.

He called in his administrative assistant to videotape what became the pre-nuptial signing ceremony. It only took about ten minutes once the video recording began, but with all the people and cameras and lighting, I thought we were shooting a commercial. There was a notary, witnesses, and the attorney, who sat near me, asking me things like, did I have sufficient time to review and consider the pre-nuptial agreement. He even asked if I had an opportunity to request changes. What changes could I have requested? Who the hell was I to ask Jeff to make changes to the agreement he had drawn up? Besides, it was straightforward enough, and nothing seemed crazy.

He read through everything I was giving up in the event we divorced in the first ten years of our marriage. He continued to tell me that on February tenth, two thousand twenty-three this agreement was null and void, and had me acknowledge that I accepted that. He told me Jeff could sell or transfer any property without me signing or being involved. I knew that too. He asked me if I thought the agreement was fair, which I guessed I did, so I told him yes.

The statement I thought was the most striking was when he asked if I was freely signing the agreement without any coercion or any influence by Jeff. *Dude, go look at my house where Sky is living* is what I wanted to say to him. I didn't need anything to influence me more than the thought of living there again. Then he asked if there were any threats of bodily harm or any type of force used to get me to sign. Jesus, I knew Jeff had his quirks, but that would be over the top.

Once we finished the questions, it was time to sign, which I did. When I walked out of the attorney's office, I felt more uneasy than I had before walking in. I couldn't help but think maybe I should have gotten a lawyer to read through that thing for me.

I got up early and got Abby ready to go to Sky's. Sky got Abby settled in to watch a movie after locking the front door. He had added a special lock up high on the door to make sure she couldn't get out. He turned to me with squinted eyes and tilted his head. "What's on your beautiful mind? You look like something's bothering you."

I shook my head. "Nothing. I'm okay."

"No, you aren't; something's wrong. Tell me. Did that fuckwad do something to you?"

My eyes prickled. Sky was the one person who knew me the best. I couldn't hide anything from him. I had never been able to. He walked over to me and ran his fingers across my jaw-line, lifting my eyes to meet his. My nose tingled and my eyes burned.

"Tell me, Nik."

"I don't want to tell you; you'll get pissed."

"I already am. He's no good, I can feel it."

"I'm going to marry him, Sky."

"Yeah, and that's really fucked up, if you ask me."

I stood in my own living room, looking around as if I were in a foreign land, as Sky grabbed my hands. "Come with me; let's talk away from her." He nodded his head in the direction of Abby. She was so busy watching Sponge Bob Square Pants that she wouldn't have cared if the house was on fire. We walked through the kitchen and out onto the screened-in back porch, sitting on the same raggedy couch that had sat in his apartment living room.

I couldn't keep the secret any longer. I told him about the pre-nup Jeff had waved around and threw in my face, how he was forcing me to sign, and how he had hollered at me when I hesitated. A single tear streamed down my face, and Sky's fingers swiped it away. Maybe I exaggerated a little, and I left out that I had already signed the damn agreement.

Slowly, Sky slid off the seat and onto his knees in front of me. With a pleading look in his eyes, he begged me to come back to him. He wrapped his arms around my hips and held me tight.

"I'm nothing without you. I love you so much, Nik. You and Abby belong here. You deserve someone who loves you, really loves you."

With tears streaming down my face, I said, "I love you too, Sky, but we can't keep going on like this."

"Don't give up on me, Nik. Please, don't give up on me."

I lowered myself onto my knees with Sky. I wrapped my hands around his neck and kissed him. He wrapped me tightly in his arms and kissed me deeply. His tongue was exploring my mouth as if it were the first time, but the familiarity was what we both desired; we both needed each other. I ran my fingers through his hair as my core shook. I needed his touch; I wanted everything about him.

I couldn't help but think about how, when we had been together, love was all we needed, and I loved Sky with all of my heart. He made me weak.

We grasped and clutched at each other with a burning passion.

"Sky, we can't do this back here."

"Come upstairs. God, I need you so bad, Nik." The physical attraction was too fiery to ignore. We quickly walked past Abby, rounding the corner to disappear up the steps into my old bedroom. With our arms crossing each other's, we worked at a feverish pace to remove our clothes while also tugging at each other's garments. Our breathing was erratic, and our obsession was unwavering. We wanted each other in the worst way; right now, right here on the bedroom floor.

Sky grasped my hair and slightly directed me downward, lowering my head to his waiting, dripping erection. Without hesitation, I cloaked him with my enthusiastic lips. I licked, sucked, slurped and choked him back into my throat as far as I could take him. I couldn't get enough of him or his taste. His scent mixed with Dove soap was driving me crazy. What the fuck was it about Dove soap?

Sky reached his fingers down between my legs as he kissed the top of my head. I was so wet down there, I could hear the noises my pussy was making, calling him, begging him to fill me. That made him even more rigid as his impatience shone through and was throbbing in my throat. I stroked up and down his shaft with my slightly parted lips, allowing him to fit firmly between them. As his pre-cum dripped over the ridge, I licked up his shaft to quickly retrieve it.

"Damn, girl," Sky cried out. His hand strummed down my face. "I missed you so much."

He ran his fingers across my slick pussy lips, rubbing my clit and making me moan.

"Don't make too much noise, Nik."

My mouth was full, and I wasn't releasing him from my mouth's grip. Sky continued to rub and massage my clit until he was able to get me to orgasm. I sucked even harder and let my teeth graze along his length as I muffled my cries. Sky jumped once he felt the teeth, but soon relaxed when I pulled back some.

He reached back and pulled a pillow down off the bed to put under my head, then lowered me down to the pillow after removing himself from my mouth. Grasping my thighs, he pressed them back and apart as he lowered his head licking his tongue across my sex. His licks got faster, and his tongue separated my lips to allow him to sink deep into me while sliding one, then two fingers deep inside my crevice.

I pulled him up to me, wrapping my mouth around his. As I consumed his mouth, my hands wrapped around his tight butt and tugged him into me.

"I need to feel you now, Sky," I begged.

He plunged deep into me with one stroke, slapping his flesh into mine. His thrusts became more powerful and fast, making a whooshing sound. He had to slow down to make sure he was in control. He took my nipples into his mouth and sucked and licked around them.

"Damn, I love you," he proclaimed as he rammed into me -- in and out. He withdrew and lowered his mouth back down to lick me, letting his tongue reach down to my ass, flicking it fast across my tight hole before sliding back up to my slit.

"Oh, shit," I cried out. My sex was on fire, waiting for him to bring me to orgasm once again.

"I can't get enough of you." Again, he sank his throbbing erection deep inside me. "Look at me, Nik; I need to see your eyes." He held my head tight to the pillow by my hair.

This time he pounded into me with force until I screamed out, "Oh, fuck me." He clasped his hand over my mouth. My back arched, and my body quivered as I reached my orgasm. Sky found his release, and he collapsed down on top of me.

He rolled off to my side, pulling me alongside him as he curled himself up against my back, not letting me go, his erection shrinking and still jerking inside me. He held me tight around my waist while snuggling in closer.

Leaving Sky after the much-needed mind-blowing rendezvous was going to be difficult. Why couldn't he have just gotten his shit together sooner? My heart ached to be with him. Every possible emotion coursed in my mind as I lay next to my ex-husband, my first love, my soul mate, trying to determine the least emotional exit strategy.

It was impossible, I concluded; our hearts were about to be ripped apart again. Tears slid down my face and over my temple, pooling at my hair that lay crumpled under my head. I questioned if my decision was the right one, but knew I needed to leave; I had to get back to Jeff's house -- my fiancé.

I gathered my things and went into the bathroom to take a shower. I was careful not to look at Sky. I didn't want him to see the tears glistening on my face. I hated that I was going to rip his heart out of his chest ... again.

Chapter 22

I wasn't sure if I-love-you sex or make-up sex was better, but having both in the same day made me one happy girl. I felt a little guilty about it, though. I couldn't help but wonder if Jeff could taste Sky on me. I had taken a shower, but Sky and I don't use condoms either. I knew I'd never tell Jeff about my sexual liaisons with Sky. If he didn't find out on his own, this secret was going to my grave. But more than anything, I knew I had to stop all sexual contact with Sky if my relationship with Jeff was going to have any chance at all.

As we lay in the bed, Jeff ran his fingers over my chest and around my breasts. "You know, I wasn't trying to upset you with the pre-nup. I didn't think you'd react the way you did."

"I probably shouldn't have gotten so emotional and just thought logically. It makes sense, and I understand why you wanted me to sign."

"So you're going to sign?"

"I already did, yesterday."

"I'm glad to hear." He leaned over and kissed my cheek. "I was doing some thinking about my groomsmen, like you mentioned. How many bridesmaids are you thinking of having?"

"Four, Jackie will be my maid of honor and three bridesmaids."

"Jackie hates me."

"Yeah," I laughed. "She does."

"I don't know why; she doesn't know me, and I sure as hell haven't done anything to her. Anyway, I'll get four men. I know Connor will be my best man. I'll probably get Jorge, Sandy, and Hunter for my other groomsmen."

"No Blake?"

"No, that won't work. I'll go with those four."

"It's your call. Make sure to confirm with them all. They have to get tuxes and shoes to match."

"Yes ma'am. Whatever you say; you're the boss."

I pushed him on his shoulder. "You're so full of shit." I laughed. I knew he was trying to appease me. As much as I liked the joking Jeff better than the vicious Jeff, I didn't want him to go over the top.

"I have another problem to deal with, and quick," I said.

"What?"

"Halloween's coming up, and I don't have a costume for Abby."

"Well, go get something. Take her to the store, let her pick out whatever she wants, and get it for her. Problem solved."

"Yeah, I'll have to find another neighborhood to go trick or treating in, too."

"Take her by your mom's neighborhood and then over by your old house. You're really over-thinking this, sweetness. She's three; do you think she really gives two shits?"

"Probably not; you're right."

"For that matter, you could buy her a bag of M&Ms and call it a night."

"That's no fun." I scowled at him. "Too bad you won't be here to spend Halloween with us."

"I'm not into trick-or-treating, unless the treat I'm begging for is between your legs."

"You dog."

We got up and dressed. I had my laptop out looking at the wedding planning checklist. Jeff sat beside me as I checked off what had been done and what wasn't going to be done. We didn't need an engagement party. The planner would be the person from the Rusty Pelican, providing we were able to get that place.

"I'm going to let you deal with the registry. Don't go crazy; we have a lot already."

"Maybe I'll ask for food; your refrigerator and pantry are always pretty empty." I laughed.

"Funny." He gave me a sarcastic smile.

"Okay, so here's one for you; officiant -- who the hell's going to marry us?"

We looked at each other, and in unison replied, "Justice of the peace."

"What about the honeymoon, any thoughts?"

"I don't care; Hawaii, Bahamas, St. Martin, Jamaica, or Italy?"

"I don't have a passport."

"It takes four to six weeks to get one. Make sure to apply this week. When we decide where we want to go, I'll get one of the assistants at work to set the trip up for us."

"Hawaii sounds really nice. Mom said she and Jim had a great time when they went. The thought of Luaus, pig roasts, and hula dancing sounds like a lot of fun to me. The closest I've been to Hawaii is watching the movie *A Perfect Getaway*."

"I really liked that movie, too. Your choice. Just let me know. I can't guarantee you'll get a chance to do all that luau roast and pig dancing stuff, though. I have better plans for our honeymoon that involve you and me naked in every nook and cranny on the islands." He winked at me. "I think you can handle most of this other stuff without me."

"Not the guest list, I can't. Start thinking about who you want to invite. When I get an idea how many people will come from out of town, I'll check with the Holiday Inn or something for a group rate."

"Too much wedding talk; we need to change the subject or I'll explode."

I leaned over to my side and kissed him. We needed to get more things worked out, but they could wait. He was right, most of it I could do without him.

Sky beat me to the costume punch, which really was a big help. He took Abby to the Halloween store and got her a princess costume complete with tiara and a wand. She wore it home and looked more like Glenda the good witch from *The Wizard of Oz*. We confirmed he'd go to the day care center for their Halloween parade and take pictures, then I'd take her out trick-or-treating.

It was weird having Jeff home during a couple days of the week. I'd gotten so used to him being gone that him being around caused me to get out of my normal routine. I did enjoy going in the basement and keeping him company while he worked out. His body was smoking hot. It glistened when it was dripping wet from sweat, and the muscles rippled as he did lat pull downs and bicep curls. Squats were another favorite of mine to watch. But the absolute best was the extra nights of sex.

He had left early that morning and would be back on Saturday afternoon. That would give me more than enough time to work on my planning list. First thing I needed to do when I got a break at work was call The Rusty Pelican to see if our date was available.

Candace and Georgia were in shock when I told them the date. I hadn't told Jackie or Mandy yet. I'd tell them after work. Same with Mom, I'd tell her later because I was in no hurry to get fussed at by any of them. I was sure all of them will run down the list of scenarios that could be prompting such a speedy wedding.

Everything seemed overwhelming; getting ready for work, focusing at work, trying to cram this damn sixteen months of planning into four, and the verbal wars when I gave updates. And now the onslaught of holidays was upon us. Thinking about all of it made me feel like an anxiety attack was imminent. How in the hell was I supposed to keep from being fired over the next few months?

Chapter 23

"Have you heard anything from the show yet?" Some days, I thought Georgia was more excited about the thought of getting on *Say Yes to the Dress* than I was.

"Nothing yet." I really hadn't expected to hear anything this soon. "But I do have good news. Someone canceled their reservation for the date we wanted so the Grand Ballroom at the Rusty Pelican is confirmed for us."

"That's great. I wish you'd looked at a couple of other places, but it's nice there too."

"Jeff was pretty insistent on them. He's the one who took me there and told me about it."

"What's in it for him, a discount?" We both laughed.

After Georgia left, her question raised some of my own. Why was he so insistent on that place? Maybe it was just somewhere he had been before and he really liked it. Maybe he had attended someone else's wedding there. Whatever the reason, I loved it, and that's what mattered.

When I got off work, Abby and I made our weekly trip to the grocery store. As I strolled up the produce aisle, my phone rang.

"Hey, Mom, what's up?"

"Hi, sweetie. I was just calling to remind you that dinner is at our house this year again."

"Yeah, I know; I remember." I could barely remember my name these days, so I was glad she had called. Reminder to self, Thanksgiving dinner was at Mom's house. "And don't forget, Gary and his family will be here, along with Jim's children and their families."

"That's a lot of people." This would be fun. I hadn't seen Gary in years. He and his wife were coming home with their three kids this year. Last time I'd seen them, they'd only had the one daughter, Bianca. I couldn't wait to see them all. I was excited to meet Jim's two sons and their families. "You don't have enough room for everyone there. I know you guys have a couple extra bedrooms, but that's still too many people for your house."

"Do you think Gary and his family could stay with you?"

"Yeah, I mean, I don't see why not. I'm sure Jeff won't mind."

"Well, to make sure, will you just ask him to make sure he doesn't mind? I'd hate to impose on him."

"Sure, I'll talk to him to make sure it's okay, but I can't imagine he'll say no. Jeez, Gary is my brother, you know?"

"Let me know what he says, dear."

"Okay, I'll talk to you later, love you."

"Love you too."

I talked to Jeff about it later that night when he called. He didn't have any objection to Gary staying with us; he wasn't sure how he'd take the noise of, as he referred to them, Gritos de dos bebés, whatever the hell that meant. I had the strongest yearning to quote Samuel Jackson from *Pulp Fiction*, 'English, motherfucker, do you speak it?' But I knew that would probably not be a wise comment after letting him know his house was going to be invaded Thanksgiving weekend. We ended our call early; he and Sandy were heading to a bar for a couple of drinks. I was so happy I'd met Sandy already. I'd have been pretty pissed if he told me he was traveling and out drinking with Sandy and I hadn't known he was a man.

The next couple of weeks flew by. Before I knew it, Thanksgiving was right around the corner. The wedding planner and I had been working hard to make sure everything was taken care of as quickly as possible. The rehearsal dinner reservation was already made, and the cake had been ordered. I was using a florist, photographer, and videographer recommended by the Rusty Pelican's planner. I'd lucked into the perfect dress for Abby. I wanted her to be the flower girl, but needed to check with Gary to see if Bianca could walk with her.

Even though we hadn't figured out where we would honeymoon yet, Mom agreed to keep Abby while we were gone. Sky said he'd take her as much as he could manage around his work schedule.

Jackie had really stepped up and was helping me a lot. She'd arranged a bridal party shopping spree -- right up her alley. They'd be looking for dresses, jewelry, and shoes. She set up my wedding website. She was also going to look into the wedding favors for me. I owed her big time.

I had started on the guest list, but had been sidetracked with shopping for the invitations. I was starting to feel like the walls were beginning to close in on me, with less than three short months until W-day.

As if the wedding wasn't enough, I had to set up two bedrooms in the house for Gary and his kids. They were bringing their portable cribs for the twins. They'd get a room to themselves and Bianca was going to sleep in with Abby. It would be like a slumber party for the two of them. That would give Gary and Carla some privacy. I couldn't wait to see them all. Too bad Jeff didn't share my enthusiasm. He agreed that they should stay with us instead of a hotel or being crammed at Mom's, he just wasn't thrilled about crying babies in the house. He also didn't seem excited about the large family gathering, but he had assured me he'd be there with me. He was supposed to get back home pretty close to the same time that Gary was expected to get into town.

My phone rang, but I didn't recognize the number. "Hello?"

"Hey Sissy, I'm calling from Carla's phone. She got a new number. What's up?"

"Gary, hey," It'd been a couple months since I talked to him. Since the babies were born, sleep for them had to be snatched whenever they could get it, at all hours of the day, so I'd been careful not to disturb them.

"Everything's fine here." I shifted my phone from one ear to the other. "When are you guys planning on leaving?"

"We plan to hit the road Wednesday morning as soon as the kids are up and fed."

"Are you going to drive?"

"No, Carla will. You know I'd lose my mind in the Orlando traffic."

"That's good, I want you all to get here safe and in one piece. I can't wait to see everyone."

"We're looking forward to seeing you all too."

"I'm going to do some shopping later. Is there anything you would like to have in the house while you're here? Maybe something for the kids?"

"You have plenty of time to shop, don't make a special trip out for us today. We can even go on Wednesday after we get there."

So he was taking the father role quite seriously, and now he somehow thought he was my dad. "I know I still have a few days, but I don't want to go out shopping after you get here."

"If you insist. Grab some chips, Twizzlers, and some Sweet tarts. Oh, and some Reese's peanut butter cups."

I wrote down the items he told me. "Um, yeah -- maybe you want some real food?"

"Whatever you or Mom fixes, will be fine."

We talked for a few more minutes, until the baby brigade demanded his attention, then we said our quick good byes.

Jeff called me after I got back from the grocery store, while I was making a peanut butter and jelly sandwich for Abby. He wasn't going to make it for Thanksgiving after all -- fucking hell. He wouldn't be home until sometime Friday. He told me the travel coordinator had problems with his travel arrangements and messed up getting him home Wednesday. I have to admit, despite my assurances to Jeff that I understood, in the back of my mind, I was skeptical about his story. I could have thrown the phone across the room -- I was so pissed.

So many things were running through my mind: He had made it clear he wasn't thrilled about the large family gathering. He knew how my mom felt about him. But he fucking told me he would be here; he'd given me his word. And he'd never had this problem with travel before. I wanted to call bullshit while on the phone, but I hated arguing with him, it just wasn't worth it. He'd become such a volatile person; if I complained, he might tell me to piss off in a half joking way or he could go to the extreme and curse me out like a stranger on the street. I felt like I had to walk on eggshells sometimes.

Tuesday was a blur. That's all I can say. My head was in a fog, and I fumed over Jeff's call throughout the day. By that night, when he called me, though, I had calmed down. He told me to get my laptop so we could Skype instead of just hear each other's voices.

"Hey, babe," I said once we were connected. Goddamn this man was so fucking gorgeous! He was leaning back in a chair with his white dress shirt unbuttoned at the neck and his tie pulled to hang loosely knotted around his neck. His hair was disheveled like the first day I'd seen him.

"Hey to you." His husky voice and smile made my stomach do flips. "How's your day been?"

"Lonely. I miss you. And I was kind of pissed all day because you won't be home until Friday."

"I'll make it up to you when I get there." A smile beamed on my face, and my heart thumped so loud he might have heard it. "How's the wedding planning?"

"Ugh, let me just say, Mr. Carrington, four months to plan is a crock of shit." I laughed. "But I'm getting there. I hope you're working on your guest list. When the invitations get delivered, I won't have time to wait before getting them sent out."

"I gotcha. I'm working on it." I think he winked. Sometimes Skype can be blurry or freeze-frame, making it difficult to see.

"So how are things with you? Do you think you'll ever stop traveling so much?"

"I do what pays the bills, baby doll."

"Yeah." I sighed and mumbled under my breath, "That sucks."

"I heard that. One day I won't have to, but until then, we just have to deal with it."

"Yeah, yeah." I pouted. "But I don't like it. Your house is too big for just me and Abby, and the creaking at night creeps me out."

"It's just settling. It's only a few years old. New houses do that." He sat forward and slipped the tie up and over his head. Tossing it into the background, he unbuttoned his shirt two more buttons, revealing his muscular chest just enough to tease me. "Enough of the small talk, I need you to do me a favor."

"Sure, name it."

"I want to watch you strip down slowly; take the laptop with you up onto the bed and masturbate for me. We are going to have mind blowing fucking Skype-sex."

I felt my face heat up. "Seriously?"

"I'm dead ass serious. Chop, chop, sweetness; don't keep me waiting." He cleared his throat as I stood up. "And, Nikki, make sure to stay where I can see you." I was so happy Abby was asleep. I hauled ass up the stairs.

"Just tell me if you need me to move and which direction." I moved the laptop to the bed and positioned it so he could watch me 'perform.' "Can you see me okay?"

"Perfectly."

It felt weird to me, stripping to a computer monitor. I knew he was watching, but it wasn't the same as him sitting on the edge of the bed watching me. Well, technically, that's exactly what he was doing. I giggled as I unbuttoned my blouse.

"Something funny I should know about?"

"No, just thinking about silly stuff; ignore me."

"Never, beautiful, I don't ever plan to ignore you. Remove the bra, please."

"I thought you were sitting back watching. I had no idea you were directing this show."

"Well, now you know -- bra please; remove it."

I reached around back and unhooked it, then slowly let each shoulder strap drop down against the skin of my forearm as I held my hands on the material covering my breasts, to keep them from being exposed. With a quick movement, I let my hands drop to my sides, and my bra dropped to the floor, exposing my hard nipples.

"God, I wish I were there. Rub your nipples and give them a good squeeze like I do."

The thought alone sent a tingle through my sex. I slid my hands up my ribcage to my tits and grasped each one in a hand, squeezing and massaging around my nipples. My sex was having a clench-fest. I wanted him so bad. I took each nipple between my forefinger and thumb and rolled them, then gave the pinch that he always did, tight enough to cause me to gasp yet not hard enough to hurt -- just fucking perfect.

"The pants, Nikki, please."

I was having a difficult time seeing him on the screen, but I was pretty sure he had his pants down and was massaging himself to my show. Jesus fucking Christ, he was going to masturbate to me. How fucking hot is that? I reached down to my waist and unbuttoned and unzipped my pants, slowly sliding them down over my hips, wriggling back and forth until they dropped to the ground and I stepped my feet out of them. I stood in just my pink lace G-string.

"You're an absolute delight, beautiful. Turn around for me."

I turned until my ass was facing the monitor. I ran my hands down over the curve of my butt cheeks.

"I could cum just looking at your sexy ass. Turn back around and take off the panties."

I did as instructed. At least he didn't have me dancing around. I stood naked in front of the computer.

"Can you see me? Can you see how hard you've got me? I'd love to be there right now, sinking my tongue into your hot, wet, pussy, then burying myself in you."

I shifted my weight from one hip to the other. His words were verbally fucking me. I leaned in a little to get a better view of him. My mouth began to salivate like a dog smelling and staring at bacon that is sitting just out of his reach. I licked my lower lip before biting it gently, thinking how much I'd love his cock in my mouth. "I wish you were here too," I managed to moan out. My left hand slid between my thighs when I stood back up, and the other cupped my left breast. It was the more sensitive of the two, and I always liked it when Jeff licked and sucked that one in particular.

"You ready to make yourself cum for me?" I could only imagine his eyes, pleading and demanding with his heated glare. "Scoot up on the bed. Prop yourself up with plenty of pillows after you get the laptop situated so I get a good view of you and your face."

I set all four pillows against the headboard, tested it out for comfort, then moved the laptop to focus in as much as I could on my pussy, while still trying to get my face. "How's that?" I asked as I leaned back against the pillows.

"That's good enough. I see everything I want to see."

"Cool." I leaned back a little more.

"That's even better right there. Damn, Nikki." I raised my head to see the screen. "Your pussy is so wet, I can see it shimmering. I'd bet it tastes good too. Why don't you taste it for me and tell me."

I ran my fingers slowly through the slick folds, parting my lips slightly for him before moving my fingers to my mouth and licking my juices off. "Very tasty; you'd approve."

"I'm sure I would. Spread your legs a little farther for me, like when I'm there and you open up for me to take you." I spread my legs as far apart as I could, then rocked my hips forward, rolling them as my sex ached for his fullness in me. I let out a low moan.

"I like that baby; my dick is rock hard. I'd give anything to be pressing into that beautiful, sweet cunt of yours." His words sent a chill through me. I was almost scared to touch my clit for fear I'd cum immediately. "Run your fingers through your wetness; I want to hear that sound."

I slid my fingers through my slit, up and down, and flicked my fingertips at my opening. The slickness made a noise that sounded like I was slapping my fingers in water.

"Close your eyes for me and let yourself just get into this. I want you to keep rubbing your fingers through your luscious lips, then slide one finger deep in your crevice." I was more into this than he could have guessed. I was nervous at first, but knowing he was jacking himself off while watching me made me go into amateur porn star mode. "You are one sexy ass bitch, Nikki." I popped my eyes open for a quick second then closed them again. He really just called me a bitch.

"Now put two fingers in your pussy for me." He watched me stroke myself with my digits. "Does that feel good?"

"Yes, but not as good as you."

"Then add a third finger or all four. Stroke hard, Nikki. I want you to fuck yourself like I would fuck you." I pounded my fingers into my hole over and over.

"Do you feel me in you?" My core tightened around my fingers, responding to his voice.

"Yeah, I do."

"Keep your eyes closed and rub your clit, baby; I want you to cum for me." I knew touching my clit was going to send me over the edge. I winced and curled the corners of my lips down before using my free hand to put a slight amount of pressure on my sensitive bud.

"Do it, baby. I'm ready to explode."

I moaned as I put more pressure on my clit and rubbed back and forth. My hips rose up off the bed, grinding into my fingers that were planted deep in my pussy. I was so close.

"Such a beautiful sight; holy shit."

His words were all I needed to push me over. "Oh, fuck … Jeff." I was moaning and panting as my release extended much longer than I had expected. The more I rubbed my clit, the more I cried out. "God-damn, baby. Fuck."

When I finally stopped touching myself, I gasped and trembled while my clit and pussy throbbed; pounding like a second heart was located down there.

"Baby doll, look at me. Look what you made me do." I looked at this absolutely breathtaking man, sweat dripping down his face and chest, and his hand covered in his cream.

"Very sexy; too bad I'm not there to help you clean up." I licked my tongue out, lapping at the air. "I'd love to feel your arms wrapped around me right now."

"If I were there, you'd feel more than my arms, that's for damn sure. Thanks for indulging me tonight. I'll have a surprise for you Friday."

"What kind of surprise?" I turned onto my side and poked my ass out toward the screen so he could get a good view.

"That would ruin the whole premise of surprise if I told you. You'll enjoy it, with or without me. I hope your brother's in the farthest room from us. I'm looking forward to ravishing you and that sweet ass of yours."

"Maybe I should stick them in the basement." I laughed.

"Not a bad idea, pussycat. I plan to make you purr, claw up the sheets, and scratch to get away while I fuck eight of your nine lives to death."

"You can't get here fast enough."

Chapter 24

Once again, I was rushing around to get ready and out the door because I'd hit the snooze one too many times. I made it to work by the skin of my teeth. I wished I'd taken the day off. We only had a half day since it was the day before Thanksgiving, and Gary was going to arrive later that afternoon.

"Did you hear anything yet?" Georgia asked as she came storming toward my desk the moment I got there.

"Nothing yet; I probably won't hear anything until after this weekend, if I even hear then."

"You need to start looking for a dress. You can't wait until the last minute."

"I know, I know." I turned to my computer and logged in. She'd piqued my interest; I had to check my email again. The last time I had checked was before I left the house. I'd included on the application my home and work email addresses so I had to constantly check both.

"Still nothing; I'll tell you what, if I don't hear from them by the end of next week, we can start trying to find somewhere around here for me to go see what they have."

"That sounds good; I'll start checking places out."

"The place my mom took me in Orlando was nice. Maybe we can add that to the list of shops."

"Text or email me the name, and I'll add it."

"Thanks. I better get to work; I've been kind of slacking the past week."

"I'm sure I'll see you before we leave today."

Candace was the smart one of us three. She'd taken the day off. I hadn't seen Tristan or Robert, so I figured they must have taken off as well.

I couldn't concentrate. It was always the same story around Thanksgiving and Christmas. You come in to work and think about everything except work. Today, my mind kept drifting to my dad. It had been a long time since I'd seen him, and I missed him. I really wanted to see him again, but I wasn't sure if he wanted to see me. I really wanted to invite him to my wedding. He probably didn't even know I had been married once already. Why did he have to be such a complete asstard and walk out of our lives?

My cellphone rang, pulling me off the path of my trip down emotional memory lane.

"Hey Gary, where are you guys?"

"Stuck in traffic around Orlando, just like I expected."

"You knew it would happen." My brother is no exception to the male species. They were driving over from Ft. Lauderdale. I told him to take Alligator Alley, but he was scared of that stretch of road with nowhere to stop. I guess I can see it; he has three young kids. Eighty miles is a long way to drive without stopping.

"Yep, we did."

"Whenever you get in is fine. I'll be home. Mom has Abby today. I'll go pick her up and head home."

"Why not just stay at Mom's and we'll meet you there?"

"That works. I'll stay and wait for you there."

"Ugh, freaking people! They get on my nerves!" I heard Carla tell him to calm down.

"Bye, Gary; drive safe. I'll see you all when you get here."

"Bye, Sissy."

I was pretty sure Mom and Jim would be completely bat-shit crazy after this weekend. There were nine grandkids all together, and they'd all be in their house tonight and tomorrow for dinner.

The next two hours were spent alternating between checking my home email on my phone and my work email. I glanced at the account I had up on my screen occasionally, but couldn't find the motivation to make any updates. I was also afraid anything I did today would result in an ass-ripping on Monday. One of those per decade was more than enough for me.

I came back from the ladies' room with thirty minutes remaining of the work day. I couldn't believe a half day seemed to be taking longer to end than a normal nine-hour day. I checked my work email one more time and still hadn't received anything. Reality was slowly setting in; Georgia may be right. I logged off and turned my monitor off. I reached in my desk to get my purse before locking all the drawers and doors. Fifteen more minutes. I was fidgeting with my phone, checking my Facebook and Twitter. It was eating me alive. I had to check my email one more time before leaving -- and there it was. I screamed. The email I had been waiting for. I jumped up out of my seat as I did the I'm-gonna-be-on-TV dance.

"Whoa there, tiger, slow down. Are you in that big of a hurry to get out of here?" I almost knocked Georgia flat.

"Oh my god! It came! I got the email."

"What's it say?"

"It says I need to confirm we can make it to the Atlanta taping on December thirteenth." I couldn't stop smiling and squealing.

"Calm down; jeez, I know it's exciting. When is that?"

I quickly pulled up the calendar app on my phone and scrolled to December. "It's a Thursday. It's a Thursday," I sang. I was bouncing around like a kid in a toy store.

"I guess on Monday we can all put in our request to take off."

"Shit, Georgia, I need to get out of here. Are you busy on Friday?"

"No, I'll be looking for an escape from my family."

"I'll call you. Let's get together Friday morning and do some Black Friday shopping before Jeff gets in town."

"Sounds like a plan to me. I'll talk to you later. Happy Thanksgiving."

"Thanks, you have a good one too."

I was bopping as I walked out to my car, dancing and walking at the same time. Dalking or Wancing; jeez, I was going crazy. *I'm fucking going to be on TV. Yeah, bitches.* I laughed as I hit the key fob to unlock my car door. I tossed my purse across to the passenger side, sat down in the driver's seat, turned the radio up loud after starting the car, and continued bobbing and celebrating that I was going to be on TV.

I parked my car in Mom's driveway, jumped out, and had to grab the side of the car to steady myself. Perhaps I jumped up too fast, or got too excited, but the brief bout of dizziness was accompanied with a slight feeling of nausea. I really didn't need to get sick now, not with Gary and his kids coming to stay with us. Once my head was back on solid ground and the dizziness subsided, I continued my merriment and went into Mom's house.

"Mom? Mom, where are you?"

"Good grief, is there a fire somewhere?" She walked out of the kitchen drying her hands on a towel. "Is everything okay?"

"Yeah, it's great. I got my email today. I'm going to be on that show."

"That's wonderful, dear."

"I want you to come with us."

"That's silly; you girls go have fun. You don't need me tagging along."

"No, I do need you. I need you to help me make sure I have the right dress. I need you to be there for me … with me."

"Well, come in the kitchen and tell me all about it, and I'll try to make arrangements with my job to be away."

I followed her into the kitchen, and we talked. Abby was taking a nap, so we weren't interrupted.

I sent a flurry of texts to Sky to ask what his schedule was. He was able to watch Abby those two days since he was able to take her to day care.

As it turned out, my mom's schedule was already free on December twelfth and thirteenth. She said she would drive out with us, but would fly back on the thirteenth in the evening. She had an open house on Saturday the fifteenth that she couldn't miss and she didn't want to be away from Jim until Sunday anyway.

Watching the way her eyes lit up when she talked about him was incredible. I wanted that kind of love. I'd had it with Sky, but things didn't work out. Was it possible for me to love Jeff as much as I loved Sky? First, I'd probably have to feel like I actually loved him at all.

"Have you heard from Gary?" I was snapped out of my musing by my mother's worrying nature.

"He called me earlier; they were stuck in traffic around Orlando last I heard."

"He'll get here pretty soon, then, I would think."

"It won't be long. Once he breaks free of the traffic, it should be smooth sailing. Any word on Jim's sons?"

"They're on their way."

"I can't wait to meet them all. Hey, I was thinking. Why don't you all come to Jeff's house and cook dinner? We have more room and the pool; plus, he has the movie theater."

"I don't know, sweetie. I'd rather do that when he's home and he invites us. I don't like the idea of invading his house."

"Don't be silly, Mom; he won't care. And seriously," I raised my eyebrows, "would you really want to be there when he is?"

"I plead the fifth."

"That's what I thought. Just come by tomorrow, and I can help cook. The kids can play and swim and have a good time."

"It's tempting," she started. "But, Nikki, I just –"

"I'll be up at six in the morning waiting for you. No more trying to find an excuse. Everyone else can come over later, after they wake up."

"Fine. I just hope he doesn't get upset."

Well, that made two of us. I'd find out when I let him know later that his house was the new Thanksgiving dinner location.

Chapter 25

He took in a deep breath and rolled his eyes. I knew what that meant, and my stomach sank in reply as I watched him on my laptop screen. After releasing what seemed like every bit of breath in his lungs in a slow sigh, he replied, "Fine, Nikki, it's fine. Just don't let the kids into the movie theater with any food, candy, or juice. And make sure their hands are clean. I don't need a bunch of sticky fingerprints all over everything."

"I will."

"And whatever you do, don't let them in my closet to touch my audio visual equipment. No one turns things on or off or operates the DVD player except you, got it?"

"I got it."

"And I hope like hell I don't come home to the house looking like a tornado went through there."

"Jesus, Jeff, it's my family, not a bunch of random people off the street."

"Do you know how they live? Because if you don't, and they let their kids just do whatever they want in their house, they'll do the same thing in mine. And that's the kind of behavior that will cause my things to get broken or become part of the great Thanksgiving mystery of why shit no longer works."

"Then I'll be extra watchful. I didn't think you'd mind this much."

"You live there too; you can have them over. I just don't want any of my shit to get fucked up. Do you get that?"

"Yes, I get it." I get that I'm sick of you talking to me like I'm a fucking child.

"So what else is new, kitten? Did your brother make it to our house okay?" So my fiancé was a tad bit neurotic.

"Yep, I met him at Mom's earlier, and they followed me here. They are getting the kids settled now."

"I'm looking forward to meeting him Friday."

"Yeah, things should be calmer by then. You'll miss Jim's side of the family, but they'll hopefully be in town for the wedding." I licked my lips and rubbed my hands together. "You know, I like Skyping better than just talking on the phone. I love looking at you."

"You're not so bad on the eyes yourself; I wish we had more time, but I understand your brother's there and you're going to be cooking early." I had an early morning and a lot of food to help cook.

We talked for a few more minutes before saying our good-byes.

When the alarm clock began blaring at 5 AM, I briefly resented that I'd offered to have Thanksgiving at our house. What in the hell was I thinking? *This is ridiculous.* But I knew my Mom. I told her six, and, to her, that meant five-thirty. I pulled myself out of the bed, rummaged through the dresser drawer, and pulled out underwear and some yoga pants. Then I rifled through Jeff's drawer and found a Florida State T-shirt. I dragged everything into the bathroom with me and took a nice warm shower.

I stepped out and towel dried my hair before I wrapped myself in the extra long towel. It was so soft, fluffy, and cozy. After drying every inch of me, I slipped on my clothes. Jeff's T-shirt had a hint of his cologne, just enough to tantalize my senses and stir the butterflies in my stomach. I inhaled his scent before slipping it over my head. I brushed out my hair before heading downstairs.

As expected, the doorbell rang around five thirty-five, right after I started the pot of coffee.

"Good morning, Mom."

"Good morning, sweetie. Are you ready for this?"

"I have to be, I guess." I helped her unload everything from her car and got it all into the kitchen. Pots and pans, food, utensils and, thank God for Mom, wine. She turned the oven on to let it warm.

We spent time washing some of the dishes that hadn't been out of storage since last year's Christmas dinner. Mom washed and pulled the paper wrapped package of stuff out of the turkey, then slathered it with butter, salt, and pepper before slipping it into the turkey body bag and tying it off with the provided zip tie. She fit the twenty-five pound bird into the roaster pan, and into the oven it went.

We sat out back with our coffee. We had about an hour before we needed to get cracking on everything else.

"I take it Jeff was fine with us all being here today?" She sipped her coffee raising her gaze to meet mine.

"Mom, if I told you he wasn't, would you leave?"

"No, I'm here now, and the turkey is in the oven. And he won't be home until tomorrow."

I couldn't help but laugh at her brazen tone. "He was fine with it. He wished he could have been here to meet everyone."

"Humph," was her normal noise of disbelief. "How is the wedding planning coming along?"

"It's coming along okay. It helps to have the planner from the Rusty Pelican."

"Well, let me know if you need anything, dear. I have a few days off next month that I can help if needed."

"Thanks. I appreciate that."

"How is Jeff helping you with all his traveling?"

"He's doing what he can. I want him to get his guest list together. He says he's working on it."

"You don't worry or wonder what he does in his free time while he's out of town? A handsome man like him; that would drive me crazy."

"No, Mom. I trust him. I have to."

"You don't have to, dear; men who travel are known to have other women stashed."

"I know what you told me about him." She was making me crazy.

She took a sip of her coffee. "I wish I could remember that woman's name that he was having the affair with when he dated Gretchen…"

"It doesn't matter; that was her, and that was the past." I was already suspicious of him not coming home until tomorrow, but for a different reason. Now this seed was being planted. No, I couldn't let her infiltrate my mind with this shit. "Maybe we should go get everything else started. When are Jim and his kids coming over?"

"They should be here around noon."

We went back into the kitchen and divided up tasks and kept cooking. I drew the short straw and got stuck with peeling and making mashed potatoes. With Mom, everything is made from scratch, no boxed just-add-water dishes for her.

About two hours into our meal preparation, the turkey smell was wrapped tight around my head; the scent was grasping my neck like in the cartoons, choking me and causing my stomach to roil.

"Are you okay, sweetie? You look a little green around the gills."

"I'm fine." I really wasn't fine. "I think it may be lack of food or something."

"Get some juice; that may help."

As I poured a small glass of juice, I couldn't help think that throwing that wretched turkey out of the house would help. The smell was giving me the old one-two punch in the nose and gut. The juice did nothing to ease my misery. I had to get out of the kitchen and away from the foul fowl. "I'm going to run upstairs and grab my phone. I'll be right back."

I took off up the stairs like a track star. The bedroom was the perfect sanctuary – no turkey, no smell, no more nausea. I picked up my phone and sent a text telling Jeff I wanted to Skype with him real quick. I grabbed my laptop and ducked into the bathroom.

"Happy Thanksgiving, babe." I had a cinnamon swirl candle burning nearby to remove the remnants of that gross ass turkey smell from my nostrils.

"Happy Thanksgiving, my beautiful baby doll. Did all of your family make it over?"

"Not all of them. Just Mom's here right now; we've been cooking since five forty-five. Can you believe it? What are you going to eat today?"

"The hotel restaurant is open, and I'll be forced to eat there for today."

"Well, I'm sure it'll be good. After all, it's Thanksgiving, so they'll probably have a feast planned for the guests."

"My feast will be tomorrow."

"Really? Are we eating out?"

"Not we sugarplum, me. I will be eating you out." My sex spasmed, and my stomach clenched, in a good way.

"I can't wait to see you."

"Me either, so why don't you give me a sneak peek and slip your pants down."

His voice, his request, caused the wetness to saturate my panties. I stood and turned the laptop so he could watch me. I locked the door, then stepped back into view, pulled his shirt just high enough, and slid my fingers under the edge of my yoga pants. Tugging slightly, I slid them down about three or four inches, just to the top of my mound.

"Come on, baby, take them off."

I wriggled them and my panties down over my hips and slid them to my ankles.

"All the way, sweetness."

I did as he requested, then let the shirt fall back down to cover me like a mini dress. I pulled at the ribbing around the neck of the shirt. "Should I take this off?"

"That would be splendid."

The shirt was pulled over my head, leaving me standing in front of my laptop in just my bra.

"Take the bra off too; I want to see your beautiful body completely naked."

The bra came off quick. I could feel my wetness on my upper thighs. The anticipation of what he might command me to do next sent a fiery heat coursing through me.

"You are magnificent." He licked his lips. "If I were there, the things I'd do to you are too many to list. Just know tomorrow and for the next five days, I plan to make sure you know how thankful I am."

"Maybe when I go out shopping, I'll get Gary and Carla some earplugs."

"That's a damn good idea. You're going to have to beg me, in between gasping for air, to stop pounding that tight pussy."

The wetness that was collecting at my upper thighs spilled down my thigh. "Can you see this?" I pointed at my leg where the drop of dew stopped its descent.

"Wipe that off and lick your fingers for me." I did as instructed, licking and sucking my finger, moaning, as if my finger were his cock. "Sit on the tub surround and turn the laptop to face you; then spread your legs so I can see your beautiful wet lips."

"Okay, but we need to hurry. My mom is going to wonder what happened to me."

"Don't talk about her right now -- this is just you and me. This will only take as long as it takes you to cum."

My sex tightened with longing as I took my position.

"You know what I want to see, so don't be shy."

I rubbed my fingers between my slick lips, pulling them apart to expose the ripe, and wet, pink hole inside. He and I moaned at the same time. My fingers toyed between my opening and my lips, not penetrating, not yet. I slid them up to my swollen clit and rubbed gently.

"Harder, baby, I want to watch you get off."

I put more pressure on my bud and rubbed until I was close to the edge then stopped. Slowly, I moved my fingers down to my opening and slid my fuck-you finger inside me. When I pulled it out, I put it in my mouth and sucked and licked it like it I wanted to do to his cock, getting all the juices off, moaning and closing my eyes.

"God damn it, Nikki, you try your best to unravel me."

I pulled my finger out of my mouth and returned it to my waiting hole, slipping two fingers in this time, then three. I plunged them inside as I rubbed my clit. I could feel my channel contracting around my fingers as I went over the edge. I kept the pressure on my clit and moaned, then called out his name. Once I removed my hands from myself, I collapsed back against the side of the sink cabinet and gasped for breath as if I had just finished running a marathon.

"Damn baby, you're so hot. I can't wait until tomorrow. And don't forget, I'll have your surprise with me."

"You're all I need. Just hurry up and get home."

We ended the call after I told him about *Say Yes to the Dress* and that I'd be out doing Black Friday shopping.

I quickly washed up before bopping back down the stairs. I walked into the kitchen to see Gary and Carla nursing cups of coffee.

"Good morning." I walked over and gave them each a hug. "Where are the kids?"

"They're in the living room. We took their breakfast in there. We set the bounce-a-bouts up for Brian and Brianna."

Holy fuck -- and the monitoring of Jeff's house began.

I walked into the living room to make sure no food had made its way to the floor. Abby and Bianca were playing with the babies and had pretty much not eaten anything.

"Are you guys going to eat any more of your cereal?"

"No, I want Nana's bird," Bianca said.

"Yeah, Nana's bird," Abby mocked.

I picked up both bowls and headed into the kitchen with them.

"They didn't eat much of anything; they're waiting for turkey, or in their words, Nana's bird."

Mom looked up at me. "Are you sure you're okay, dear? Now your cheeks look flushed." *Oh, Mom, let it go. I just masturbated for my fiancé.*

"I'm feeling fine." I walked over by the stove and was slapped hard by the aroma of that fucking creature in there called turkey. "Well, except the fact that something about this turkey is making my stomach turn every time I get a good deep whiff."

"Perhaps you should shuck the corn at the table so you're away from the stove, dear."

"Isn't that farmer talk? Shucking corn?" I grabbed the bags and laughed at 'shucking corn' as I made my way to the table. "Where are we, Iowa?"

"Iowa is the potato state, idiot. Idaho is corn," Gary chimed in.

"No, jackass, Iowa is corn, and Idaho is potatoes. Jeez, Mom, why didn't you teach him anything?"

Carla laughed, but Mom didn't seem quite as amused.

"Perhaps I should have taught you that I didn't give birth to a jackass." Gary turned to me and stuck his tongue out. "But your sister is right; Iowa is the corn state, not Idaho."

"Who cares, get to shucking, Farmhand Nicolette." Gary smiled as he flipped me off behind Mom's back.

I decided to let it go...for now. But as soon as Mom turned her back to me, I flipped him off right back. I smiled as I thought about the fact that the finger I used to flip him off had been in my pussy just a short time ago. The smile stayed on my face as I proceeded with my shucking duties.

Jim arrived with his two sons and their families just before noon. I welcomed them in and took them on a tour of the first floor and showed them the pool. Justin, Jim's oldest son, and his wife, Lisa, decided to take the kids for a swim before we ate. Gary had Bianca's swimsuit with them. Fortunately for Justin and Johnny's boys, even though they didn't have swim trunks, they'd worn shorts. Carla took the girls up to change while the boys ripped their shirts over their heads, tossed them on the floor, and darted out the sliding glass door like a pack of wolves.

Johnny, Jim's younger son, and his wife, Karen, sat in the kitchen with us and talked but made sure they had a good view of the pool. Their kids were all at least ten years old.

Karen, Lisa, and I set the dining room table while Carla pinch-hit for me on cooking duties. We set places for twelve at the large table, letting Justin's two older kids and Johnny's oldest sit with us. Then we set up the folding table in the waste of space area for the four younger kids to sit there. I think we all were hoping Gary's twins would take a nap so they could eat in peace.

During prayer, which was led by Mom, everyone bent their heads except Gary and me. We made faces at each other across the table until we heard Mom say, "And please Lord, bless my two babies, who are rude and disrespectful." We both said Amen with everyone else then laughed.

Dinner was really good, all except the turkey. I couldn't stand the smell, even fully cooked, so I ate all the vegetables, potatoes and a piece of pumpkin pie.

"I'll get everything cleaned up; you guys can go in the living room and relax," I said.

"I'll help you," Carla said.

As everyone was filing out of the dining room and making their way to the living room, Carla and I made quick work of clearing the dishes from the table. I had her set them on the counter as I loaded the dishwasher.

By the time we got done in the kitchen, the kids were begging to go swimming again.

I noticed Jim was asleep in the living room. "Looks like the turkey got the best of him," I said to Mom and Gary.

"He'll be full of piss and vinegar in about an hour. I don't think we'll stay too much longer after the kids finish swimming." Mom folded her arms and sighed.

"Is something bothering you, Mom?" Gary walked over and put his arm around her shoulders.

"I just have this feeling…" She dropped her arms to her side. "Well, I can't help but wonder with Nikki getting married, if your father will make his way back to the surface."

"It's funny you bring him up. I was thinking I should at least reach out to him. If he wants to come, fine. If not, that's fine too."

"Well, you both are better than me, because I just don't give two fucks about him. He could die and I wouldn't give a shit or attend his funeral."

Chapter 26

It was close to eight o'clock when everyone except Gary, Carla, and their kids left. I took Abby up to give her a bath, got her pajamas on, and tucked her into bed. I was exhausted. I sent a quick text to Georgia to see if we were still on for tomorrow's rat-race shopping and meet-up. She baled on me.

By the time I went back downstairs, Carla and Gary had their twins tucked in bed, and six year old Bianca was lying on the living room floor fighting to keep her eyes open. Carla had her head on Gary's chest as they sat watching Cartoon Network, the channel of choice today instead of football.

"Are you up for some Black Friday shopping tomorrow morning, Carla?"

She lifted her head and looked at me with sleepy eyes. "How early are you thinking about leaving?"

"Not too early, probably around six."

"Yeah, sure, why not?" She looked at Gary. "You don't mind, do you, honey?"

"As long as I'm not being forced to go, I don't mind. You guys have fun."

"I'll have Abby with me, so we won't be out long."

"Get the hell out of here! You can't shop in that madness with her. Leave her here and I'll take care of her," Gary replied.

"Are you sure? That's four kids."

"I'll be fine, trust me. I'll probably end up at Mom's before you get back anyway."

"Cool, I'm going to sleep so I have the energy to fight the crowds." I went over and gave them each a hug. "Goodnight."

"Goodnight," they both called at the same time. They were a very cute couple and complemented each other well.

"Do you want me to take Bianca up?"

"Sure, thank you," Carla said. "B, go with Aunt Nikki."

Bianca gave them both a hug and kiss, then I picked her up onto my hip. She was much heavier than Abby.

When the alarm went off, I thought I was still dreaming. I moved in slow motion to get it to turn off. It would've been cruel and unusual punishment to wake Abby up and drag her out of her bed.

I was leaning against the counter sending a text to Jeff, letting him know my decision to brave the insanity, when Carla stumbled down the stairs. She looked almost like she was sleep-walking toward the smell of brewing coffee.

"This is going to suck; I'm just saying it now," Carla said with a stoic, straight face. I reached for a cup for her and set it on the counter.

"Do you have anywhere you want to go?"

"A toy store; anywhere, I don't care." She poured her coffee and refilled my cup.

We finished our coffee and each took a cup with us.

While we spent the day shopping, laughing, and having a great time talking, I filled her in on bits and pieces of my relationship with Jeff. She didn't offer up any judgmental comments or make it seem like what I was doing was ridiculous. But she did ask that one bothersome question that stumped me: 'Do you love him?' Of course I replied yes because what else was I supposed to say? No, I don't love him, but what the fuck, he wants to marry me for God knows what reason and he has a lot of money, so why not? That wouldn't go over too well.

When we reached the breaking point of shopping, she called Gary and found out he was still at Jeff's house, so we drove back there. He was trying to get everyone and everything out of the foyer and loaded up in his car to go to Mom's. We helped him, and all of us went over.

I had lost track of time when I heard my phone chime, signaling an incoming phone call.

"Hey, are you home?"

"Yes, I'm home. And I'm not too happy about the way the house looks. The kitchen is a mess and something was spilled in the living room. I didn't think I asked for too much, darlin'." I slinked out of the house and took a seat in a chair in the backyard while I listened.

"I'm sorry. We were out shopping. I didn't check the house before I left. Gary watched the kids. That's my fault." *Fuck!* Why hadn't I done a check of everything before I left?

"Obviously I was wrong." He continued talking to me and completely ignored what I had just said. "I didn't want stains on the carpet or a sink full of dishes. Perhaps you just didn't have a good understanding of what the fuck I had asked of you." My stomach sank as Jeff scolded me.

"I'll be right there. Just let me --" He hung up on me. My eyes stung with tears, and my knee bounced out of control. I had to regain my composure before walking back into the house. I couldn't let them see me looking out of sorts and being able to deduce what had happened on this call.

After a few deep breaths, I rose from the chair and tucked my phone into my pocket. I put on my happy face and returned to the house like nothing was wrong.

"I need to go home for a bit; Jeff's back from his trip."

"That's cool; why don't you leave Abby with us? She and Bianca are having a good time. We'll bring her with us when we come back," Gary offered.

"Are you sure?"

"Positive; leave her and go see your man," Carla added with a wink.

"Okay, I'll see you guys later." I gave everyone a hug goodbye, told Abby I was leaving, and headed for Jeff's house.

The fifteen-minute drive was gut-wrenching. My mind was racing a mile a minute. I didn't want to fight, and I didn't want to get hollered at any more.

I unlocked the door and walked into the house to hear Jeff talking. He turned in his chair and saw me standing in the foyer, then hung up his phone.

"Hi, babe," I said, my voice shaking with trepidation.

"Hey, come in here. Where's Abby?"

"Gary kept her at Mom's." I walked with slow, small steps, edging my way into the kitchen, looking at the dishes left in the sink. "I'm really sorry; I swear –"

"It's not like it can't be cleaned up. Come over here." Okay, did I mention that my fiancé is neurotic? I walked over to him, and he scooped me into his arms and lowered his lips onto mine, consuming me as he held me tight to him, murmuring into my mouth, "I missed you."

He helped to maneuver my body so I was straddling his lap. His fingers were dragging down my back, and his strong hands were palming my ass cheeks, pulling me into him tight. His need was overwhelming. My flower responded and was silently begging for him, burning and aching to feel him as my hips moved forward.

"Not in the house today, baby. I don't want any interruptions. I don't want to be heard, and I damn sure don't want to be found."

He lifted me off of him and set me on the floor. I looked down at his impressive package waiting to be unwrapped, noticing the wet spot on the front of his pants. "Is that from me?"

He ran his fingers between my legs, feeling my crotch through my pants. My legs spread for him. I could feel the moisture in my panties. "That's compliments of you." He rubbed his fingers against his thumb, then stood and took my hand and led me out to the pool house.

I had never been in there; I never had a need or desire to go in there. There was a storage area with pool supplies and behind that was a door. Jeff led the way through the neatly stacked items and tools, then unlocked the door. We walked through the door, and I was shocked. There was a small studio apartment set-up. There was a bed, a sofa, a kitchenette, and a bathroom.

He led me to the bed, sat down, and tugged me down onto him. He laid back and pulled me with him as our mouths fused together. His fingers abraded my hard nipples, causing my stomach to clench and my thighs to clamp together. His hand slid down my torso, over my hips and down across to my mound. His hands quickly unfastened the button and zipper of my pants. I reached down and helped shove off my pants and panties. Our lips parted.

Jeff knelt above me, pulling his shirt over his head and tossing it onto the floor, and then tossing my garments over with it. He lifted my shirt off over my head and unfastened my bra. I lay there, naked, waiting for him to use me however he wanted.

"I have your surprise out here, baby."

"Okay." I was a little apprehensive. I had never been a huge fan of surprises.

"Close your eyes." He stood from the bed, and as he walked into the bathroom. I closed my eyes tight. I felt him press into the bed. "Lie back and spread those luscious thighs for me, and make sure you don't open your big brown eyes."

I loved when he ordered me and instructed what he wanted me to do. I felt his warm breath on my over-sensitive skin. I could have felt the breeze of a gnat's wings flying in the air above me. His warm, moist tongue lapped at my folds, then the breath returned. His tongue stroked across my bud before I felt his heated breath on me. He dipped his tongue deep into my folds to my channel, licking at the opening before disappearing, making me want more.

"You're making me crazy, Jeff."

"You've already driven me out of my mind; welcome to the party. Keep your eyes closed."

His tongue lapped and sucked at my clit while my body curled in toward him. He was going to make me cum like this. But he pulled away, my body eventually relaxing as I waited in anticipation of his next touch.

He scraped his fingers up my inner thigh to my flower, parted my lips gently, then ran his tongue from my tight knot up to my bud, slipping his finger inside me. My hips rose slightly off the bed to meet his hand.

"You're so wet. You always are." I heard him slurp and peeked to see his finger in his mouth. I closed my eyes. "And you taste so fucking good, sweet Nikki." His finger found its way back inside me again. "My beautiful baby doll."

I felt something cool rubbing on my bud, not his warm tongue, and his finger stayed lodged deep in my crevice. I was confused and wanted to open my eyes, but resisted the temptation. Then there was a click, and the vibration began. Holy hot fuckness to death, he'd brought me a vibrator.

"You like that, baby?"

"Yeah," I moaned as my hips gyrated.

"Good. I want you to use this when you make yourself cum for me. Take it; you hold it." My hands reached blindly down toward my clit. He steadied them up to the handle. I knew without opening my eyes that he had bought me the wand. *Oh, joy!*

His fingers thrust in and out as the vibration on my clit pushed me closer and closer to tipping over the edge.

He pulled them out, and his tongue resumed probing my cleft beneath the vibrating head. His hands slid under my ass, lifting me up to his skilled mouth like he was serving my pussy on a platter to himself. A bolt of lightning shot through me. I began to perspire. My heart raced as my stomach muscles contracted, curling my back off the mattress. "Good fucking God, Jeff." Every muscle in my body stiffened as I reached my climax. The vibration on my swollen clit had me orgasming non-stop. It became nearly unbearable, yet felt so good at the same time.

Jeff pried the wand from my hands. "Looks like we have a winner here." He laughed. "You can open your eyes. Are you ready for me now, baby?" He looked so delicious with his jeans hung low on his hips and his muscles rippling.

I was panting and writhing on the bed. "I've been ready for you."

"I like that." He stood up and slid his pants down, revealing his cock to me.

"Come here." I motioned for him to bring that beast up to my mouth. The drip of pre-cum resting on the tip was hanging on for dear life, waiting for me to lick it off. I engulfed his length in my mouth and watched his head roll back.

He lifted his head, stroked his hand through my hair, and gazed down at me. "Jesus, Nikki, if I don't feel your pussy squeezing around me soon, my head is going to burst."

I pulled my mouth back off him. "We can't have that." My legs spread wide, and my sex ached for him. He positioned himself in front of me and pushed himself into me, stretching and filling me. He moaned through clenched teeth as he slid his length deep into my core. He dragged back through my gripping walls, then plunged back in fast.

His hands clasped mine, holding them over my head, tight to the bed while he lowered his mouth, hovering just above mine, licking my lips, thrashing with my tongue. I could taste myself on him as he continued thrusting. "Damn, baby, you feel so fucking good."

His raspy voice made me spasm and pushed me closer to losing control.

He released my hands and moved his arms under my knees and pushed them forward, forcing my knees to nearly touch my ears and my greedy pussy to take all of him.

"Fuck me hard, Jeff, fuck me really hard." He impaled me deep and hard, and our wet skin collided over and over. "Damn!" I went over the edge with him ramming into me. "Shit, don't stop, don't you fucking stop!" I wanted him to use me until I was unconscious. I couldn't get enough of him. He pounded in me for what seemed like fifteen more minutes.

"I can't take it anymore; I'm going to cum."

"Give it to me, baby."

"Uh," he grunted out through his pained I'm-cumming face. I found my final release as his hot cum filled me.

He collapsed on top of me, and we both struggled to catch our breath. I had a little more difficulty trying to breathe under his weight. He must have sensed it because he rolled off and laid beside me, draping me with his powerful arm and pulling me tight to him.

Sometime later, I jumped and realized we had fallen asleep. Everyone was going to come home and wonder where we were. I hoped everything was okay with Abby. I had to get showered and back to the house to check my phone. My mind was racing. Then his large hand extended over my thigh and pulled me back into him. I fell into his embrace and back under his spell. I didn't give a damn about anything else for the next thirty minutes except Jeff and the encore performance.

Chapter 27

The weekend was unbelievable. The past five days with Jeff made me feel like we had grown closer. We had Sunday and Monday practically all to ourselves after Gary and his family left.

It felt weird. I had a hard time admitting the feeling. I had always thought there would only be one true love in my life. As much as I loved Sky, the thought of ever loving another man that much hadn't seemed possible. Not that I loved Jeff like I loved Sky, but I was falling. And fast. Yet, as good as this feeling was, I couldn't help but feel kind of guilty. In a strange way, I felt like I was betraying Sky. I still loved him. I had never expected I would be able to love anyone else as long as he was alive.

There was so much I still didn't know about Jeff, though. What if I ended up finding out something that was a complete deal breaker? And I often wondered why he didn't ever talk about his family. Maybe he didn't have any living family. One day, I'd ask.

The wedding planning was falling behind. I felt so overwhelmed with the details and the upcoming trip to Atlanta. Thank God for Candace's cousin; she had a friend who worked at a large hotel chain and was able to get us a discount on three rooms. I had to get as much done as possible before we left because Christmas was going to cause some planning activities to completely halt.

The wedding invitations would be in by the end of the week, and Jeff still hadn't given me his guest list. I'd have to make that priority number two on the weekend and work on other things. I still had no idea what wedding favors to pick. The choices were too many.

We hadn't talked about the honeymoon too much, but Jeff tossed out a couple of ideas. Hawaii and Jamaica were my top two choices. I'd never been to either. I liked the idea of Jamaica, but Hawaii sounded better for a honeymoon. I planned on wrapping that decision up when he came home for the following weekend, then he could get whoever from his job to get everything set up.

I didn't have the person who was going to officiate the ceremony lined up yet, I had no idea how many hotel rooms to reserve, I didn't have a dress yet, but in thirteen days I'd be in Atlanta, and the DJ was still up in the air. I was going fucking crazy and had just over two months to get this all done.

My concentration was for shit at work. It seemed I was doing just enough to keep from drawing attention to myself. I'd managed to go unscathed through the week so far and had finally made it to Friday. Caffeine was the official word of the day -- coffee, and lots of it. I grabbed my mug off my desk. I stood way too fast and got lightheaded. The late-night Skype and wand sessions were taking a toll on me. I had to get more rest. After regaining my wits, I headed to the break room and ran into Tristan.

He gave me his normal happy-go-lucky smile. "Are you going to make it for happy hour tonight?"

"I'm not sure. I want to, but I really need to keep working on this wedding."

"You also need to take a break every now and then. You're going to go insane sweating the details."

"The details are what either makes it a success or flop. But maybe I'll just come out for an hour."

"That'll be cool. I'll let the others know." He walked away. He was right; the planning was eating me alive. The break, even for an hour, would do me good.

By five o'clock, I was spent. "All work and no play will make Jill a dull girl," Georgia said trying to lighten my mood some.

"I know, but time is getting away from me."

"I'll help you next week. I'll have some time."

"I'll kiss the ground you walk on. I need help. Jackie's been so tied up with work, she doesn't have much time right now, either. She's got some time after we get back from Atlanta."

"Don't worry; it'll all work out. Let's go get a drink. We both need one."

I ordered a Bud Light. I was scared if I started drinking mixed drinks, I'd close the place down, have to be poured into a cab, and shipped to Jeff's house. Luckily for me, Georgia only stayed for an hour, so when she left, I went out with her.

Sky picked up Abby after school and was keeping her until Sunday. I really needed the break from her so I could concentrate on this wedding. I got home and spent more time on the guest list. I had seventy-eight people I wanted to invite. I did include an invitation for my dad. That left Jeff with over one hundred for his list.

I was startled awake by Jeff's hand stroking down my hair and face. "Good morning, baby doll."

"What …" I yawned, "What time is it?"

"It's ten fifteen."

"Oh my god, I fell asleep last night staring at this list. I came upstairs at seven thirty."

"Yeah, I tried to call you but got no answer."

"I'm so sorry. Damn it. And I wanted to get this done last night, too."

"Don't apologize; if you're tired, you're tired." He kissed my forehead. "Let's go get something to eat. We'll go out."

"Sounds good to me." I stood from the bed and instantly was bowled over by a wave of nausea and dizziness.

"Are you okay?"

"Yeah, I'll be fine. I just got dizzy for a minute."

"I don't think that's normal, is it? I mean, I haven't seen you do that before."

"It's happened a couple times. I'm okay, though." Once it subsided, I grabbed my clean things from my drawer to go take a shower.

"I'm starving." I looked over my shoulder at Jeff sitting on the edge of the bed with his head resting in his hands. "We need to talk about the guest list."

"We will, just hurry up."

I went into the bathroom and after making sure the water was perfect, stepped into the shower. "Babe, can you go get me some Maalox? I have the worst indigestion."

"Yeah."

A few minutes later while I was drying myself off, Jeff walked in with the antacids and held his hand up to my mouth while I licked them off him like a horse taking sugar cubes. It took a few minutes for them to calm my stomach down, but then I felt good as new.

"I'm ready."

He pulled me into him tight, wrapped his arms around my waist, and stared into my eyes. "Damn, you're beautiful."

I felt myself flush. "Thank you."

He crooked his neck down and ran his fingers from my lower back, up my spine, over each vertebra, up my neck, raising goose bumps on my skin, and through my hair. His lips skimmed mine. My lips parted in anticipation of him. He licked at my lips with light brushes of his tongue before he consumed me. The heat coursed through my body like wildfire. I wanted him so bad -- right here, right now. Then he released his lips from mine; and was still hovering over me when he whispered, "We have all day, but first, we need food. Later I look forward to hearing you beg me to take you, then hearing you beg me to stop."

I cleared my throat as I fought my urge to begin the begging right now. "Let me get dressed real quick. We need to go before we don't leave." I slipped on my garments, then I clasped his hand in mine and walked to the door.

Jeff surprised me by taking the drive to Island Way Grill in Clearwater Beach. Their brunch was exquisite. The whole ride there, I was craving scrambled eggs and pancakes, but instead had pancakes, ham, wings, and shrimp. The smell of the eggs made me want to hurl so I avoided them like the plague. I tried almost every sweet pastry that was out and enjoyed a couple mimosas. By the time we left, I was stuffed and had a nice buzz.

We walked along the beach for a few minutes before deciding to make the drive back.

The ride was quiet until I broke the silence, "How are you coming along with the guest list?"

"I have about sixty people on it. How's yours?"

"I have seventy-eight. I can't think of anyone else."

"I feel the same, so maybe we have a smaller wedding than we planned."

"That's fine with me as long as we each have everyone there we want."

He glanced at me and reached to place his large hand over mine. "As long as we're there, that's all that matters. Fuck everyone else."

Hmm, well, isn't that special. "Yeah." I sighed. "So you gave me Hawaii and Jamaica to choose from for the honeymoon. I think I want to go to Hawaii."

"I was hoping you'd pick there."

"By the way, what are you going to do the weekend I'm in Atlanta?"

"I didn't realize you'd be there the whole weekend. I'll think of something, I guess."

"You guys need to get to finding tuxes. It's not like any of you besides Connor are 'off the rack' size."

"He's supposed to be setting that up. I'll check with him later."

"I have too much to do in two months time. And Christmas is right around the corner, which makes things even more difficult."

"Relax; do what you can do."

"Easy for you to say; you're not here running around like a chicken with no head, trying to work, trying to make arrangements and phone calls, hoping you're doing what you're supposed to be while hoping you don't get fired."

"You can only do so much. The wedding will be perfect no matter what. And if I tell you I'm going to do something, don't second guess me. I don't need you to fucking lose your shit on me."

"I'm sorry, I didn't mean to snap. I'm just so tired, and everything is getting on my nerves. I'm turning into a damn wreck. The stress is killing me."

"I have the perfect stress relief for you. You will be rejuvenated in no time. I have this perfect private oasis for you." He laughed.

I knew what that meant, and I was ready to let the begging commence.

Chapter 28

The weekend went by so fast. The next week and a half went even faster. Georgia was so much help. We got the invitations all mailed out, and she helped me come up with a first cut of a play-list for the DJ. Her brother had agreed to take on the DJ role. I'd never heard him, but she swore he was very good and I wouldn't be disappointed. Jeff assured me he would review the playlist on the weekend after they got their tux fittings done. I made sure to include his requested groups and songs. I had heard a few of the songs, but some of the group names I didn't know. He told me to make sure all the line dancing songs were put together so that shit could get done and over with all at once.

Before I knew it, it was Wednesday the twelfth and we were on the road. The ride was quick and without any issues. We had to be at the store on Thursday the thirteenth. My stomach was churning with excitement and anxiety. I wanted to jump up and down screaming with joy and at the same time wanted to cry fearing that I would leave without a gown. I didn't even know what style I wanted. A ball gown, mermaid -- I had no fucking idea. I was thinking I needed an off-white gown, but what if the one I loved only came in white? I wanted to go throw up!

Mom and I were set up to share a room. I was so tired that by the time we got checked in, and I finished my brief conversation with Jeff, I laid down in my bed and fell asleep.

Before I knew it, it was morning. I was not woken up by an alarm clock, instead it was my mom whispering in my ear. "Are you ready to find your dress, sweetie?"

I stretched and sat up, still tired. I needed coffee, which mom had sitting on the nightstand beside me. She was fully clothed and ready to go. The hotel clock next to my coffee read seven forty-five.

"The others are up already, we're just waiting for you to get ready." Mom sipped her coffee.

"Okay, I'll get a quick shower and make up my face. Are we getting anything to eat?"

"They have some pastries downstairs, we can grab something on our way out."

"Awesome," I sang as I stood. The dizziness caught me off guard and I immediately sat on the edge of the bed.

"I really think you should go get a check-up, dear."

"I will. After we get back, I'll make an appointment."

"Good. Is there anything I can help you get?"

"Can you grab my make-up bag out of my carry-on suitcase? I can get my clothes out of the other bag."

She took the make-up into the bathroom, then sat back down at the small table with the remote in her hand. "I'll be done in a jiffy."

"We have time. If you need me or feel dizzy, please call for me."

"I think I'm fine." I ducked into the bathroom and took my shower, dressed, and applied my make-up. I pulled my towel-dried hair back into a loose side ponytail.

"I guess I'm ready." She frowned when I raised my eyebrows at her. I slung my purse on my shoulder and picked up my coffee.

"Relax, dear; it's just a dress." We walked out and she pulled the room door closed tight. We stopped by and rounded up the rest of my crew, then went to the lobby so each of us could get a pastry before we walked down to wait for Jackie to get the car.

"What if we can't agree on a dress, Mom? What if I love something and you all hate it? And what if I find something I like but my boobs are too small and I can't get it? What if Jeff hates the gown I pick?"

"Sweetie, you get the dress that makes you happy. You'll know it when you find it. You'll be beautiful, and Jeff will love it." Jackie brought the car around and picked us up, then drove the few minutes over to the shop. She dropped us all off out front while she went to park the car.

I wrapped my arms around my mom and tears flowed uncontrollably. "I love you, Mom." I hated that I was being so emotional over finding a damn dress.

"I love you too, dear." Her arms held me tight to her. "Let's go and say yes to a dress."

I smiled, but the tears still trickled down my face as I caught a glimpse of the sales lady walking toward us.

"Hi, ladies; so who's the bride?"

I raised my hand slowly wiping at my eyes and nose.

"Well, good grief, is this a happy occasion?"

"Yes, it is. It really is," I said. "I'm Nikki."

"Great to meet you, Nikki. So the camera crew will be here shortly. Once they arrive, I'll greet y'all and ask who the bride is. Once you acknowledge you are, you'll do your introduction: give your name, your age, and where you're from. Then I'll ask who all you brought with you and you'll go around and introduce everyone. Everything okay so far?"

"Yes."

"Great; then, after the introductions, I'd like you to tell everyone who you're marrying and how you met your fiancé. After that, we'll talk about when the wedding is. You can tell me in months or years or days and tell me a little about the venue. I'll ask you if you have any idea what style dress you're looking for. Do you have a particular style in mind?"

"I have no idea. I looked at some dresses online, but it's so hard to tell. I think I want an off-white gown. This is my second marriage." Jackie walked in and found us. She squeezed in near Georgia.

"We will do our best to find your dress, but don't rule out the white gowns just because this is wedding number two. Pick what you love."

"Who's the maid of honor; is she here?" Jackie lifted her hand. "What's your name?"

"Jackie."

"Do you have any ideas, as far as style, what you think would look best on the bride?"

"A black gown with a black veil." She rolled her eyes. "Just kidding. I think she would look stunning in a fitted gown; nothing that looks real southern belle-like."

"When we get to that segment where I ask Nikki about the style she's looking for, I'd like you to speak up and state what you think. Anyone have a different opinion?"

My mom raised her hand. "I'm the bride's mother. I like the ball gown southern belle look. I'd at least like her to try that on."

"Great; we'll get you to speak up on style too." She shifted her eyes back toward me. "What's your budget for your gown?"

"Thirty-five hundred dollars."

Jackie put her hand over her mouth and mumbled, "Jeff's cheap ass." I gave her a pointed glance to shut her up.

We eventually made our way back into the studio, where we all began browsing through what seemed like endless gowns. I knew it would be a long shot, but if by some miracle I was able to find a dress that fit me perfectly, then I could take it with me that day and put a great big fat check mark next to that item on my list.

The scene in the studio was chaos. We weren't the only bridal party in there. I don't know if Jackie, Georgia, and Candace decided to ham it up for the fuck of it or if they really were on opposite ends of the spectrum, but they were a mess. My poor mom was beside herself and clammed up, refusing to comment. Mandy was no help, honestly. She liked everything and couldn't think of one thing to say to help me decide.

After trying on everyone else's selections, I tried on the gown I'd picked. I knew as soon as it was fastened in the dressing room and I spun to see my reflection that it was the dress for me.

The gown was simple, yet elegant. It was form-fitting and fit me as if I were the model they'd used to make it. The straps were a wide lace that wrapped around my shoulders almost halter style. The lace continued down throughout the length of the gown and down to the train. My boobs fit perfectly and the sweetheart neckline enhanced my cleavage -- I had cleavage. It was clinging to my figure all the way down to my mid-thigh, where it began to flare out ever so slightly. It was just sheer enough to see my legs once the flaring began. The best thing was that it fit me perfectly, no alterations, no modifications, nothing. *Bag that bitch and I'm out.* And I knew Jeff would like it -- no, he would love it.

Mom tried to get me to pick a veil, but I declined. I was going to get my hair done and would find something to use for an accent, but I didn't think a veil would look right with that dress anyway.

Once we finished with my appointment, we went to get something to eat before Mom had to catch her flight. Jackie knew this great BBQ restaurant, Fox Brothers, so we all agreed to go there. I can say those ribs and pulled pork were the absolute best I'd ever eaten. It was so cool when the owners came by and asked how everything was. They had to be proud of that place. It was worth the wait in line.

Once we finished, we drove to the hotel to get Moms' bags, then drove to the airport to drop her off, and then headed back to our hotel to get ready for the rest of the night.

I made a quick call to Jeff and let him know how things went. He tried to get me to put the dress on and send him a selfie, but that wasn't happening.

We all changed our clothes and took a cab to Vanquish. Taking a cab was the smartest decision we made because by the time we left, not one of us would have been able to drive. It wasn't overly crowded for a Thursday night, but we had a good time. I was surprised any of us even remembered the hotel we were staying in.

Instead of making it down to breakfast with everyone else, I spent my morning snuggled up with my cool new porcelain boyfriend in the bathroom. I felt like I was going to die. My actual stomach was the only thing left in me to come out. "I swear I'm never drinking again," I groaned to myself. Tears streamed down my face as I talked to myself between dry heaves. "I'm so stupid." What the fuck was I thinking? The crazy thing is, I didn't think I'd drank so much that I'd be sick.

I heard a faint chime of an incoming text. Great, just what I needed. I crawled on my hands and knees into the bedroom to get my purse. Every time I set my hand or knee down onto the carpet, I was overcome by queasiness and a pounding in my head that felt like it was going to split in two. I dug through my purse and pulled my phone out. It was nine in the morning, and the message was from Jeff.

Jeff: How was your night?

Me: We had a good time. This morning, just shoot me.

Jeff: Don't tell me you drank too much.

Me: Yeah I did.

Jeff: That's fucked up. Call me later.

Me: K

I crawled as fast as I could back into the bathroom in time for another dry heave that left my stomach tied in a knot. I made my way back into the bedroom and dragged myself back into bed. I felt like shit. I'd had times when I'd drunk too much before, but I had never felt this bad. Maybe something I'd eaten in the bar didn't sit well in my stomach. And my head felt like a bomb that was going to detonate into pieces. Whatever was to blame, I would not be having a repeat performance of this tomorrow morning. We had been told about another club we planned to try out tonight, Opera, but I couldn't even think of going out or drinking another drop of alcohol right then.

I woke to an eerie silence. My stomach felt a million times better, and my head felt closer to normal. I got out of the bed and was hit with a bout of dizziness that made me stagger. I needed food, but before that, I needed lots and lots of water. My mouth was drier than hot pavement in the summer sun. I ripped the plastic wrap off one of the cups by the sink, filled it, and drank every drop before refilling it again.

I made my way back into the room and picked up my phone. It was almost two o'clock. I couldn't believe my entourage had left me alone for so long. I could have died in here. Well, maybe I was being overly dramatic. I scrolled through and had no calls, but did have a text from Jackie and Georgia. I decided to call Jeff first before figuring out where the girls were.

"Hey babe."

"Hey. How are you feeling?" He sounded like he was just getting up from a nap.

"I feel so much better now. Good God, I wanted to just die earlier."

"When are you guys coming back? Saturday or Sunday?"

"We were planning on Sunday. Is that okay still?"

"It's fine, but I'd love to see you tomorrow. I miss you being here with me."

"I miss you too, baby."

"Maybe you can convince the road-trippers to come home early."

"I'm sure I can, I'd rather be in your arms tomorrow."

"Let me know. I have to run, our tux appointment is in an hour and a half."

"Okay, I'll talk to you later."

Now to find these bitches. I decided to call Jackie instead of sending a text. They were all over in Candace and Georgia's room waiting for me to wake up from my alcohol-induced coma. We decided to go get something to eat and talk about what we were going to do that night. I planned to also let them know I thought we should leave the next morning instead of waiting till Sunday.

Chapter 29

Friday night at Opera was fun, and it was crowded. I drank nothing except Ginger Ale all night. Saturday morning, we were all eager to get back home. We loaded up the car, paid our hotel bills, said goodbye to Atlanta and were on our way back to lovely Tampa -- home sweet home. I sent a text to Jeff letting him know we were on the road.

We made it back home in six and a half hours after one stop for gas and a couple bathroom breaks. After dropping everyone off, I couldn't get home fast enough. I pulled into the driveway, but noticed Jeff's car wasn't there. I checked my phone and realized he had never replied to my text earlier. That was weird; he never just didn't reply. He had been home on Friday when I'd last talked to him. Should I call the police and file a missing person's report? Or just sit here worrying myself stupid until he showed up or I found out he was dead? I sent him a text letting him know I was home, then went upstairs to put on my swimsuit. I decided to lay out by the pool while I waited to hear from him.

Soft lips slanting onto mine startled me awake. "Hey there." His eyes were filled with white-hot desire. He needed me as much as I needed him.

"Hey," was the only word I could utter before his mouth covered mine again. When he released my mouth, I was able to ask, "What time is it?"

"Five thirty. I sent you a text that I was on my way home, but you must have fallen asleep."

"I'm so glad you're here. I missed you." I wanted to tell him I loved him. And I did, with all my heart. I knew I had fallen in love with him. I knew it when I was in Atlanta away from him, missing him. There was no denying it anymore. But I was scared to tell him. I wasn't sure if he felt the same way, and I wasn't willing to allow myself to be left hanging from a limb. I had been a fool and said it before, when I really didn't love him, so when he hadn't said it back, it didn't bother me. But now, if I said it and he didn't say it back, I'd be devastated.

He pulled me up into his tight embrace. He wrapped me in his arms while his tongue claimed me, marked me as his territory. I had hoped we'd make it up to the bedroom, but he took me poolside in the lounge chair again. Every ounce of passion I felt for him was conveyed through my touch and my gaze while I opened myself to him. I would have crawled across a hot desert to feel him. And when we found our release together, the love in my heart was so intense, I wrapped him in my arms and held him tight, never wanting to let him go.

He whispered in my ear, "I only have to be away for two days this week. I'll be gone Tuesday and Wednesday."

"That's good. And Sky is taking Abby Saturday and keeping her until Christmas afternoon, since I had her on Thanksgiving."

"Well, we should let her open one present on Friday night before she leaves. She can open the rest when she comes back home."

"I don't know …"

"Ah, come on, spoil sport Mommy, she can have one gift early. What's it going to hurt?"

"Okay, only one."

"And you get one too."

"I've got all I need right now." I slid my hands down his body and grabbed two handfuls of his sexy, round ass. He leaned in and kissed me.

"I feel the same. But I have one thing I want you to have early. It's killing me not to give it to you right now."

"Well, you have to wait; I still have to finish my shopping before we do any gift exchange."

My mind raced; my mom hadn't mentioned anything about Christmas plans. And if she had, I'd forgotten. I needed to call her and find out what she and Jim were up to. My to-do list was growing. For every one task I could check off as complete, two more managed to creep up on me.

The rest of the weekend and week raced by. I barely got the decorations and tree up and my shopping done, but I did manage to find jewelry to match my dress and also found my shoes. Mom and Jim were going out of town the week of Christmas so we planned to stop by to see them on Sunday. And I was surprised to hear Sky tell me to bring Abby by before ten Saturday morning; he was going to take her to visit his mom for the weekend.

Friday night, we had our early Christmas. Abby was in heaven when she was handed her present from Jeff. "Go ahead Abby, open it," he urged.

She looked at him with her big brown eyes and smiled from ear to ear. She loved presents. She began ripping at the edges of the paper.

"Help her, babe; I think you have too much tape on it." Jeff knelt down beside Abby, and using her tiny fingers, he showed her how to get her fingers under the flap of paper and pull it. Of course, you know I had my camera phone out taking video. It was so cute.

Her eyes widened and she screamed, "Look!" She held up a new doll.

"You got a new baby." I smiled at Jeff. My heart was overflowing with his kindness and thoughtfulness.

"What do you say, Abby?"

"Thank you, Mr. Jeff." She jumped up and wrapped her tiny arms around him and kissed him on the cheek. What a fantastic day; my family was coming together.

"You're welcome, sweetie." He hugged her with one arm. "What are you going to name her?"

Abby looked at me with a puzzled look, then smiled. "I don't know."

"Maybe Daddy can help you think of a nice name for your baby."

"Yeah, Daddy can help me."

She scampered off carrying her doll.

"That was so sweet of you."

"We won't tell anyone that Jeff does 'sweet' shit, right?" He made sure to throw the air quotes up when he said sweet.

"Never."

I convinced Jeff to wait to do our exchange on Christmas Eve, just the two of us. He wasn't happy, but he agreed.

Abby stayed up for about another hour before I settled her and her new baby into bed. We had to get up early, and I didn't want to be late getting to Sky's.

The alarm startled me awake. I was pretty deep into sleep. The kind of deep sleep that you hear the alarm and think it's the phone, then you think it's the doorbell, then you don't know what the fuck it is, and finally, you have the brilliant revelation that 'oh yeah, it's the stupid alarm.'

I sat up on the edge of the bed for a few minutes before prying my ass up and going into the bathroom to brush my teeth and comb my hair. I crept back into the bedroom to put on my jean shorts and T-shirt.

"Hurry back," Jeff said as he looked up at me.

"I will." Who in their right mind wouldn't hurry back to a man like him?

I went and got Abby ready and grabbed her new doll and the bag we had already packed. We ran downstairs into the kitchen. I tossed an Eggo waffle in the toaster for her while I finished getting her shoes tied. Once the waffle popped up, I put it on a plate, got it buttered, put syrup on it, and poured her a glass of juice. The waffle smell was different. It didn't smell as appealing as it had in the past.

After she was finished, I wiped her hands and mouth to make sure she wasn't sticky. We ran out the door and got in the car.

My heart was racing the entire drive. My eyes flashed between watching the road and watching the clock. I knew I was cutting it close and was going to get there right at ten o'clock, if I made it on time at all. I parked the car out front with one minute to spare. Sky walked out the door as we parked and came down the sidewalk with his keys in his hand.

"Nik! Nikki! God, Nik, you have to be okay." Sky was slapping my face. What had I done to him that he was hitting me?

I heard sirens blaring. My vision was blurry, and I couldn't tell what was going on. I kept thinking someone must have gotten into an accident nearby because the sirens kept getting louder -- then they stopped.

I realized I was lying on the ground and Sky was holding my head. "What … What happened?"

"You passed out, Nik. You don't remember? You told me you felt funny and just fell out." I tried to lift myself up but felt like a fifty-pound weight was resting on my chest, holding me down.

"Just lie there for one moment, ma'am; we're going to get you in the ambulance, and we'll take your vitals there." *Ambulance? What in the everlasting fuck?* "Can you tell me your full name?"

"Nikki Carmichael. But I don't need an ambulance." They lifted me and laid me on the stretcher. I guess they didn't hear me.

"Nik, where's Jeff?"

"Home."

"Where's your phone?"

"The car."

"Which hospital are you taking her to?"

"General."

"I'm following right behind you, Nik."

The ambulance ride was a quiz of my life. They asked everything on my health history, family history, if I took drugs, drank excessively, and they kept fucking asking me what my name was. *Will someone please write that shit down so you can stop asking me?*

I was taken into the Emergency Room and moved into a bay. The first question they asked me was what my name was. Within minutes, both Sky and Jeff were there by my side.

"Where's Abby?"

"The neighbor has her; you know her, Connie."

I nodded my approval. Connie loved Abby and had watched her on a few occasions for me when I lived in the house, so I knew she was in good hands. The nurse came in and took my vitals and looked confused by both Sky and Jeff being in the bay with me. Jeff was standing beside me holding my hand.

"Who's the husband or boyfriend?"

"I'm the ex-husband." Sky spoke up first.

"I'm the fiancé," Jeff growled. The vicious glares that the two of them exchanged were unnerving.

I had just noticed I had an IV stuck in my hand. I didn't remember that happening. The nurse hooked up the blood pressure monitor to me and told me the results were normal.

"Did you eat breakfast this morning?"

"No."

"You're going through the IV pretty fast; that's a sign of dehydration. We want to run some blood tests on you to eliminate some other common, yet more critical, reasons for fainting."

She disappeared, and about five hours later -- not really but it seemed like it -- she came back in with a case of tubes, a rubber band to tie me off, and the needle. She removed four vials of blood, then promised to return in a few minutes. We all knew that was a lie.

The doctor came in shortly after she left. He asked a lot of the same questions everyone else already had asked me, starting with my name. I wanted to scream 'check the chart, fuckwad' but I played his little game and answered the questions.

"Do you need anything, baby doll?"

"I'm ready to go. I feel better. I want to go."

"Well, we need to get the blood test results back and make sure there isn't any serious underlying condition before we release you. I'll stop back in a few minutes. While we wait, we'll get you up to get an EKG done."

Then it hit me. "Sky, oh my god, I'm so sorry. You don't have to stay; I know you wanted to get going to see your mom."

"I already told her I'd be late."

Jeff rolled his eyes and squeezed my hand tighter. I could tell he wanted to say something but was biting his tongue. The nurse came in and wheeled me and my bed down the hall into the elevator. Jeff stayed by my side while Sky sat in the bay, waiting for me to return. Once I came back down, we were all quiet. The tension between Jeff and Sky was so thick it could have been cut with a knife.

The doctor came back in about forty-five minutes later and announced he had some results from the EKG and blood tests. My heart sank, and a tear leaked from the corner of my eye. I was hoping he'd come in and say they'd found nothing, and tell me to go home and eat a steak.

He said the EKG was normal, no heart concerns and no arrhythmia. He told us they couldn't definitively say dehydration or blood sugar or even low blood pressure weren't the problems because by the time they ran the blood test, I had been on the IV and that could have stabilized my blood sugar. And my blood pressure was normal both in the ambulance and in the hospital.

"Have you felt the lightheadedness or dizziness before today?"

"Yes, a few times, at work and at home. I just figured it was because of not eating right, not sleeping enough, and maybe not drinking enough water."

Jeff and I looked at each other. He had a disapproving frown on his face. Then I glanced over at Sky.

The doctor began reading down the list of things that he had been able to eliminate -- no to mono, that was a good thing. There were no indications of anemia. "Although it's possible stress and anxiety could have played a part in the fainting spell, and lack of sleep is always a problem, if it persists. But I believe the reason was more likely a classic case of compression of the inferior vena cava leading to postural hypotension."

"What exactly does that mean?" Jeff asked.

"It's common with people who carry extra weight, that's not your situation though." He laughed to himself as if he were a standup comedian. "It's also common amongst expectant women. Congratulations, Nikki, you're pregnant."

I dropped my head, and Jeff dropped my hand. *Oh my god! Fuck!* Exactly what I wasn't expecting and what Jeff *didn't* want.

"Wow…, just, fucking, wow," Sky said as he stood there shaking his head.

"This doesn't go any farther than this room." Jeff glared at Sky. "You got it? *We'll* make the announcement after the wedding, but no one knows about this before."

"Shit," I said in disbelief.

"This isn't the usual response we see," the doctor interrupted.

"I can't fucking believe this!" Jeff practically screamed.

"Rebekka's on her way here; what are you going to tell her? What's the brilliant excuse why Nik's in the hospital?"

"Shut the fuck up, Sky," Jeff snapped back at him.

"Jeff, I'm sorry. I swear I didn't do it on purpose." Tears were streaming down my face. "Jeff, look at me, please. I'm begging you."

He walked over to the large window facing God knows what. He ran his hands down his face. "Fuck my goddamn life."

The End of Book 1

About the Author

Desiree was born and raised in Iowa – corn country. She married her high school sweetheart and moved to the Philadelphia area. She's been happily married for over twenty-five years. She's the mother of two sons and a daughter.

She's a Project Manager by day, writer of erotica by night. She also is an avid reader and blogger.

Desiree also enjoys traveling and spending time at the beach.

For over two years she's been working to get her thoughts in print. She finally is writing what she wants to write. Twisted by Desire is her debut novel.

A Note from Desiree

Thank you for reading my book. I hope you enjoyed reading it as much as I enjoyed writing it. I'm honored and humbled that you chose to share your time reading Nikki and Jeff's story. Their twisted life is far from over.

If you did enjoy book one, I'd be forever grateful if you'd be kind enough to leave a review on Amazon and Goodreads for me.

If you'd like to send me direct feedback, please email me at desirecox69@gmail.com. I'd love to hear from you and will respond to each email I receive.

You can also connect and communicate with me through my other social media sites:

Facebook Author Page

Website

Amazon

Goodreads

Twitter

Pinterest

Google+

Other Available Books by Desiree ...

Jaded By Desire - Book 2 in the Lust, Desire, and Love Trilogy available now.

Buy Link

Reclaimed By Desire - Book 3 in the Lust, Desire, and Love Trilogy available now.

Buy Link

Wickedly Exotic Spring Erotic Wonderland Box Set - "Fantasy Come True," available now.

Buy Link

Affairs of the Heart Box Set – "Unselfish Love," available now.

Buy Link

Sensual and Sinful Cravings – An Erotic Anthology – "The Ten Year Reunion – How It All Began," available now.

Buy Link